The Queen's Card

THE QUEEN'S CARD

Copyright © 2025 by Erin Archer

All rights reserved. Printed in the United States of America.

No part of this book may be used or reproduced in any manner whatsoever without written permission of the author except in the case of brief quotations in a book review. This book is a work of fiction. Names, characters, businesses, organizations, places, events and incidents are either the product of the author's imagination or are used fictitiously. Any resemblance to actual persons, living or dead, events, or locales is entirely coincidental.

NO AI TRAINING: Without in any way limiting the author's and publisher's exclusive rights under copyright, any use of this publication to "train" generative artificial intelligence (AI) technologies to generate text is expressly prohibited. The author reserves all rights to license uses of this work for generative AI training and development of machine learning language models.

Published by Night Waltz Press

Cover Design by Fay Lane
Editing by Sarah Valingo

ISBN (ebook): 978-1-966315-00-1
ISBN (paperback): 978-1-966315-01-8
ISBN (hardcover): 978-1-966315-02-5

First Edition: February 2025

THE QUEEN'S CARD

For my husband

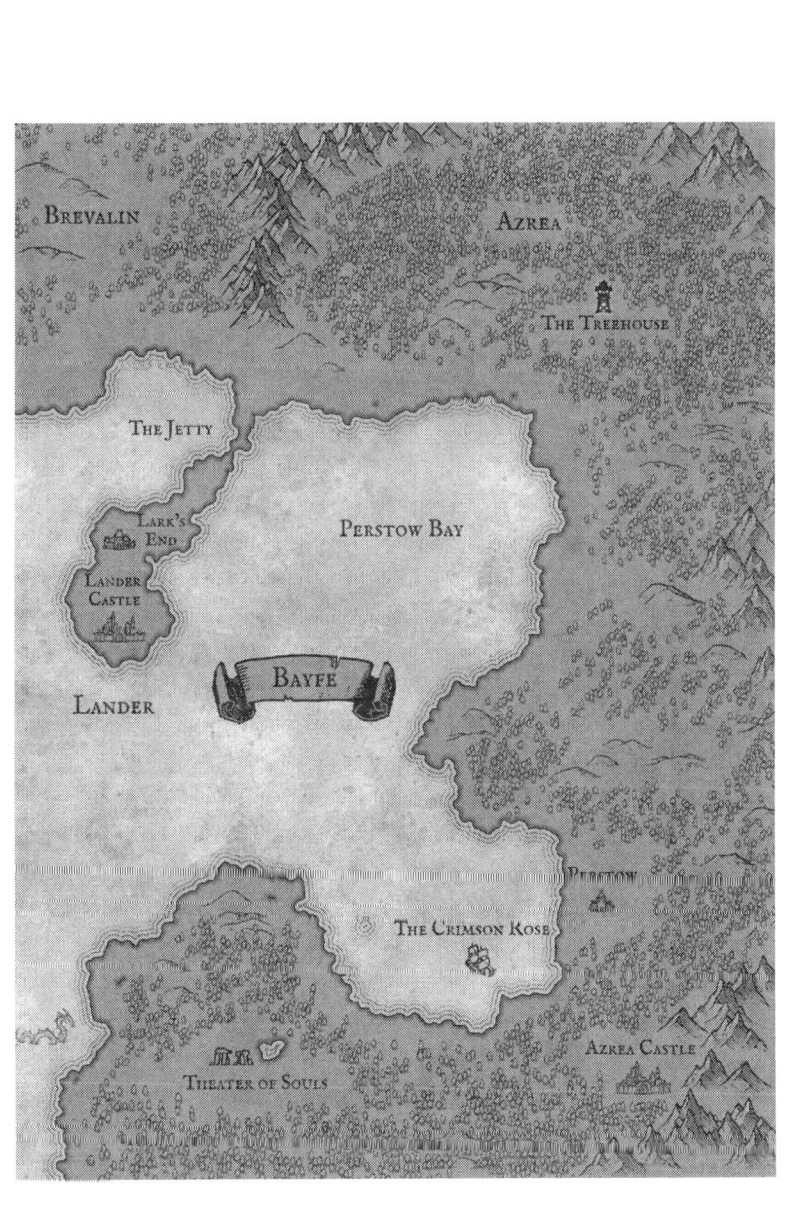

Prologue

No one notices the danger but me. A thin wisp of dark fog curls around my ankles. It's hardly visible beneath the dim glow of the torches on the ballroom balcony, but the prickling caress gives away its presence. It's *shadow* magic, and doesn't belong in Lander.

Dread coils in my stomach as I kick my foot to dispel it, but it quickly reforms. With a mind of its own, its snakes away from me and slithers across the balcony. To my horror, it pulls shadows from everywhere to form a thick, dark cloud. It fans out when it reaches the archway leading into the party.

I need to stop it before it reaches the ballroom.

But how?

Frantic, I chase after it, past a pair of my fellow guards, who stare at me in confusion. They can't see the magic. It slips into the massive room, disappearing between flowing skirts and shiny boots.

Great, I lost track of it.

The crowd has doubled since I sought the fresh sea air. Brevalin courtiers, our guests, fill the room. They're here to celebrate the upcoming alliance between our kingdoms. The Brevalin king is noticeably absent, apparently not well enough to travel.

Tension is rising between the two fae kingdoms that border us, the mortal kingdom. It's time for us to pick a side. If we're not allied when the tension finally snaps, we may not survive the fallout.

The din of the crowd quiets when musicians in the corner play a lilting tune. Elbowing my way through partygoers pairing off to dance, I give up on looking for the shadow and scan the room for my sister, Elyse. There are two others like me: my sister and Ambrose. But *unlike* me, they both have *keeper* magic.

I loathe the thought of relying on Elyse, especially now. We argued earlier tonight when she said I haven't proven myself to the king yet. Doesn't she know I'm trying?

She could help me, but she won't.

Tonight, I may need her, but someday, I'll prove my loyalty to my king. I'll become a keeper, too.

I dart between the carved pillars and under the massive seashell-adorned chandeliers until I spot her. She's standing just to the left of King Adrian and his daughter, Princess Dulcinea, who is perched on the dais, presiding over the ball.

The king sits stiffly on his throne, his fingers tapping against the armrests anxiously. On his right, the princess leans in to her betrothed, Prince Reid of Brevalin, who is equally captivated by his bride. She's resplendent in a blue velvet gown that compliments her gray eyes. Her long, dark blonde hair is pinned just behind her shoulder. He's handsome in an emerald green doublet, his dark hair shorn close to the scalp. His hand rests on hers, and when he leans in and whispers something in her ear, her eyes light up.

None of them notice anything amiss.

THE QUEEN'S CARD

I try to catch my sister's eye, but she's watching the pair as they rise and descend the stairs on the far side of the dais to join the revelers.

I continue swerving around dancing couples until I reach the set of stairs closest to the dais. The guard narrows his eyes at me.

I try to move around him, but he steps in front of me.

"Move!" I hiss, but he just crosses his arms.

"Don't bother the king. He's busy."

Fury rises within me.

He can't see the threat that's racing through the ballroom as we argue.

I don't have time for this.

I elbow him hard in the stomach and he grunts, reaching his hand out to grab my uniform. I dodge him, and when I'm a few feet away from my sister, the massive wooden doors leading to the rest of the castle suddenly burst open, smacking against the stone walls.

From where I stand, I see the shadow fog again. They crossed the entire ballroom and are now merging with a dark cloud at the threshold of the open doors. Behind it, the half-dozen guards stationed at the entrance lay unmoving in the hallway.

Everyone turns to see who emerges from the darkness.

It's Queen Roma.

Her black velvet cloak billows around her on a non-existent breeze. Her pale features are sharp, and her eyes are as dark as her hair. She's the ruthless Queen of Azrea, the kingdom excluded from this alliance and the greatest threat to our future.

As the other Lander guards close in, I watch the enemy queen, a smile curling on her red lips.

"King Adrian," the queen says, tilting her head toward the dais, "forgive my tardiness, but it seems someone misplaced my invitation." She steps forward, and the crowd visibly cowers.

Our king stands, his lips pursed. From the corner of my eye, I spot Heath, head of the Lander Guard, skirting around the perimeter, whispering commands to his guards as he makes his way toward the queen.

"Queen Roma, this is…unexpected." His jaw ticks. "I assume you know what we're celebrating tonight?"

"Oh, so it wasn't misplaced, then?" Her laugh is light, but it makes my blood run cold.

When the king responds only by clenching his fists, she tuts and lets her gaze wander, spotting the prince standing in front of his bride in the center of the room. The prince shields the princess from the queen's view, his hand on the pommel of the sword at his hip.

"Well, shall I assume any negotiation we had is void?"

"Negotiations have been long over. Now, if you'll excuse us, we'd like to celebrate—"

"—well, since I'm here," the queen interrupts. A hush falls over the crowd. "I have something I'd like to show you and your lovely daughter. Call it a *reminder* of the past." Her voice sends shivers all the way to my toes.

She takes another step, but Heath appears in front of her, his guards flanking him. Four guards surround the princess in a practiced maneuver, ready to sweep her from the room.

The queen smirks but stays where she is.

"Leave us," the prince says, his voice low in warning. He steps toward the queen.

A condescending smile forms on the queen's face. "Prince Reid, it seems you're keen to defend this useless, insignificant kingdom already." She clicks her tongue, and with one graceful sweep of her hand, she disappears in a cloud of darkness, then reappears in the middle of the room.

The crowd shrinks away as she stands face to face with the prince. "What a waste of power." She sneers, and one long, gloved finger trails under his chin. He stiffens, visibly restraining himself.

She takes a step back to address the room, rolling up the long sleeves of her cloak. From an inner pocket, she pulls out a single tarot card.

The room falls silent; we all know which one it is.

It's the *Death* card.

A former fortune teller, her identity lies with using tarot cards to navigate the future.

She turns her gaze to where the princess stands, barely visible behind her guards as she twirls the card in her hand. The card shows a raven perched on a human skull with a crescent moon behind it.

The king's voice thunders across the room. "Is that a threat?"

Heath unsheathes his sword and his guards follow suit.

"Oh, Adrian," the queen croons. "I hope the wedding invitation gets tome this time. It's in two weeks, isn't it? I'll be there. You can count on it."

Without warning, she lifts her hands and aims at the princess. Curling tendrils of shadowed fog race through the air, undeterred by the guard's slashing swords. Dulci screams and the king's fury echoes off the walls. The air crackles and the queen's eyes light with malice.

"Kneel to me, or your princess will die."

Heath launches himself at her, his sword raised as his guards close in. Despite a well-aimed strike to her chest, the sword passes through. The shadows dissipate.

My heart sinks.

Lander is no longer safe against our greatest enemy.

Chapter 1

The moon is out tonight, but so are the shadows. They're different from regular shadows. They're not the ones cast by a cluster of trees or the distorted shape of the exterior stone wall. I mean the ones that move, that slither and slink in the night. It's like they have a mind of their own. Ones like those from the deadly, ruthless queen who threatened my kingdom only a few days ago.

I see them every night now, a complex web of spindly fingered tendrils that slither in different directions. They cover the entire beach and disappear at dawn.

Are these from the queen herself?

I walk the perimeter ward first before wandering the beach to observe the shadows. I keep hoping to find a central location where they're all coming from, but it's like trying to follow a single string in a tangled heap of yarn the size of the castle.

It's maddening trying to guard the kingdom from something I can't catch or destroy. Plus, it's invisible to all other mortals.

They don't see the threat at all and they perceive only what they can see.

Which is why I'm out here alone, sneaking under my sister's nose to investigate. She'd kill me if she knew I was out here following them.

I'm still a mortal, training to be a *Keeper of the Wards*, a member of a secret society within the Lander guard. We can wield magic through our keeper rings, and we're tasked with protecting the mortal crown, something we've already failed to do.

I inherited the title and a ring, along with my sister, but I haven't earned my magic yet. Once I prove my loyalty, I'll unlock the keeper magic within my ring and earn my keeper status. Then I will belong to something meaningful, and I can keep the princess safe.

Until then, I am powerless. I am no one. I belong nowhere.

And time is not on my side. How am I going to earn my place among the keepers when our enemy is on our doorstep, threatening the princess?

Sweat beads on my forehead despite a chill in the evening air. I've circled the beach twice already, careful not to step on the shadows. As I suspected, there's not a single blemish on Ambrose's ward. The absence of a tear or a hole does nothing to assuage my worry. The shadows are still getting in somehow. But how?

I need to abandon my effort if I'm going to show up for my responsibilities tonight, even if it's only observing, not casting. Tonight, Ambrose is my guard partner—the other keeper that my sister, Elyse, and I grew up with—who smashed my heart into a thousand pieces.

It was a year ago, and that's ancient history, right?

Still, he's not my favorite person to share a shift with.

I'm careful not to slip on the rocky outcrop as I traverse above the water's edge. One misstep and I'll tumble into the cold, dark water of the bay. Just a few more steps, and I'll reach the glamoured alcove only the keepers can access. It's on the exterior wall surrounding the beach encompassing Lander. On the other side of the wall is a dirt path through the grassy dunes to the village of Lark's End, and to the castle. Our kingdom is small, it's a spoon-shaped island connected to the mainland by a jetty.

The night in the ballroom plays on repeat in my head as I reach the exterior wall. I follow the strongest ribbon-like shadow as it moves past me like water flowing down a river. When it reaches the stone wall, it separates into smaller sections and squeezes through the gaps in the stone.

Confused, I dart through the hidden alcove to watch it reform on the other side.

That's *not* good.

I retreat, stumbling back through the glamored alcove, my mind racing.

If the shadows can pass through the ward *and* the wall, could I have stopped the queen's threat even if I had access to keeper magic?

Why does the Queen of Azrea want Lander, anyway? She's already attacked once, twenty years ago; our land is forever marked by the barren patches along the island where nothing grows. Azrea and Lander had had a tenuous relationship at best, but now? Azrea is our greatest enemy.

We're small with meager resources and, most importantly, *mortal*, with an apparently faulty protection ward. My sister thinks it's just Queen Roma's pride that made us the target of her ire, that King Adrian chose to align with the other kingdom in the realm that could pose a threat to Azrea.

I shove my hands in my pockets and continue down the beach. Without warning, a shadowed tendril seizes my ankle in its icy grip and pulls. My ankle rolls and lodges in a gap between two rocks. I lurch forward, my knees landing hard on a jagged stone and so do my open palms.

When I lean down, the tendril lets go, recoiling back into a nearby bush. I wince, trying to yank my foot from where it's wedged.

This is what I get for losing focus.

A wave of pain washes over me, so I pivot instead to unlace my boot. With a sharp inhale, I gingerly pull my foot out. It throbs, and when I try to put any weight on it, a sharp pinch shoots up my leg.

I lift my head and let out a huff, wondering how the hell I'll make it to my shift in time. Ambrose will be grousing about it all night I'm sure.

Suddenly hating the idea, I hobble awkwardly up the shore. My thighs burn with exertion by the time I reach the cobblestones of the town roads. Turning down the nearest alley, I can tell where I am even before I see the sign for *The Whale & The Whisk*. The princess loves the cinnamon pecan buns here so I stop by often. As I lean against the white limestone facade of the building, I peer into the windows. During the day, the display shows golden, flaky pastries topped with berries or dusted with sugar, but now it reflects the darkening sky.

The town is mostly empty, Landerians tucked safely in their beds. I push a wayward curl of hair out of my eyes and curse the distance to the guest house we refer to as the *Carriage House*. It's one of several guest accommodations on the castle grounds, a rarely used converted carriage storage building. It's also the least likely place on the grounds where Princess Dulci would be, which is why we've been hiding her there every night since that disastrous ball. We can't take any chances with Azreans getting that close again.

Elyse convinced the king to let us cast an illusion and escort the princess out of the castle each night. That's a feat because only Heath knows, not even the rest of the guards know.

But to me, it's not enough. I want to know how and why the shadows appeared, and I won't rest until I figure it out.

THE QUEEN'S CARD

In the meantime, Prince Reid left for Brevalin immediately after the incident. I overheard Heath saying the prince promised to speak to his father, King Baylor, about sending soldiers to secure Lander Castle for the wedding. However, there has been no word yet. The silence is less than reassuring.

Footsteps just ahead catch my attention. Under the soft glow of the streetlamps, I see a flash of a cobalt uniform that mirrors mine. I whistle sharply and the figure turns.

I know exactly who it is before I even see his face. No other guard is built like Taryn; he has broad shoulders and is impossibly tall. He lingers in the corner of every room he walks into, silent and scowling, which he's doing now. When he sees me, I wave. He lumbers over, clearly displeased to interact with me.

"Taryn, have you seen Ambrose? My ankle, it's—"

"Mira, there you are!" Ambrose appears around the corner. We both turn to see him bob into view. His long, lean legs eat up the distance between us in a few strides. Dirt flecks his blue uniform, smudging Lander's St. James' family crest of a deer on his lapel. His brown hair, a bit too long on the top, tousles in the wind. I fight back the unwanted urge to run my fingers through it.

"You're late. What happened?" He takes a step closer, and I flush when I smell leather and the damp earth. *His* scent.

His eyes finally land on my bootless foot.

"I rolled it," I admit. The creepy shadows tripped me, but I'm not about to admit that.

He sighs. "Alright, come on." He leans down and, without warning, lifts me off my feet and into his arms.

My heart races at the sudden closeness, but if he feels anything like I do right now, he doesn't show it.

He's all business now.

I feel the tell-tale sign of his magic as a calming, tingling sensation washes over my foot. It's as if I just stepped into a cool stream. I wiggle my bare toes and let out a sigh, relaxing in his hold.

"Where's your other boot?" Ambrose asks.

"It's on the beach."

Ambrose turns to Taryn. "Can you retrieve it for me?"

Taryn doesn't answer but stalks off toward the beach, eager, I'm sure, to be away from us. We take off toward the castle grounds, and although I'm no longer injured, I still sense that he adjusts the rhythm of his gait to avoid jostling me.

Suddenly, I feel sheepish about indulging in the closeness.

"I can walk from here," I mumble half-heartedly.

"Don't be ridiculous," he says, his voice a low rumble. "You're missing a shoe."

I open my mouth to argue, but nothing comes out. Instead, I just stare at his profile, fixated on the familiar; the tiny scar an inch from his ear from when we once fell through brambles, and his slightly crooked nose.

"Were you doing what I *think* you were doing?" he says, his voice low.

I chew on the inside of my lip. I can't admit that I went down to look at the shadows, especially after Elyse specifically told me *not* to. I don't want to tell him that I'm examining his handiwork on our ward, either.

"I needed some fresh air," I say instead, which isn't *really* a lie.

"Mmhmm," he says, unconvinced.

Desperate to deflect, I blurt the first thing that comes to mind.

"Doesn't it bother you that we never found out how the queen got through the ward?"

The weight of that statement falls heavy between us. What I want to ask is, *doesn't it bother you that we can't do anything to stop her?*

THE QUEEN'S CARD

He grumbles, and another long moment passes. "Of course it does," He finally says, "but we don't have time to dwell on it right now."

I bristle in his arms. I used to appreciate his bluntness. Now it grates on me.

"But what if they can still get in? What if they try again?"

He sighs. "If they do, then we'll stop them before they get anywhere near the princess. *That's* our job right now."

The rest of the sentence remains unsaid: we must keep the princess safe at all costs, even if it means the rest of Lander is at risk.

"Besides," he continues, "it's not like there's a shortage of guards. They have to be good for something."

I snort and he chuckles, though the reprieve in humor is short lived.

I hate the idea that Azreans could be here right now, lying in wait to strike again.

"I just have a bad feeling about it," I concede, deciding that bickering with Ambrose won't get me very far.

He nods. "I know. We all do."

I take a deep breath and instead focus on the dark outlines of the tree canopies we pass and the sound of the waves crashing along the rocks.

We stay silent, lost in our thoughts.

***

We wind up the path leading to the castle grounds, the sprawling town behind us. The manicured path to the Carriage House sits right along the edge of a slow-moving stream, the cool, clear water knee-deep.

When the structure comes into view, Ambrose gently sets me down.

"Can you stand?"

I nod, testing my weight on my newly healed ankle. It's still tender but I can put weight on it. He nods and turns toward the building, raising his hands.

I watch in envy as a dark orange ribbons of magic flows from his fingers in a small but steady stream. Rather than touching the building, it forms an outline around it, encasing it in a faint, glowing bubble. I imagine summoning magic must feel powerful.

His task tonight is specific: maintain a protective ward over the Carriage House that hides the princess's presence. I'm also guarding her overnight, but I'm not allowed to do it alone. I have to have Elyse or Ambrose with me.

"She should be here soon," Ambrose says, dropping his arms at his sides.

I nod but don't meet his gaze. Instead I turn and walk along the stream that flows nearby. This spot is the respite I didn't know I needed, a place of calm to quiet my frazzled nerves. I live in a comfortable enough room at the castle as a keeper, much more comfortable than the other guards, but I prefer the seclusion of here, it's serene.

I sit on the rough-hewn stone ledge along the perimeter of the stream, watching the water flow lazily past me. I take off my only remaining boot and dip my feet in. The water is like a soothing balm, and I relax, soaking up the moonlight.

I twist the ring on my index finger absently. It's a simple gold band, plain except for the rune symbol for *protection* inscribed on the inside.

It's the symbol for keeper magic; our duty to protect.

Soft purple petals from the wisteria blossoms that grow along the wall behind me float past, a few sticking to my legs.

THE QUEEN'S CARD

We just have to survive until the royal wedding. And even when that day comes, we have to keep the princess alive. Who knows what tricks Queen Roma will employ to keep the princess from saying *I do*?

Chapter 2

We should move the wedding to Brevalin. I had the idea last night. It solves all our problems. Queen Roma expects us to host the wedding in Lander, and we already know she slipped through our wards. She could do it again. Having it elsewhere gives us the element of surprise and a much stronger army.

We may not know how the queen plans to hurt her, but this would help keep the princess safe.

If the king agrees, could it be enough to save Dulci and earn me keeper magic?

The sun warms my back as I traverse the cobbled stone path with both boots—Taryn eventually appeared with my abandoned boot last night. I wind through the gardens behind the Carriage House. It's the scenic route to the castle, which allows me enough time to rehearse my pitch to my sister. She's the keeper's leader, so the king defers to her.

Gulls swoop and dive above me, floating on the sea breeze. As I get closer to the castle, the stomp of hooves and shouting reaches my ears.

I take off, leaving my quiet solitude behind. When I emerge from the brambles and onto the main road, it's to a flurry of activity; a half a dozen carriages in a procession amble toward the front gates. Large green fronds poke out from one of the carriage windows. It must be the decorations for the wedding.

I follow them, though at a distance. I have to squint against the sunlight gleaming off the wrought-iron gate. The air feels colder up here at the highest point on the island. Higher still are the battlements where the roving guards nod to let me in. I watch each carriage searched and approved as I dash through the lush courtyard just inside the walls. I pass the perfectly sculpted topiaries and shrubs, colorful flowers, and swaying willow trees my sister and I used to hide in.

I love Lander Castle, with its coral-tinted limestone facade and seahorse-shaped hand pulls at the massive oak front door. It fits within the nature surrounding it, like a seashell found on shore. The foyer is grand and taller than the trees outside, spanning several floors with a dome-shaped ceiling. Massive stained-glass windows reflect a kaleidoscope of colors across the floor. My gaze wanders to the intricate chandelier above me where clusters of stringed seashells and pearls sway and tinkle like bells when the wind catches them.

But the lights don't catch my eye today, and I don't linger in case I get caught in the sea of servants swarming each carriage, bringing in large blue vases, sparkling baubles, and giant candles.

I take the corridor to the left of the main staircase. It leads to the guard tower, where my sister should be. The higher I climb the rough stone steps, the quieter it is and the cooler the air, though my heart beats loudly in my ears. In my rush, I haven't even considered how I'll tell her. I've always struggled with speaking eloquently, so I will opt for directness.

We should move the wedding to Brevalin. We can use the element of surprise and the might of their army. If you agree, you can take credit for the idea.

I'll leave that last part out.

The wind whips my hair wildly when I emerge at the top, where the open-air corridor leads across a battlement to the tower. I pause and grip the parapet, my stomach swooping uncontrollably. It's several floors above the ground floor, a long way to fall.

When a familiar pair of guards catch my eye, I shout across to them. "Is Elyse here?"

They stare at me but don't reply. The taller of the two, a man with a thin mustache, wrinkles his nose before shaking his head.

That's not surprising. I trust them about as much as they trust me.

But on the bright side, at least I don't have to traverse the walkway. I don't care for heights. Suddenly directionless, I turn back the way I came, pausing in the doorway to the interior stairs. I stop and allow myself a moment to take in the view.

It's a clear day, so I can see the kingdom blanketed in forest across the bay to the northwest, Brevalin. Generations of magical families call *Bayfe*, the continent made up of our three kingdoms, home, though a sordid history of betrayal and manipulation long since drove a wedge between our kingdoms.

We're closed off from the others and know next to nothing of how the other kingdoms live. Travel between the kingdoms is rare with the mounting tension caused by Queen Roma's rise to power. The other kingdom's culture is a mystery to us.

We know Brevalin has green magic, and Azrea uses shadow magic. It makes Lander the only mortal, non-magic kingdom. Our king claims Brevalin sees our alliance as just what they need to tip the scales in their favor.

But it doesn't matter why they agreed. What matters is that they did.

We need their protection.

My eyes linger on the jetty connecting us to the mainland; the other kingdoms. It reminds me how small we are. In fact, the jetty was only a sliver of an entire section of our island lost in a battle with Azrea years ago. That, along with the pock-marked landscape leading to Lark's End where her shadow magic touched our soil, are the scars we bear of their might, and their cruelty.

Until that point, Lander kept to itself; a closely guarded kingdom that needed no magic to function. We have survived years of failed attempts at occupation and enemy rule. Even though our mortal kings have taken pride in our continued independence without the benefit of magic, ironically enough, they have had *our* magic, keeper magic, to protect them all along.

And as a Landerian, it's something I'm honored to do. I want to make my king and myself proud.

Azrea, the kingdom to the southeast, is the most dangerous kingdom of all. The same dark fog I saw at the party hangs around the mountain peak, only adding to the ominous, eerie emotions it evokes.

The longer I stand here, the more bravado and energy seep out of me, so I turn and wind down the staircase, letting my feet take me back to my room. These halls are so familiar that I don't need to consciously navigate them, so I let my mind wander.

I'm about to reach the corridor to my room when someone turns the corner so sharply that I jump back in alarm.

"Heath?"

The gruff man huffs in annoyance, his crisp blue uniform a little too tight around the shoulders. As he's Lander's Head Guard and King Adrian's Second in Command, he is one of the few in the king's circle that knows of the keepers.

"Watch where you're going, would you?" He veers around me.

I know I should run it through my sister first, but the words tumble out before I can stop them.

"We should have the wedding in Brevalin," I blurt.

He stops mid-stride and turns to face me. "What?"

"If we do, then the ceremony will be far away from the queen's sight. She'll never suspect it and Brevalin's army can assist in protection."

He appraises me briefly before replying, perhaps deciding whether I'm worth responding to.

"No," he says flatly. He turns on his heel, clearly done with this interaction.

"Why not?" Panic within me rises. "We never found out how the queen got through the wards. This is a good plan—"

"It's a foolish plan that depends entirely on another kingdom's security. I refuse to let us be at the mercy of Brevalin until they sign the alliance. At least here we have control."

He stalks off.

"Wait!" I call, but he disappears around the corner before I get the chance to point out that we don't have control *here*.

I continue toward my room, deflated. I knew he wouldn't take me seriously and I shouldn't have said anything. Maybe I should have let my sister ask the king.

I pause with my hand on the doorknob, hating the idea of sulking alone; it feels like accepting failure. And besides, I'm not tired despite staying up all night.

The best way around it is through it. That's what our mother used to say.

I just need to think of another one. I push the thought of my sister's ire from my mind and cycle through every practical option, along with some of the impractical ones. What are the chances I'd be able to go in front of the king?

I shake my head, dismissing that insane idea.

When I feel overwhelmed, like right now, I go for a run. Dane, Lander's Head Scholar, suggested it, and I hated it initially, but running helps me clear my head. It forces me to steady my breathing and focus on the cadence of my steps, not the overwhelming anxiety I constantly try to shove down.

After a hasty snack and an outfit change, I take off from the front steps, careful to dodge the massive piles left from unpacking the supply carriages. I run toward the delicately carved stone path around the rose garden. Moving feels good. My foot is tight from last night's injury but after a few minutes, it stretches out.

I run past the stables, the greenhouse, and the corridors to the interior courtyard, where groundskeepers trim the hedges surrounding a fountain decorated in vibrant blue and white shells.

By the time I finish my second lap, the pile of decor has dwindled. I stop to catch my breath when I spot Ambrose striding toward the stables with a cylindrical case strapped to his back.

Those are for maps. Where is he going with that?

I wipe the sweat from my brow, the sun now high in the sky.

"Good day for a run."

I whirl around and see Dane squinting at me in the sunlight.

Dane is the only one in the kingdom remotely qualified to give the three of us guidance on our magic. It's all theoretical, as he's not a keeper, but without his research, advice, and an unusual amount of patience, we wouldn't have a clue how keeper magic works. I've already tried to ask him what I need to do to earn my magic, but he is as elusive as the others. He's Ambrose's father, but he's also the closest thing Elyse and I have to a father, too. Our mother was the only keeper in the last twenty years, but she died before she could mentor us in our new roles. I was young when she died. It hurts that I don't remember her smile or the sound of her voice, but there will always be a place in my heart where her memory lingers, even if it's no longer a tangible one.

He appears from behind me, putting his hands in the pockets of his faded green trousers. He smiles at me, the corners of his eyes crinkling.

"I'm following your advice," I say, exhaling and putting my hands on my hips.

"Well, I have excellent advice."

We both chuckle. My gaze lands back on Ambrose's retreating form. "What do you think he's up to?"

Dane shifts, standing a little straighter. I catch his eye and watch as a frown forms. He knows something.

"We're traveling to Brevalin tomorrow night," he says, sounding falsely casual, but I know him well enough to sense anxiety.

"Why?" I say evenly, though now it's my turn to sound false.

"To iron out logistics for after the wedding, where the princess will stay, schedules for travel, that sort of thing. Plus, we want to get a better look at the castle to determine future security."

"Oh," I pause, struggling to find the right words. Wouldn't the king want Ambrose to stay here to maintain our largest ward, the one that covers the entire island? "Don't we need to focus on surviving the wedding first?"

Dane frowns. "It's an order, Mira. I follow the king's wishes."

He makes a hasty retreat, knowing well enough that if he sticks around, I'll pepper him with more questions.

There's something he's not telling me. Why would the king prioritize this when an imminent threat is around the corner? We should be strategizing and preparing for all outcomes.

Then it occurs to me that maybe they are, they're just not including me. It shouldn't hurt as much as it does. If Ambrose knows, then our leader must be the one keeping me in the dark. And I know why.

I blow out a breath and head toward the front door. I've spent all morning tracking her down, but I'll keep trying until I find her.

Chapter 3

I can't find Elyse anywhere. She's not in her room, anywhere on the grounds, or in the scholar's tower, where she often has her nose stuck in a book. It must be a sister's instinct, since I have a knack for dodging her when I know she's mad at me.

Seeking a distraction, I look for the one person I shouldn't confide in but who excels at making the best of any situation: Princess Dulci.

Certain she'll be in her chambers now that it's daylight, I trudge up the stone steps to the west tower that's shrouded behind Elyse's protective ward.

When I arrive at the top of the stairs, I feel the magic; it's like walking through a silk curtain. I traverse the corridors and pass pockets of afternoon sun beaming through the windows. The princess's guards part when they see me, revealing the door to her rooms.

I tossed and turned last night worrying about her. I've known Princess Dulcinea my whole life. We used to play together as children, tracking dirt through the halls of the castle and hiding behind heavy curtains. I know my place, though; she's the princess, and I swore to protect her and her father. And though I can't admit it aloud, I consider her my closest friend. It's why it's so important that I prove myself. I care about the royal family; it's not just out of duty. I want to live up to their expectations of me.

I hover in front of the door and can see it's ajar. Dulci has a fondness for peonies, and her chambers reflect it. Soft pink carpets cover the otherwise cold stone floor, and the lavish four-poster bed boasts hand-stitched drapery meant to mimic hundreds of flower petals. There's always a soft, floral scent permeating the rooms.

She sits in her plush armchair, her legs tucked underneath her. Her blonde hair falls gracefully to one side, freshly brushed. She's staring out the giant window, the sunlight illuminating her face. Through her window, it's an unencumbered view of the bay and the sea beyond, along with the terracotta roofs of the cottages and shops in town. She looks distracted, and an embroidery hoop lies abandoned on her lap, the needle still held between two fingers.

"Hey, Dulce."

She startles, but beams at me. "Don't sneak up on me!"

I manage a small smile. "It's not my fault you're daydreaming."

She lets out a mock huff. When she unfurls herself from her chair and places her embroidery on the table, I glimpse the recent addition to her outfit. I've seen it up close, but it's still mesmerizing. A rose gold band with a pale pink diamond catches the sunlight. I feign momentary blindness.

"Watch where you shine that thing!" I tease.

She laughs, and it's like the tinkling of a bell.

"He did well, didn't he?" Her eyes crinkle in the corners.

I nod. "It's perfect for you. Almost as if you told the prince exactly what you wanted."

"It's better to tell him what I want than for him to fail trying to guess."

THE QUEEN'S CARD

Dulci is always direct about what she wants, and I admire that. It makes her far more formidable than the picture of a demure princess everyone expects her to be.

"Was he like you imagined?" The party was the first time they'd seen each other since childhood.

Her eyes light up. "Even better."

We both chuckle, but then fall into an uneasy silence as we continue to dance around the real subject troubling us.

It's an indescribable weight that hangs around us.

"Did you see the decorations that arrived this morning?" I ask.

She smiles, but it doesn't reach her eyes. "Right on time. I want the castle to be a forested wonderland by the time they finish."

That explains the fronds to mimic the lush, thick forests of Brevalin.

She pops a berry in her mouth from a bowl on the table between us. My eyes snag on a nearly full cup of tea. I recognize the metallic swirls of silver in the gray liquid.

"You're not drinking the *night bloom* tea." I point at it.

She makes a face at me. "Have you ever tasted it? It's horrible."

I purse my lips at her, unamused. "I'm sure, but you have to drink it."

She sighs and takes the cup, drinking it all in one gulp. She flourishes her hands as if for praise.

"It's for your own good." I shrug, not rising to the bait.

We brew the tea from night blooms found in the castle's *night garden*, a small greenhouse hidden in an inner courtyard. When Ferne, the castle healer, mixes it with her herbs, it forms an elixir to keep Dulci from succumbing to unwanted enchantments. In short, it's a precaution. I make a mental note to check in with Ferne about her stores and how soon she needs me to harvest more. She can harvest them herself, but it gives me something productive to do.

Dulci leans back in her chair. "I know," she concedes, letting her gaze wander to her balcony and the open air. "And so is spending every night in a loft that smells like hay."

I purse my lips. "I know it's not ideal, but we can't take the risk."

"It's just," she continues, the mask of lightheartedness finally slipping away, "the decorations, the food, it feels like it doesn't matter anymore. After the queen's threat..." she gazes back at me and blows out a breath. "I'll be lucky to get through the ceremony alive."

I reach over and grab her hand, giving it a reassuring squeeze. "You can't think like that! You *will* get married and secure the alliance. Everything's going to turn out alright."

She nods half-heartedly. "Why does she care about Lander, anyway?"

I watch as her eyes glaze over. I know exactly where her mind is going; back to that night.

I have no answer for her. The queen attempted a negotiation for Lander to become an extension of Azrea several times, but the king has always refused.

"I don't know," I finally say, "but we won't let her sabotage this anymore than she already has."

She nods, squeezing my hand back. "I'm glad you came to see me; you're the only one who's honest with me."

My heart tightens in my chest. I'm not being honest at all. Although I reassure her, I'm just as filled with doubt. But I can't let her see it. I'm not the one in genuine danger here; she is. I want to ask her if she fears the queen's impending threat, getting married, or the kingdom's future. But it's not my place, no matter how much I want to be close to her.

A shout coming from outside interrupts my thoughts. Dulci and I hear it simultaneously, and we bolt to the balcony for a better look. Two Lander guards in the courtyard below stride toward our balcony, where a handsome Brevalin servant lingers. He leans against a column where two ravens circle overhead.

We're too far away to hear the conversation, but a Lander guard touches the pommel of his sword threateningly.

"I didn't realize the prince left servants here to assist."

Dulci snorts. "Looks like that one's not assisting at all."

She turns and walks back in, settling back down on the couch. The Brevalin servant puts his hands up placatingly, and I notice for the first time how large he is. With a barrel chest, he seems much more suited as a guard or a soldier.

As if my thoughts conjure his attention, he lifts his gaze toward the balcony, tilting his head as if in curiosity. Unease creeps unbidden up my spine. He's looking right at me.

***

The green beans are soggy tonight. I stab one with a fork and hold it up. Exhaling, I eat it anyway, just for something to do. I move the vegetables around my plate, swirling them in watered-down gravy. I try to distract myself with the usual din of the hall. Silverware clangs against plates and tin cups tap against the wooden tables as conversations blur together.

I'm in the farthest corner of the dining hall from the door. Cobalt-clad guards fill the rest of the subterranean room, but I might as well be alone for all the attention they pay me. We don't train with them or live with them. They know *nothing* about the keepers, they just think we're entitled and aloof; hence Taryn's reaction to retrieving my shoe. To them, we're just advisors within the guard with a chip on our shoulders.

So, when Elyse keeps me in the dark about what she and Ambrose are doing, it makes being alone that much worse.

Apparently, I'm not worthy to be included.

When the door from the hall opens, my eyes snap to the newcomer. It's not Ambrose; he's probably still busy packing for his trip. I recognize that brown braid anywhere. It's my sister, finally making an appearance.

Elyse makes a beeline for our table, completely bypassing the food line. Her mouth is open to speak when she sits, but I beat her to it.

"Where have you been?" I snap, the entire day's worth of irritation bubbling over. I wave my fork around and gravy splatters onto the table.

"Me?" she says, incredulous, "I had things to do. And don't snap at me." She leans in, brushing her curly bangs away from her eyes. "You told Heath we should move the wedding?"

I swallow but nod. I knew the consequence of telling him first, and it's still worth it to me. "Yes, but I went to look for you first. I just ran into him."

"Well, he's furious. He gave me a piece of his mind." she hisses.

"At least I'm doing something!"

She opens her mouth to argue, but seems to think better of it. Instead, she sighs and rubs at her temples.

"Mira, you need to slow down. You don't always have to be *doing* something to make a difference. I swear your impulsiveness will give me a—"

"What does that even mean? Doing something—anything—is better than doing nothing." I hiss, frustration rising in me. "What would you rather I do while Ambrose is off on a secret mission and you're doing"—I wave my hands around, my fork long abandoned—"whatever it is you're doing? It's not like I'm included. I'm not *one* of you."

She purses her lips. "Of course you're one of us. You can see the shadows—"

"Yes, the only magic I'm granted is the ability to *see* threats I can do nothing about!"

She blows out a long breath. "It's not a secret mission."

"There's no way it's just to iron out logistics." I lean in, further lowering my voice. "Not with everything else going on. Why would the king risk Ambrose leaving Lander unless he's planning something?"

She frowns at me. A long, tense silence stretches between us.

She huffs. "If there's a plan, I don't know about it. The king needs the strongest caster with large-scale wards. I chose Ambrose; he's the obvious choice."

"But what about *our* ward?"

"I can cover it once he leaves."

There it is; I should have expected it.

This all boils down to magic, the one thing I can't bring to the table. They don't need me at all. Magic would be the only skill I can offer my kingdom.

And I don't have it.

"I know what you're thinking," her voice softens, like she's talking to a small child, "but magic isn't what makes you belong; you already do. We need you here. Stay alert and stop running around trying to stir things up. There's plenty you can do here…"

I stop listening and instead close my eyes and take a long, slow breath. There's no point in arguing anymore; I'm not one of them. I will never be one of them until I have magic.

I stand from the table and take a moment to study Elyse's features in the warm light. We share the slight upturn of our noses and the apples of our cheeks, something we both got from our mother. But that's where the similarities end. She has everything I want and don't have: access to magic, the king's respect, and some semblance of control over her own life.

She may be my sister, but she's also our leader; the only one the king listens to. She's the one who's holding me back and holding her success over my head. She could help me earn my place, but she doesn't want to.

Now I know better than to think she'd trust me to have the kingdom's best interest in mind when she thinks I'm just doing this to *stir things up*.

I turn to leave. When I hear her calling my name, I ignore it.

Chapter 4

The sun peeks just over the horizon, casting a pale pink haze across the grounds. My shift just started, so I'm roving between the scholar's tower and the king's wing, which means I can see the entire northern section of the castle.

I stay within the scholar's tower to avoid the other guards, and because it feels familiar. I spent most of my childhood among the shelves of delicate manuscripts and small wooden tables, where Dane's handful of scholars study the kingdom's history. And although I don't care for research, the company of books is preferable most days than trying to make stilted conversation with whoever else is on duty.

As our primary goal is to keep the kingdom safe, we maintain the protective ward around the island. Our work is secret; no Landerian even knows they exist within a strong, well-guarded bubble. It's dull work watching something that hardly moves save for the occasional shimmer from a strong breeze, making the edges appear like an iridescent soap bubble. But that's all I do, unless it's my night to guard the princess.

When the door to the scholar's tower opens, a familiar head of salt-and-pepper hair appears.

"Hey, Dane." My smile is genuine when he strides up to me, squeezing my shoulder.

"See anything interesting?" he says, following my gaze out the window.

I shake my head. "Nothing except watching them hack away at the hedges."

We both gaze toward the largest courtyard, where a groundskeeper shapes a topiary into a lion, the symbol for Brevalin.

He chuckles and so do I. Then puts his hands in his pockets and takes a step forward, pivoting to face me.

"I heard about your run-in with Heath yesterday."

I groan, bracing myself for a lecture.

"I need you to do something for me." He pauses, searching my gaze. "When we leave tonight, I need you to stop sneaking out to investigate the shadows on the beach." He gives me a knowing glance. "You know I know everything that goes on. Mira, we don't know how dangerous it is."

If Dane knows, then does Elyse know too? Why didn't she say anything about it last night?

I think about the way it yanked my ankle and tripped me, but I don't mention it.

I open my mouth to argue, but he continues, "And no more bothering Heath with your ideas. Your candor didn't impress the king."

I chew my lip, disappointment sinking in my stomach like a stone. It's the opposite reaction that I wanted from the king. I didn't think that suggesting other locations for the wedding or investigating a legitimate threat would earn a reprimand.

Was it because I went straight to Heath?

"Okay," I concede.

His green eyes soften. "Thanks Mira, I knew I could count on you."

***

Dusk settles over the castle by the time the party to Brevalin leaves. I spot four Lander guards below from the window in one of the inner corridors, already on their mounts. They wait impatiently for Ambrose to cinch his horse's saddlebags closed. After consulting with the guards at the gate, they finally ride through, disappearing down the jetty toward the mainland.

I chew my lip, my mind spinning. The rational part of me races through ideas, trying to grasp onto something tangible. There must be something else I can do, something else that proves my loyalty, something that won't backfire.

By now, the castle is quiet. Despite the glow of the sconces on the walls, shadows crowd the corners and creep their long fingers across the halls, eating up the space. Lost in my thoughts, I wander back to my room.

Maybe Ferne will have ideas on how to strengthen the night bloom tea for the princess.

I turn the corner and smack face first into a wall of dark green.

My feet slip out from under me, my heels grazing the floor as I fall backward. Suddenly, one strong arm grabs my hand, the other wraps around my back. Despite the assistance, I still brace for impact, squeezing my eyes shut. Any moment now, I expect to hit my head on the hard stone floor. When I don't, I open my eyes and my breath hitches.

It's him, the Brevalin servant. The one built like a soldier. And his face is inches from mine. Though shadows partially hide his features, his eyes are deep, fathomless pools of brown, appraising and assessing me. My gaze travels to his dark hair, the top is much longer than the sides. It looks so soft. Certain that my mouth is hanging open, I shut it.

He's holding me, suspended in the air a foot from the ground in a dramatic dip as if we're dancing. Butterflies flip in my stomach, suddenly awkwardly aware of how physically close I am to a stranger. But his attention is magnetic, and he smells like leather and freshly tilled soil, which is somehow the sexiest thing I've ever smelled.

He pulls me to my feet with surprising grace. With his broad shoulders, he towers over me. Once I'm steady, he drops his arms and steps back, his concern morphing into irritation.

"You should watch where you're going." His voice is low.

And just like that, the attraction evaporates.

"Me?" I huff. "What are *you* doing scurrying around?"

He narrows his eyes. "I don't scurry. Now, if you'll excuse me."

He steps around me, passing right under the glow of a sconce. When his features come into focus, a familiar feeling washes over me.

My chest seizes up, and an overwhelming sense of dread washes over me.

He's around the corner and out of sight before I finally realize who it is.

But it can't be, can it?

As I take off down the hall toward my sister's room, I know I'm right.

It's Queen of Azrea's Second in Command, known only as the *Raven*, the bird he can shift into, is notorious for being cunning and ruthless. He's loose in our castle and I won't let him stay.

THE QUEEN'S CARD

***

"There's no way," Elyse says, folding her arms over her chest. She didn't let me into her room, so now I'm forced to argue with her in the hallway.

"Elyse, I wouldn't tell you if I wasn't positive. It's him." I hiss. "I swear it is."

She raises an eyebrow, her expression dripping with condescension. I bristle.

"Mira," she blows out a breath, "I know you're upset at me for not including you, but—"

"—this has nothing to do with that!" I shout, all my pent-up fury and anger boiling over. "He's here! He's dressed as a Brevalin servant! Who knows what he's up to—"

"—what would possess the Raven to do that?" she hisses, matching my anger now. "The commander who rips out mortal hearts with his talons? And you're saying our wards didn't catch him? If, by some miracle it didn't, then any Lander guard worth their salt would have recognized him and caught him already!"

We both stand there, fuming.

"So, you really don't believe me?" I ask, my voice low.

She sighs dramatically. "I just think you're upset and hurt, and you want to feel like you can contribute. But I don't have time to indulge in this"—she gestures vaguely at me—"whatever this is."

"Fine, don't believe me." I spin on my heel and walk away. Hot tears fall, and I angrily swipe at them.

If she doesn't believe me, then I'll prove it. I know what I saw.

★★★

When I spot him again, the moon is high in the sky. He's loitering in one of the inner courtyards. Is he waiting for something, or someone? It's one of the last places I looked since I assumed he'd go for the armory or the king's chambers first. The other guards gave me strange looks when I stalked past, and I knew they'd never believe my discovery even if I told them. Now, they're nowhere to be found. Either they're oblivious, distracted, or he's somehow sneaking past them.

The night garden is in the farthest greenhouse from where I stand, on the opposite end of the courtyard from the princess's tower. It's not much to speak of: a small greenhouse no larger than one room, with barely enough space for two people to maneuver around the plants. I see him striding toward it, but he disappears behind the foliage surrounding the entrance.

I can't tell if he went in or not.

Anxiety and curiosity tug at me in equal measures.

Is this plan insane? Probably.

But I can't just ignore this threat, even if my sister does. She can't see him, not that she'd believe me long enough to even try.

This is my chance to prove my loyalty. It's my duty as a keeper. I'll report it to the king and earn my keeper magic.

I just need to get close enough to contain him. Maybe I can lock him in the greenhouse?

I take a few steps closer, squinting for any sign of movement.

Why is he here?

And what is he doing in the night garden?

As quietly as possible, I follow him, my feet padding softly on the plush grass. My heart thuds loudly in my ears when I peer in, but I see nothing except the outlines of plants.

I know this is reckless, and I don't have a plan if I confront him, but no one else is doing it.

Someone needs to stop him.

Taking a deep breath, I push the door open. The air is thick and warm inside, fragrant from the dozen species of flowers. Taking a tentative step, I pass the shrubs of gray night bloom lilies, no taller than my knees. I strain my ears to pick up any sound in the small space, but I hear nothing. I take another step, scanning the rows of pots littering the metal worktable with abandoned gardening tools.

Still nothing.

One more step, then I feel it. Terror snakes around my lungs and squeezes. I gasp, feeling the air move from a flutter of black wings behind me and footfalls in the dirt. I turn around and my heart drops.

An enormous figure appears in the greenhouse doorway, massive wings sprung from his shoulder blades. He comes right at me.

Instinctively, I back up, desperate to keep my distance. He's shed his stolen uniform, and most of his body is swathed in darkness. When his eyes find mine, it's like a cat cornering a mouse.

It's him, it's the Raven. I knew it!

I plant my feet. "Don't come any closer!"

It doesn't stop his advance.

I scan the room. Can I throw something to distract him, then dart for the door?

He lunges for me, and in the next instant, his massive, gloved hand covers my mouth. I stifle a scream as he turns me around, wrapping his arms around me and pinning me against his body. I swallow my fear, desperately wishing I thought this through.

I need to focus. I need a plan.

I can't bite through the gloves; they're way too thick. I kick backward, and I hit something. He grunts but he doesn't loosen his hold. He flaps his black wings, the whoosh of air whips errant strands of hair into my eyes.

The last thing I think of is Elyse. I wish she trusted me. I was right, after all, and I just stepped into the path of the most dangerous man in the kingdom.

My heart hammers in my chest and I struggle to breathe until my vision turns dark.

Chapter 5

A fire crackles nearby as I come to. My body feels impossibly heavy but warm, so I don't move. I could stay in my bed longer, letting the popping of embers lull me back to sleep. It's so calming, and the pillow beneath me is so soft. I try to shift, but there's a dull ache behind my eyes. It's an effort to move my head from side to side. Vaguely, I remember the sound of wings.

When did I hear that?

My mouth suddenly feels parched, so I wrangle my limbs to move. When I finally open my eyes, I see the flames in a hearth, but I don't have one in my room. I'm not in the castle.

I scramble off the bed. My legs tangle in the sheets, and I pitch sideways. I hit the bare wooden floor with a jarring thump, and pain radiates down my left side.

I clamber to my feet and blink several times, desperate for my eyes to focus. The room is small and sparsely adorned. A hearth takes up the entire opposite wall. There's a window with closed drapes to the right of the bed, and I see a door in the corner. I race to it, but it's locked. I jiggle the handle, each passing second more frantic than the next. Abandoning the door, I turn to the window and rip open the drapes. What I see makes my jaw drop.

I squint out into the setting sun. It's not what's the most frightening. I'm staring out into a sea of green foliage, canopies of unfamiliar trees. I look down. The drop is several stories high.

Sweat beads on my brow and in my palms. Without warning, everything comes back to me.

The Raven.

Oh, no.

If I'm not in the castle, then there's only one place he'd take me: back to Azrea, Queen Roma's kingdom.

I'm in enemy territory.

And Azrea is no place for a Landerian; mortals are no match for their shadow magic.

I scramble back, my legs hitting the bed. My heart pounds loudly in my head. I squeeze my eyes shut, recalling the moment he took me.

I was in the night garden. How did we get here and how do I get back home?

Uneasiness coils in my stomach. I turn back and scan the room again. I see the bed, the door, the fire, a small table, and my boots.

My boots!

Ignoring the uncomfortable thought of him taking them off in the first place, I rush to the fireplace and yank them on.

Looking down at myself, I'm wearing the same clothes I wore that night, specks of dirt still on my long-sleeved shirt and trousers.

I scan the fireplace, spotting a block of wood as thick as a book. It's warm, but it hasn't caught fire yet. If this is my only weapon, I could get a good swing in. I get to my feet and stride to the door. It takes a few good shoves and a well-aimed kick, but the door finally gives in and slams into the wall.

So much for a quiet exit.

I steel my nerves and lift the wood over my shoulder, darting out of the room. The cramped hallway is dark, but I follow the glow of another fire. I emerge into a sitting room with oversized leather chairs, one with a blanket draped over the headrest.

The other side of the room has a modest wooden table with a discarded plate and metal cup. No utensils, I frown. That would be too easy to slip into my pocket.

"A piece of wood, really?" Says a voice behind me. I jump back as he emerges from a doorway behind me, an apple in his hand.

I blink at him, stunned.

Hearing him speak is unnerving. After attacking and kidnapping me, I expected behavior akin to a feral animal, not human speech.

I don't answer, and he gestures to my makeshift weapon. I stand up a little straighter and grip the wood, itching to take a swing. Splinters dig into my palms.

He holds his hands up placatingly, an apple in one of them. He lowers the other slowly to pull something from the inner pocket of his jacket.

That's when I spot it. My ring. It's my ring.

I stare at my fingers, dumbfounded. In my haste, I didn't even realize it was missing.

I narrow my eyes. Did he steal it from me when I was unconscious?

He sees my eyes snap back to his. A smirk curls on his lips, and he takes a slow, languorous bite of the apple. The arrogance is astounding.

But I expected it from an Azrean, especially one that works for the queen.

They're all the same; wealthy, arrogant, and hate mortals.

My mind races, trying to calculate a way to snatch it out of his hand. He raises his brows as if baiting me to respond. When I don't, he finally breaks the silence.

"Were you looking for this?" He tosses it gently and catches it in his palm. I tense.

He has no right to touch it. It's mine and I'm taking it with me when I run.

I wind up and take a swing, but he steps back at the last second. Momentum tips me forward, so I drop the wood and lunge for him instead. He holds it easily out of my reach. I swat at it a few times, and I feel my cheeks reddening at his obvious amusement.

"Give—it—back!" I shout between swipes of my hand, but he's impossibly tall. I must look like a kitten with a string right now. Finally, I give up, swiftly retreating to snatch up the piece of wood and to get some distance between us, fury and embarrassment welling up inside me.

I stare daggers at him and the air loses the hint of playfulness. We both stand, staring at it each.

"Why did you take me?" I ask, my voice uneven and breathy.

"Because you're meddling in things that don't concern you."

"Your presence in Lander concerns me."

"Well," he says, pocketing my ring, "we're no longer *in* Lander."

I figured that out already.

"What are you going to do with me?" I ask, standing up a little taller.

"I thought about killing you," he says casually as he leans back on the wooden table, "but I settled on keeping you for leverage. You must be valuable to a mortal king."

I don't miss the subtle curling of his lips.

I stiffen. If he truly wanted me for leverage, then he picked the *worst* mortal to kidnap. I won't lay down and accept this turn of events; I'm getting back to Lander as soon as I make it to the front door.

I hate to leave my ring with him. It's part of me; part of my heritage. It makes me feel close to my mother.

But I'm limited on choices.

My eyes shoot to the door, trying to calculate if I can make it there before he grabs me. But he follows my gaze. He doesn't make a move to block the door, instead taking another indulgent bite of his apple.

"I wouldn't do that if I were you."

"What? *Not* try to escape when someone kidnaps you?"

He takes another bite, chewing slowly. His eyes rove over me as if he wants to memorize me. Heat rises to my cheeks.

"Believe me, it's much safer here than out there," he cocks his head toward the door.

I doubt it.

He pushes off from the table and takes a step toward me. I stumble back with the sudden movement. But when he stands before me, he doesn't attack. Unlucky for him, I don't wait to see what he's doing or why.

Thwack.

Lunging forward on my toes, I smack him across the face with a plank of wood. It cracks against his cheek and whips his head to the side. I turn and bolt for the door, dropping my weapon.

When I reach the door, I hear his growl. It makes the hairs on the back of my neck stand up. I turn back to face him, preparing for a blow, but he's leaning against the table, working his jaw. All traces of his casual demeanor are gone; now he looks venomous. The place where I hit him is bright red. We stare at each other for a long, tense moment.

"I'll take my chances." I swing the door open and dash into the night.

A moment later, my stomach feels like it lodges itself in my throat.

Because I'm free falling.

Out of a damn treehouse.

***

Everything hurts. I'm sprawled out on the forest floor, and I take several minutes to catch my breath, my lungs screaming for air.

Dense darkness covers the forest, obscuring the moon and the night sky. My mind conjures the terrifying shadows Queen Roma commanded.

Would I find them here in her forest?

Or worse, the goblin guards that follow her every command?

I know nothing of Azrea's terrain. Frustration prickles at me, cursing my lackluster education.

I focus instead on what I can hear and feel to quell my rising panic.

The wind whistles through trees. Something hard on the ground digs into my back. I shift a little and my shoulder blades ache. I must have landed on a tree root. But where my hand lands, the ground cover is spongy.

I let myself lay for a few more moments before I force myself up. My stomach rumbles in protest, and although I don't wish I was back in that house, I wish I thought to steal something that holds water. Or even that apple.

With nothing but slivers of moonlight to guide me, I slowly get up. I feel around until I find a tree trunk and use it to haul myself to my feet. When I look up, I see where I'd fallen from; the outline of the treehouse is barely discernible through the thick canopy. I don't estimate how far I dropped; I'm just lucky to be alive. I shouldn't be surprised that a man who can shift into a *bird* lives in a tree. I just need to put one foot in front of the other.

The best way around it is through it.

I take off at a grueling pace, pumping my arms in time with my legs, imagining I'm going for another run around Lander Castle. I have no sense of direction, but if I put distance between us, I consider it a win. I don't last long before my legs burn with the effort, so I slow down to walk. Adrenaline leaks out of me, and exhaustion takes its place.

Who knows how long I've been gone? Elyse is undoubtedly furious at me, but that's the least of my worries. What's going to happen if I can't make it back before the wedding?

I need to stop the queen from hurting Dulci. But right now, I need to wait until morning so that I can see where the hell I am. Then I can come up with some semblance of a plan to get back across the border into Lander.

I stop under a tree with thick branches at eye level. I grip the bark, my palms tender. The last thing I want to do is climb a tree but I can't risk falling asleep on the forest floor, where I could fall prey to anything walking by. Straining with the effort, I use gnarled knots in the trunk to hoist myself onto the branch. My limbs scream in protest, but I ascend into the tree's foliage. The higher I climb, the better I feel.

By now, the canopy must hide me well enough from anything below. I can barely see the ground. I wedge between a fork in two branches, looping my leg over. This way, I can at least lay back against the trunk and feel relatively secure. The effort leaves me winded and drained. I need to rest; then, I can figure everything else out.

Chapter 6

Raucous laughter jolts me awake. I swing precariously on my tree perch. Several pairs of footsteps echo in the night. When I look down, it confirms my nightmare. Half a dozen Azrean goblin guards walk just underneath my hiding place, making rude gestures that look a lot like ripping something apart.

My hand flies to my mouth to keep from screaming.

They're much more terrifying than I'd imagined. Large tusks protrude from bottom lips, and horned helmets sit atop each goblin's head. Their studded armor has sharp points, and while some carry torches to light the way, others have crude weapons to beat, bludgeon, or slice. I squeeze my eyes shut, willing myself to be smaller, to take up as little space as possible.

I just need to wait until they leave. If they don't hear me, then I can stay off their radar a little longer. That wish was short lived, though.

Soft rustling in the leaves right in front of me makes me gasp, then *he* appears on the branch in front of me. One eyebrow raised, he leans forward from his perch, closing the distance between us. I don't move; I have no room.

The rustling catches their attention, and one goblin bumps into another several feet from the tree. They all look up, scanning the trees until their gaze lands on the one I'm in.

The Raven catches my eye and looks furious.

"A bird," a goblin grumbles below.

"No, *bigger*." This goblin's voice is close; he stands just underneath me. He squints into the night, his dark eyes scanning my hiding place. My heart thuds in my ears, and for a moment, I think he can hear it. I bite down with such force that I taste blood.

Movement catches my eye. The Raven extends a hand to me. After a few moments, he wiggles his fingers in a *come here* motion. I shake my head.

Another goblin stands behind the first. They both stare up the tree. Could they see me? They all loiter under me, including the first that dismissed his companion.

The seconds stretch on, and I may pass out from fright when one of them tests the weight of the lowest branch and begins to climb.

No, no, no, no.

"Unless you want to see how fast they can climb, come with me," the Raven whispers over the excited grunting below.

"I'm not going anywhere with you," I hiss.

"Voices!" the climbing goblin shouts to his companions below.

I grit my teeth but say nothing, panicking as I watch the goblin climb higher. Searching the ground, I see no place for a safe landing, so instead I look up into the tree canopy. How high can I climb before he catches me?

I turn to meet the Raven's gaze again and shoot him another glare. Without him, I wouldn't be in this mess, but is following him my only option?

"I'm your only chance at getting out alive," he snaps. "They'll take you straight to the queen." I don't move and he purses his lips. "Come on," gestures again. Then he sighs, "I don't bite."

I wrinkle my nose in disgust, this time looking down. The climbing goblin is mere feet from me. His dark eyes meet mine, and he flashes his sharp teeth. He reaches out and grabs my ankle. "Got you," he shouts excitedly. I scramble up and kick wildly; his grip is bruising.

Suddenly, a sharp, high-pitched whistle from the Raven startles both myself and the goblin, enough that he lets go. He looks around, spots me, and lunges again.

"Last chance," the Raven hisses. "Come with me or face the queen."

Finally, I give in. Anything to get away from the goblins, but that means suddenly he's the lesser of two terrible fates. Black wings surround me, flapping wildly. Then we take off into the night.

★★★

I never thought I'd be so relieved to see the inside of this treehouse. But that thought only lasts a moment. When I get my bearings, I realize I'm tied to a chair at his dining table. I look down in horror to see the black tendrils of shadow holding me so tightly that I scarcely breathe.

Cabinets slam as I hear rummaging coming from the other room. Here appears a few moments later with a plate of rolls, cheese, and a handful of nuts and fruit.

Who brings snacks to an interrogation?

He releases one of my arms from the bruising grip but stays just out of my reach.

"Eat."

THE QUEEN'S CARD

I stare down at the plate but make no move to touch it. Why would he offer me food? Why would he think I'd trust him?

I shake my head. Of course, my stomach chooses this moment to growl loudly.

One brow lifts. He clearly hears my hunger, but he doesn't push it.

"I don't starve my guests," he says pointedly.

I bite back a retort. I'm not a guest.

Then he waves his hand lazily and a tendril of shadow binds my arm back to my side.

Dammit.

"So," he breaks the tension, "what did we learn about opening the front door and *scurrying* off into the night?"

I snort, the condescension grating on me. I can't hold back my irritation now. "There was no scurrying." I say. He has the nerve to use the same phrase I used when I found him stalking around the castle. "I fell out of your stupid tree."

He takes a roll from the plate then leans back in his chair so that the front two legs suspend midair. He watches me as he takes a bite.

Birds have no table manners.

"Then you should be more observant."

I blow out a breath, and an errant curl falls into my face. I desperately want to wipe it away with the back of my hand.

"We need to have a chat."

"About what?" I narrow my eyes.

He finishes a roll and helps himself to a piece of dried fruit.

"You're going to tell me where the entrance to the caves is." He leans back again to watch me.

This catches me off guard.

What caves?

I tilt my head, as if looking at him from a different angle would help me glean new insight.

"The caves in Lander." He drums his fingers on the table. "How do I get in?"

Does Lander even have any caves?

I can't decide if I should admit that I don't know or if I should bluff. Maybe I can try to negotiate a way out of this? I must take too long to answer because he slams his hand down on the table so hard it makes me flinch.

"Now!" he snaps. The shadow tendrils grip impossibly tighter and my lungs struggle under the pressure.

"I don't know what you're talking about!" I bite back, gasping for air.

"Don't play coy. It doesn't suit you," he says, narrowing his eyes.

"I'm not being coy." I really don't know.

"You work for the king, don't you?"

I say nothing.

He waves his fingers and a shadow tendril curls around my throat. I gulp as it slowly squeezes until I'm gasping for breath. I finally manage a small nod.

He loosens his tendril's hold on my throat just enough for me to take a shallow breath, but he's still appraising me.

His scrutiny sends prickles of discomfort down my spine. Suddenly desperate to redirect, I blurt, "How did you get through the wards?"

I can't tell if the misdirection works until I realize the bonds around my neck don't squeeze.

His lip curls into a smug smile. "I have my ways."

I resist an eye-roll.

He leans forward. "We could go back and forth all night, but you're *going* to help me. Here," he pulls my ring out from his pocket.

I lunge for it, but the bonds keep me from moving an inch.

"I'll make you a deal. You take me to the caves, and I'll give you your ring back."

"Why would I help you?" I say, still struggling against my bonds.

He dressed up as a Brevalin servant and stalked around the castle halls. He's already gotten away with more than enough.

"You want your ring back, don't you? The rest is none of your business."

"It is when our enemy breaks into our castle, and—" the realization hits me so suddenly that I forget to breathe. I know exactly where the shadow magic came from that night, and every night after. It was *him*, combing the beach for an entrance to these supposed caves.

That must mean he knows how the queen got through the wards. He's getting through them, too.

What other kinds of magic can he do?

I need to know how he did it so that I can keep him out. But I can't do that in my current state. I need to convince him I'm going to help him.

"Fine," I bite out, feigning defeat. "I'll help you find the caves if you give me back my ring."

Once I get my ring back, I'll let him take me back to Lander, where I can find Heath and Elyse. Elyse can cast a ward and Heath can detain him. Then I can go back to stopping the queen from making good on her threat.

And thank the saints he doesn't know what that ring means.

He leans in, the smell of coffee grounds and pine waft over. "That's better."

I blush furiously, for purely the unwarranted invasion of personal space. Not for the way he smells. Or the sudden intensity in his eyes. Because I pointedly ignore *that*.

The shadows that bind me to my chair loosen enough for him to grab my wrist before they tighten around my chest again. Before I can stop him, he rolls up my sleeve and sweeps his thumb across the inside of my forearm, just below my elbow. A shiver runs down my spine, then I feel a stab of white hot pain. I shriek and thrash, trying to jerk my arm back, but he holds it steadily. The burn intensifies for another agonizing moment before it subsides and he finally loosens his grip.

I look down, expecting to see an angry imprint of his fingers, swollen and burned, but it's so much worse. To my horror, a black mark appears, a small symbol of two interlocking crescent moons, their points facing opposite each other, twisted to create the letter x. It's barely larger than my thumbnail.

I swipe my branded arm at him, which he easily dodges.

"What did you do?" I yell, trying and failing to launch my entire body weight forward. I take a swing at his face again, but he grabs my wrist.

"It's a *shadow mark*," he says, forcing my arm down so that he can re-bind it. "It's to ensure that you keep up your end of the bargain."

Now that I'm once again tethered to the chair, I am forced to confront the magnitude of what he's just done.

What can he force me to do, or force me to be?

He's no longer just an enemy of my land; he's now *my* enemy. And he's just as dangerous as I heard he'd be. At least we're no longer dancing around the truth with his arrogance. He's showing his cards now.

What have I done?

"As promised," he says, waving his hand lazily. The shadow holding me dissipates and I take in greedy lungfuls of air. I hear the gentle *tink* of my ring when he puts it down on the table. Without looking at him, I snatch it and jam it onto my finger.

He stands and gives me one last look.

THE QUEEN'S CARD

"Get some sleep. We leave first thing in the morning. And don't think about running again." He points to my arm. "I'll know."

And with that, he strides across the living room and up a set of stairs, tugging on the sleeve of his tunic. So he must have a matching mark on his arm.

I can't move. I can't think, but I'm no longer tied to the chair. He just left me to my own devices in his house. I look down at the mark, tracing the delicate lines. So far, all he told me is that he could track me, but can it force me to bend to his will? I don't know what to do about it, but I can't just give up.

I need a plan. Forcing myself to move, I rise from the table and make a beeline for his kitchen. It's small, but upon further inspection, I find a canteen, which I promptly fill. The water from the carafe is cool.

It's past nightfall and I can't risk leaving again in the darkness. And I need sleep, just an hour or two. Tomorrow will come too soon. I need to be ready.

So many things can go wrong, but I can't think about that right now. I'm so exhausted and angry that I can barely think at all. All I can do is survive tonight.

Chapter 7

I awake to a storm outside. It's still dark, but the light pink hues of dawn appear through the trees. Damn, I slept longer than I intended to.

I locked myself in this room earlier tonight. I tried to calm down, but fury had begun anew every time I looked down at the mark on my arm. I had paced, alternating between plotting his murder and flinging myself out the window just to see what he would have done. To see what this mark would have forced me to do.

He's *marked* me.

I don't know what it means, but it doesn't matter. He's marked me as his to bend to his will.

When I finally laid down on the bed, sleep claimed me instantly.

But now I listen to the howling wind that sweeps rain across the window. If I step out into a downpour, I'll freeze before I make it home.

I know I'm not safe here, but at least I have my ring back. I spent more time last night than I'd like to admit pleading with it, trying to cast something, but nothing happened.

Would confronting our greatest enemy's second in command count as proving my loyalty? I let out a long breath, allowing one more moment of frustration before I force myself to move.

Sitting up is a chore, and my limbs scream in protest. I untangle and stretch, testing which parts of me hurt the most. So far, it's my back, sore from where I landed on a tree root. I breathe and lean against the headboard, the downy softness and warmth begging me for just another moment of sleep. But I can't give in.

A few hours ago, I'd convinced myself that he wouldn't murder me in my sleep because he needed me to lead him to the caves. But still I wedged a chair under the door to make me feel better. He had gotten through the ward; he had gotten close enough that he could have hurt Dulci or the king, even if finding the caves had preoccupied him.

When it comes to the Raven; it seems there is merit to the rumors of his ruthlessness. My mind wanders to the chatter in the castle. The rumors of his sharp talons that can rip and tear mortals apart. How else would he gain the respect of the entire realm?

I lift my hands and inspect them. Dirt cakes my fingernails, and my palms are tender and red, but I continue to stare as if magic would spring from it. I imagine ribbons of blue or green magic swirling and dancing, looping in the air as light as feathers. Elyse and Ambrose have different colored magic, maybe mine will too. I can still indulge in the fantasy. I can almost feel it.

But I know it's not real.

I run through my options. He can take me to Lander, but after witnessing his abilities, I know escaping is impossible. Did I truly expect to contact Elyse or Heath without him knowing? And I can't risk him going straight to the king or the princess and harming them.

If I run, I'd have to leave now. The rain will soak me to the bones in minutes. I don't know where I am in Azrea, how far it'll take to get to the border, or even which direction that is. And who knows what other dangers lurk here.

But he's planning to take me back tomorrow, which cuts out the need to navigate my own way home. I'd be able to find out how he got in and if I could miraculously escape, then I could finally fix the ward. Well, Elyse would have to fix the ward.

I could spend all day debating, but I need to decide one way or another. And I know one thing: I can't trust him, even if taking me home is in his best interest. I can't risk bringing an enemy to the king's front door.

I need to leave right now.

With a water canteen and a pocketful of nuts, I lace up my boots and grip the edge of the window. A gust of wind sprays me with rain. I peer over the edge and the ground looks much farther away. Now that I'm looking down, my stomach tightens with anxiety. But that's not the only thing I feel; a curious tugging pulls at me, as if to force me to stay inside. I cast it aside as just nerves. I sway a little, fear sinking its claws in me. Why couldn't his lair be on the ground?

The branches are slick and sway when the wind picks up. I shove down my panic and focus on what I need to do: reach the nearest limb and inch my body out of the window toward the tree trunk. Easy and not at all reckless.

I dry my hands on my pants and take a deep breath.

As a child, Elyse and I practically lived in the willow tree on the far side of the castle grounds. We'd spent hours hiding, playing in the low-hanging fronds, and climbing until we couldn't see the ground. This is like climbing that tree, except a lot more dangerous.

Without another thought, I lean over and grasp at the branch. It shakes under my grip, and a few leaves shed water droplets. I hoist myself onto the window ledge and shift my weight, grabbing the branch with my hands and leaning over. I inch as far as I can along the branch, then jump toward the tree trunk. My grip slips, and for a horrible moment, I think my fingers will give way, and I'll fall again. But I don't, and despite my fingers protesting, I hold on. I swing my legs and use the momentum to move closer to the trunk. I extend my foot, almost close enough to step into a knot protruding from the trunk.

I just need to focus. It's as easy as just reaching with my toe and—

He clears his throat. I scream and let go, the all too familiar rush of wind now whipping against me. How did he even get in my room? In a blur of black feathers, he leaps out my open window after me. For a moment, I'm suspended in free fall until I feel the grip of his strong arms. Dark wings flap. I never hit the ground.

When his wings unfold, I hit something hard. I topple backward into a chair with so much force that I teeter back on two chair legs. Waving my arms forces me forward, and my palms smack into a dining table.

"Stop jumping out of my cabin!" he shouts.

He sounds as angry as I am, but I'm the one here stuck against my will and unable to outrun him. He stalks toward the table with all the agility of a panther stalking its prey, his stare so intense that he looks one moment away from shifting and swiping his talons at me.

Tendrils of shadow cascade from his fingertips and curl around me, pulling me against the chair. Fury rolls off me at being restrained again.

How the hell did he know?

"The mark," he points at my arm.

Was that the tugging that I felt? Was it pulling me back to him?

He slams his hand down on the table, making me jump. I glare at him.

He opens his mouth to say something but seems to think better of it. Instead, he cracks his knuckles and sits.

"Why," he forces his voice to sound even, "did you run? I'm taking you back home."

I scoff. "I don't trust you. Why would I trust someone who hates mortals?"

He narrows his eyes at me. "Who said I hate mortals?"

"Everyone in Azrea hates mortals."

His jaw ticks but before he can reply, he suddenly doubles over. He grits his teeth and fists his hand on the table. The shadows binding me to the chair dissipate.

What is happening?

"Run," he says through a clenched jaw.

He doesn't need to tell me twice. This time I don't run to the door, instead I run across the living room and into a hallway. Before I make it to the room I'd woken up in, I hear a sharp crack. I whirl around, tucking myself into the shadows, and look back at him.

She emerges from a cyclone of darkness.

Chapter 8

She's here, in his treehouse. Queen Roma stands mere feet from where I stood moments ago. Her straight black hair is shiny and sleek, and it moves like silk when she turns her head to scan the room. Her eyes are dark and the thin lines of her eyebrows furrow in suppressed anger. I cup my hand over my mouth to suppress a scream. I don't even let myself breathe.

"Why aren't you in Lander?" she demands, peering down at him while he clutches his chest. "You know I hate *projecting*." She lifts her hand and wiggles blackened, shriveled fingers.

Oh, my god. What's wrong with her fingers?

"Needed—rest" he grunts, taking shallow breaths.

"So, you found the entrance to the caves and thought you'd take a break before reporting back to me?"

He shakes his head, remaining bowed.

"Since when do you need to be told twice?" she hisses.

"Perhaps he needs a break. He looks paler than usual," a low voice interjects.

Who is that?

The queen snaps her head back toward the kitchen, but there's no one else there.

"Quiet, Mirror!" she snaps, "unless you want me to remove your voice?"

The voice, wherever he is, doesn't reply.

Queen Roma turns back to the Raven, who averts his gaze.

"I'm sure I don't need to remind you what's at stake here." She leans down and puts one slender, blackened finger underneath his chin to tilt his face to meet hers. "You have three days to find the caves, or I'll take away the one thing you love."

With that, black shadows swirl at her feet and circle her. When they dissipate, she's gone.

Neither of us move or speak for a long time. When he finally unfurls from what was certainly a cramped position, he searches me out in the shadows. I don't mean to, but I let his gaze find mine. I don't want to see the suffering in his eyes, to see the sorrow there.

He's supposed to be nothing but pure malice and cruelty.

He's not supposed to be a victim, too.

★★★

I hide in the room he's put me in, desperate to be alone with my thoughts. His queen mentioned magic I don't understand; projecting. Maybe it's how she appeared in the treehouse. Is it also how she got through the wards?

Why did he hide me from his queen? The Raven must be contradicting his queen's wishes, but why?

THE QUEEN'S CARD

I've been pacing and processing all through the morning. The sun rises and hangs high in the sky by the time a knock on the door pulls me out of my thoughts.

When I don't answer, I hear him set something down just outside the closed door. I don't move; just because I saw a moment of vulnerability doesn't mean I think he's any less dangerous. I didn't hear him walk away, though I didn't hear him approach either. I wait another moment before tiptoeing to the door and throwing it open.

I look down to see a plate piled high with scrambled eggs, blueberries, and sausage that smells so good it makes my mouth water. I pick up the plate with both hands and realize he left me no utensils.

That's not surprising.

"I didn't poison it," he says gruffly.

I startle when I see him leaning against the opposite wall, his arms crossed. How long has he been standing there?

He stares for another moment before reaching over and grabbing a blueberry off my plate. He pops it in his mouth. "See? No poison. Just blueberries."

When my stomach growls, I relent, turning and kicking the door shut. He blocks the door with his foot and takes a tentative step inside, a fork in his hand.

"You're giving me a weapon?" I ask, my eyebrow raised.

"A fork," he amends. "Consider it a peace offering. No stabbing though. It's a house rule."

I gaze up, and I see a hint of amusement behind his deadpan expression.

I chew the inside of my lip. Unsure of my next meal, I snatch it. I'll need my strength. I cross the room but keep him in my sights. He stands at the threshold, his posture stiff. I place the plate on the wooden table next to the bed before turning to look at him.

"I don't know your name," he says, breaking the silence.

"Well, I know yours," I say. "Do you prefer Raven? Or—"

"Bael," he says curtly.

I nod. *Bael.* I chew my lip before revealing my name.

"Mira."

"Well, Mira, you're going to help me defy the queen."

I clench my fist around the fork. Did I hear that right? This is another step backward in my plan, and I've wasted enough time as it is.

"No," I say firmly, bracing myself to fight off his shadows.

"You know I can just make you," he says, cracking his knuckles impatiently.

I swallow but continue on.

"We had a deal, Bael." I lift my arm up to flash the ugly mark. "You need to honor it, unless fairies don't follow through with things they say they'll do!"

He scoffs. "You expect me to honor our bargain after you tried to run? I thought keepers had some kind of code that includes not ambushing and attacking unprovoked?"

"You kidnapped me!" I shout, and I'm on my feet, brandishing the fork, fury rising within me. That's until dread washes over me.

I tense up. He knows I'm a keeper?

He senses the sudden shift in me. When he smiles, it's all teeth. "I know what a keeper ring looks like."

My breaths come in short bursts. He knows about keepers. Does that mean that he knows I don't have magic?

My eyes dart to the window again.

I've underestimated him, and I don't know how to navigate this.

"Don't even think about it."

THE QUEEN'S CARD

I take a step toward the window. He raises a hand, and I brace myself to be crushed and constricted like before. When his shadows race across the room toward me, a large coil of it wrenches my arm forward. Tendrils like shadowed fingers pull the ring from off my finger. I watch it land in his palm.

"No!" I lunge forward, but smack into what feels like a wall.

He holds my ring between two fingers tauntingly.

"I'll make you another deal—"

"—No more deals!" I rage, pounding my fists against the shield, the fork from my hand clattering onto the floor.

"Fine, I'll amend our current one," he says. "I'll unlock the magic in this thing," he glances back at the ring, "if you help me retrieve something from the castle."

My fists drop to my side.

Did I hear that right?

He can't seriously know how to do that. No one knows except the king. And why would I trust him when he's the enemy?

He raises an eyebrow knowingly. "The rune is incomplete. That's why the ring has no magic."

"How do you...?"

"If you had keeper magic, you'd have attacked me with it by now."

My stomach drops like a stone. He's right. I would have. A keeper would only refrain from using magic against the enemy if they didn't have any.

I'm powerless and out of options.

"How?" I ask slowly.

He shakes his head. "Only if you agree."

"Fine," I purse my lips, wishing for magic more than anything in this moment.

A curious tingling erupts in my arm, exactly where the mark is. I look down at it warily.

"We're going to break into the castle and steal something."

Oh, no.

"You want me to steal from the Queen of Azrea?" I ask incredulously.

"It's not stealing if they don't belong to her."

"They?"

"She has...someone I love," he pauses, a range of emotions crossing his expression.

Fury.

Shame.

Determination.

I thought he was loyal to her, but is she controlling him instead?

The revelation is uncomfortable, so I try to cast it aside, along with the growing lump of worry in my throat. Whoever this is must be important enough for him to defy his queen.

"How?"

He doesn't answer. I try a new tactic.

"Where in the castle is she keeping them?"

"I can't tell you," he says. "Her coercion keeps me from speaking of them."

I remember the pain it brought him when she appeared in his treehouse. Is that what would happen if he spoke of them?

"That's not a lot to go on," I say slowly.

"I know that," he huffs, running his hand along his stubble.

My chest heaves as I try to take in a deep lungful of air. "Why should I trust you? You don't exactly have a record of being trustworthy."

"I don't claim to be trustworthy, but now you have just as much at stake as I do. And besides, helping me is for the good of all of Bayfe. The queen took someone whose life is worth mine tenfold."

"What does that mean?" I snap.

He ignores my question.

"We leave tonight, so you should eat." He points at the plate on the bedside table. "There's someone we need to see."

Chapter 9

The queen took someone whose life is worth mine tenfold. That's what he said before leaving me to my thoughts. I ate my fill and paced all afternoon until I decided it must be a lover who the queen took. It's hard to imagine him with a lover, but it's even harder to picture him with a family.

A low, simmering rage forms in my stomach at the mere thought of him. I hate that he gets to change the rules when it suits him, and that he knows more about my ring than I do.

My mind wanders back to the Azrean Queen and her blackened fingers. If I make it back to Lander, I need to tell Heath what I've learned. She must be projecting through our wards and it's clearly weakening her to do so.

I finally succumb to exhaustion and it's not until the sun dips below the horizon that I hear another knock on the door.

"Where are we going?" I grouse, though I don't care, as long as it means leaving this room. He leads me to the front door. When he opens it, a rush of cool air hits me.

He doesn't answer. Instead, he stands behind me and wraps his arms around me. I thrash in his hold immediately.

"Hold on."

That's all the warning I get before his massive wings emerge from his back and we pitch forward through the open door. I brace myself, remembering my recent fall.

Instead, we fly straight up through the treetops and emerge into the open night air, the stars blinking brightly.

Wind rushes past us, and his black feathers blur when his wings flap. I force my eyes open to get my bearings. Much like the first time we flew, my back is flush against his chest. I grip his muscular arms that hold me at the waist, adrenaline making my stomach somersault and my eyes water as the wind rushes past.

We leave behind the dense canopy of forest for the night sky, and I get an unobstructed view of Azrea, something I needed the two times I tried to escape on foot. The kingdom is vast, enough to make Lander feel even smaller. The thick forest thins as we soar along a cliff side, towering over deep, blackwater. Seeing the bay tugs at my heart, and I feel it: the call to home. It's in the rhythmic crashing of waves below and the smell of the air, salty from the ocean just beyond. Lander is close.

We fly south toward the harbor city of Perstow, the capital of Azrea that sprawls beneath rolling hills and rocky outcrops. Further south is the looming mountain range, with the largest known as the *Forbidden Mountain*. It's where Azrea Castle is located, where Queen Roma presides over her kingdom.

Instead I focus on the pockets of inky black waves as they lap against the shore. As we descend, I see boats gently rocking in the marina, while a few bob further out into the water.

As we near the shoreline, outlines of steep, black gables and tall chimneys race toward us. Rows of tall, slender buildings stand like thin, spindly fingers reaching for the heavens. Clusters of buildings that span city blocks bear pockmarked walls, and some walls have imploded.

Everything in this city has sharp edges, crooked lines and fractures. It's nothing like Lander's smooth architecture that mimics the waves of the sea.

But that's not what's so curious; a thick, dark fog nearly covers every cobblestone street. Like the shadows she cast the night of the party, these curling tendrils are everywhere, swirling and spreading. Pockets of light cast from streetlamps barely illuminate darkened storefront windows and darkened alleyways. I watch a shadowed figure stride purposefully down the street, kicking up the fog that swirls around his feet.

When Bael sets me down onto a quiet cobblestone road, I resist the urge to kick away the shadows that remind me so much of smoke, just to see the ground beneath me. Instead, I take a deep breath and a *giant* step away from him.

Everything here makes my insides churn as if we've stepped into an alternate universe, not just another kingdom across the water. It's as if someone painted a cityscape without ever seeing one; the details aren't quite right.

A shiver of discomfort runs down my spine. All the buildings tilt slightly, and the shadows they create are too long, stretched and exaggerated. It reminds me of the shadows that Bael used to tie me to a chair just yesterday.

Bael turns and appraises me, tucking his wings out of sight and putting his hands in his pockets.

"Not what you expected?" he asks, gesturing around.

I frown, wondering how cordial I need to be to keep up this facade of a temporary truce.

I decide to lean into it for now. Maybe I'll learn something I can use later.

THE QUEEN'S CARD

I squint down the street, taking in the shadowed buildings. Doors and windows are in various states of disrepair and covered in soot.

"No," I say truthfully. I expected the capital city to be large and crowded, but not rundown. "Isn't Azrea wealthy?" I had assumed that meant all Azrea.

He snorts derisively. "Hardly. Azrea deteriorated after the queen took over. They can hardly cast, so they're left to fend for themselves."

The click of Bael's shoes as he kicks up fog distracts me. He gestures for me to follow, and I take off after him, trying to match his brisk pace.

"Their shadow magic deteriorated?"

"*Air magic*," he corrects.

I blink at him, confused. "But I thought Azreans only had shadow magic?"

"You know nothing of Azrea, do you?"

I narrow my eyes at him and shove down my instinct to get defensive.

My expression makes him chuckle, though it's void of mirth. "Only the queen has shadow magic. Azreans had air magic until she took the throne. Now they just have a faded, weak version of it."

"So the shadows..."

"Are her own twisted brand of magic," he answers.

If he has shadow magic too, then it must be due to his association with his queen.

So how did she weaken her people, and why would she want to?

We round the corner of a building where a chip in the stone is as large as my head. Along the crumbling brick is the painting of a giant tarot card with a dancing skeleton. I stop to gape at it.

"What's this?" I ask, taking in the deep pools of black in the skeleton's eyes. One ivory, bony hand reaches toward the sky; its body arched as if dancing under the moonlight.

"The dancing skeleton? The artist took some creative liberties with the Death card."

I'd only seen the card when the queen showed the crowd the night she threatened Dulci.

"What does it mean?"

He smiles but it doesn't reach his eyes. "It represents the death of your old self, or the end of an era. It's the queen's favored card, so she's made it her symbol for Azrea."

I conjure an image of it from that night, but I struggle to remember what was on it.

"I think it's a reminder of the power she holds now," he continues. "It's the death of the old ways under her late husband. But this painter drew the skeleton dancing, rather than a raven on a skull."

When I blink up at him, he sighs. "This mural is for the *Night Waltz*."

I'm still lost. "The *what*?"

"It's the festival in autumn when the queen siphons magic from her people to fuel her own magic."

"How?" I frown.

"She casts a glamor for the crowds to indulge in, so that it's impossible to resist. It's like a one-night escape."

"So, the more they indulge, the more they feed her power?" I guess.

He nods.

So, that's how she does it. What kind of queen steals magic from her own people, then neglects them when their magic becomes weak?

It's like flies caught in a spider web.

"That's horrible." I chew on my lip.

He inclines his head. "The Night Waltz always is."

I turn to look at the mural again. "So why paint this? As a reminder of their suffering?"

THE QUEEN'S CARD

He turns to face it again, putting his hands in his pockets. "They see it as a symbol of hope. The *Danse Macabre* imagery—dancing skeletons leading us to our graves—is a symbol of the inevitability in death, that no matter your station, death will come for you. That means the queen, too."

Then it clicks. This is a subtle rebellion against their queen.

They're taking a symbol the queen uses to oppress them and showing that death comes for her, too.

I turn to look at him. I didn't miss the way he says *they*, not *we*. He doesn't see himself as one of them, does he? And he's certainly being forthcoming when sharing his disdain for his queen.

But maybe he doesn't see her as his queen. I mentally file all this new information to dissect later.

"I didn't know that Azreans lived like this," I say, more to myself than to him.

He nods, then we continue our walk in silence.

What else do Azreans have to do to survive their oppressive queen's reign? What else are they doing to rebel against her?

I hate to admit it, but maybe there's more to Azrea than I thought.

And if I know this little, then what about the rest of the realm? Keepers are supposed to know these things, aren't they?

The reality of it stings. I don't know because I'm not one, not yet.

There's so much I don't understand about the tension between the realms. Would there even be tension between the two fae realms if the Queen of Azrea wasn't driven by her own greed? Is that why she wants control of Brevalin, too? To tap into their magic?

When I turn my head, I see my reflection, albeit distorted, through the grimy window of a children's toy shop. Shadows hide most of my face, and I feel more like an interloper than ever.

Bael gestures for us to continue.

"You never told me where we're going," I say, shuffling to keep up with his long strides, needing to take two steps for each one of his.

"To see someone who can help."

"Who?" I prod.

"You're awfully chatty tonight." He lifts a brow at me.

I shrug, feigning genuine curiosity, which isn't far from the truth.

"The last person I want to go to with this," he finally answers. "Listen, you need to keep your guard up when we get there. And let me speak; we'll give him just enough context and nothing more."

Unease coils in my stomach like a snake waiting to strike. It sounds to me like we're walking right into danger. Who is more dangerous than him?

I nod but chew my lip as we follow the road until it veers left toward the harbor. We pass scattered groups of Azreans heading in the same direction as us. Most are men in dirty trousers and work boots, though we pass a curious group with a pair of finely dressed women escorted by men in sharp suit jackets, smoking cigars that mingle with the clouds of fog that swirl around them. They certainly stick out this close to the harbor. But no matter who passes us, they take one look at Bael and avert their gaze. Some give us such a wide berth that they dart out of the alleyway to let us pass. If the size of this city speaks to how large Azrea truly is, then Bael's influence is much farther-reaching than I ever realized.

So, who are we meeting who instills this type of wariness in Bael, if others regard Bael like this?

We continue walking, winding farther through the maze of streets. It's grimy in this neighborhood. A thick layer of soot covers everything, perhaps from warehouses nearby. He winds his way through crooked gaps between buildings, each alleyway getting darker and smaller.

THE QUEEN'S CARD

We emerge a few minutes later onto a nearly deserted street lined with dim streetlamps. Just beyond where we stand, the street opens up, a welcome relief from the tight alleyways. In front of me lies Perstow Bay, the blackwater merging with the night sky.

A long wooden dock connects the berths for docked merchant boats, some weathered and appearing piecemeal, all swaying rhythmically. I spot no less than a dozen goblin guards pacing up and down the dock, sneering at passersby.

Beyond them is a large vessel floating in the harbor, too far away from the harbor to swim to. Lights from the decks bob as people mingle on three separate decks. What kind of boat is that?

"That's where we're going," he says, finishing my thought. "*The Crimson Rose.*"

"What is it?"

"The biggest floating gambling den in Perstow Bay."

***

We don't traverse the docks to wait for a boat like the other gamblers. Instead, he leads me back into the shadows to crouch behind an office with large windows on the street corner. We watch the guards pass us, heading in the other direction. Bael turns and jerks his head toward the docks, and I follow, our breaths sharp in the night air. I squint beneath the flickering streetlamps to watch the guards as they shrink in the distance.

"I take it you don't want to stop for a chat?" I ask, tilting my head toward the goblins.

"My whereabouts are my business."

Bael nudges me toward a dock several feet from us, where a small queue of drunk partiers hover, waiting for a ride. Without a word, he pushes past them to the front of the line. A few of them grumble under their breath, but once they recognize Bael, they let us pass. Anxiously, we wait and I watch a man conjure a jacket for his companion with just the wave of his hand. It forms using the fog around our feet.

I can't stop staring; it's the first time I've seen Azrean air magic.

When the boat arrives, Bael doesn't wait for the ferryman to extend his hand. He steps in and turns to grip my hand, pulling me close. When the ferryman realizes who climbed into his boat, he nods and we take off, leaving the rest of the crowd on land. There's room for another half dozen passengers, but Bael clearly doesn't want eavesdroppers. I watch the docks shrink as the boat cuts through the waves, magically propelled. I grip the edges of the wooden bench as frigid water sprays over us and mist swirls around us.

When I turn my head to the distorted view of Lander, I let my mind indulge a ridiculous idea. I could jump right now and swim home. I'm not a strong swimmer, and the water is freezing, but it's so close. I'm sure Bael would dive in after me and haul me right back to the treehouse if his damn mark didn't yank me back first.

"You wouldn't survive it," Bael whispers in my ear. I look up to see him watching me closely. Is that obvious what I'm thinking?

Instead I ignore him and turn my attention to the large boat as we approach. Revelers cluster on the balconies, their laughter echoing. The bottom half of the boat is completely obscured by fog.

What do we need at an Azrean gambling den? I couldn't begin to guess.

Chapter 10

As we approach the den, excited energy radiates off the ship. When we get close enough, Bael stands. In one graceful movement, he steps onto the rocking wooden platform that floats beside the entrance. With feet planted, his hand grips mine while his other travels to my elbow, lifting me up and off the boat. My stomach lurches as my feet land on the walkway.

We walk down the gangway to the ship's deck. Large, stoic guards stationed on either side of a pair of double doors eye us until they recognize Bael. They nod before opening the doors, handing Bael a pair of black silken masquerade masks.

When the doors swing open, I cough as a cloud of brightly-colored smoke hits me in the face. It's everywhere and it's bursting with color; red puffs of smoke from fingertips touching a lover's face or green smoke curling around piles of coins in the middle of tables.

The chandelier swinging from the ceiling provides little light in such a large space. Onstage, a singer in a midnight blue dress serenades the room. Her voice is like velvet.

It's mesmerizing here: a dark room with bursts of color hidden away in a crowded city of darkness.

"Is this air magic?" I whisper.

He nods. "It's more like smoke, now."

Smoke magic?

"It's better than drawing from the fog outside."

"Why?"

He tilts his head, appraising me. "The fog outside is *her* magic. The more they pull from it, the more she can control them. So," he leans down, "they use smoke instead. It's easy to manipulate and it doesn't rely on her."

Before I can let that sink in, Bael holds out a mask. At first, I flinch.

"Do you want to draw more attention to us?"

I huff but allow him to put the mask on me. He's gentle as he pushes a few errant strands of hair before tying the fabric. I adjust it so that I can see through the eyeholes. I feel ridiculous, but he's right; everyone else is wearing one.

He leads me to a small booth in the corner. We sink into the low cushions, disappearing into the shadows.

I perch on the edge of the seat and he slides in next to me. It's the first time we're this close to each other without restraints, or in flight. I focus elsewhere to avoid overthinking our proximity.

The atmosphere is contagious; scantily clad women in silks make their rounds, flirting and encouraging the patrons to open their wallets. I can see why they retreat into the dark recesses of a gambling den; here, they finally have control. I want to look away, but I can't. It feels like I'm intruding on something intimate.

As a woman in gold drapes herself on the lap of a man holding a pair of cards; I gape. She lifts her hand and a goblet levitates above the man's head. He smiles and leans back, his mouth open. The goblet tips and

THE QUEEN'S CARD

pours wine directly into his mouth. When he finishes, he grips her closer to him. She giggles as he leans in, his tongue licking up the column of her throat.

My cheeks flush and suddenly I'm too hot. Desperate to look anywhere else, I watch as Bael leans over the table to grab two flutes of something bubbly off a passing tray.

When he puts one in my hand, I'm suddenly keenly aware of Bael's warm body brushing against mine. How did he get so close to me so fast? I drink it all just for something to do.

Several young men lean back in their chairs at a table nearby, whistling and eyeing the singer. The smoke from their cigars waft toward the ceiling. A pair of men in a shadowed corner speak in hushed tones, and I watch something change hands under the table.

A woman with long flowing hair joins them, sidling next to the man. He bristles for a moment until recognition crosses his face, then he drapes an arm lazily across her shoulders. What he doesn't catch—while he continues a conversation with his companion—is that the woman flicks her fingers and a folded bill from his jacket pocket soars toward her open palm. She tucks the stolen money into her cleavage.

All around me, people mingle and touch, using their magic uninhibited, away from their greedy queen. It feels that much more dangerous that I'm here with him, hidden in the dark.

Bael puts another drink in front of me and I'm relieved to find that it's water. Taking a sip, I watch the crowd again. I choke on my water when I feel Bael's piercing eyes inches from mine, amusement in his features.

My face turns pink as I put the drink back on the table. "So, what do we do now?" I whisper.

"Now, we wait," he says, leaning back and casually draping his arm around my shoulders. I tense up at the movement, but when other revelers notice our presence, namely his presence, I reluctantly lean into it. Only for now, only until we get out.

"So, what did you do?" He asks, his voice low in my ear.

"What?" I turn to look at him.

"You must have pissed off your king. Why else would he revoke your keeper magic?"

I feel my cheeks flush with embarrassment.

"I didn't piss him off," I snap. "I just haven't..." I trail off, realizing I had taken the bait. I purse my lips to keep from continuing.

"Ah," he says, taking a sip of his drink. "You're not a keeper yet." He tuts condescendingly. "That means you still have time to change your mind."

I bristle. "Why would I want to do that?"

He snorts in derision. "Why would you want to be one? They're self-righteous, ignorant, and dangerous, with no idea how their magic even works. A product of your despicable king."

My jaw drops. How dare he!

"Do not insult my king in front of me," I hiss. "And it's not like yours is any better! You *and* your queen are angry and hateful. Mortals don't deserve—"

"I didn't say I hated mortals, remember? I hate the mortal king."

This renders me speechless.

We sit in silence, stewing in our emotions. Why am I letting him upset me? It doesn't matter what he thinks. I need to refocus on why I'm here.

The longer I'm in Azrea, the more complicated the path back home becomes. But, despite this detour, I can still salvage it.

If this visit with *whoever* it is we're here to see can unlock my magic, then I'll use it to get back home, bargain or no bargain. And with my magic, I can stop the queen from fulfilling her threat.

THE QUEEN'S CARD

A tiny, nagging voice in the back of my head whispers that I shouldn't let temptation win. This isn't the way to go about finally getting my magic. There's a ceremony, after all, the act of receiving magic. But isn't stopping the queen's threat the real goal?

If this works, I can do just that; protect Dulci with keeper magic. It's a win-win, isn't it?

Guilt and indecision swirl around in my stomach, warring for my attention.

When Bael turns to me and grabs my hand, I jump at the contact.

"Come on, let's go." He yanks me up, not particularly gently.

We turn, traversing through the tables to the hallway behind the stage. The air is thicker here and I wrinkle my nose as I fall into step next to Bael. When we reach a large wooden door at the end of the hall, two guards materialize from the shadows. They stare us down and I fight the urge to turn and run, until they realize who's standing next to me. Bael clears his throat and after exchanging looks, the guards part to let us in.

We enter a surprisingly spacious room with a large window overlooking the black water. We stop just short of a pair of cracked and faded armchairs that sit across from a dark wooden desk. A giant ledger sits open, and a dark figure holds a quill. He has a sharp jawline beneath the shadows, dotted with stubble. Tan, lean arms flex as he runs his fingers down the page.

"Liam, you haven't changed a bit. Your nose is always in your ledger," Bael says.

The man behind the desk finally looks up. He and Bael stare at each other for a beat too long before a sly grin pulls at the man's lips. He walks around the desk to greet Bael. They briefly embrace, and the man grips the back of Bael's neck, gazing into his face like a brother.

Who is this man?

"Time is money. Haven't seen you in ages, Bael. Where have you been hiding?"

Before Bael can answer, the man turns to look at me. His eyes rove over me slowly, and nervous energy buzzes in my stomach at the intensity of his scrutiny.

"And who's this?" He cocks his eyebrow and turns back to Bael.

"A friend," Bael answers coolly.

"Does this friend have a name?" His voice is husky, like a dagger to the throat, dangerous and thrilling all at once.

Before I can reply, Bael answers for me. "We both know you don't care about pleasantries."

The man walks back behind his desk and picks up a cigar from the ashtray on his desk. As he leans back in his chair, he takes a long drag, blowing smoke rings. After a long moment, he puts the cigar down and rests his expensive looking leather shoes on the desk.

"You're wrong, my friend. Sit," he says, pointing to the armchairs across from him.

We both sink into the armchairs. I fidget with brass rivets along the leather of the arm. The room suddenly feels too small.

"So, where are you from?" he asks, swirling a finger lazily in the air. The smoke rings floating above our heads spin.

"Lander," Bael answers for me, his tone carefully detached.

This man notices it.

"From Lander? That's a surprise." His gaze lingers on Bael pointedly before turning back to me. "Now tell me, has our queen slithered her way in yet?"

I raise my eyebrows.

He snorts derisively when I don't respond. "I suppose she would have shouted it from the top of her ivory tower by now if she had. Good. *Divine right*, my ass."

THE QUEEN'S CARD

My jaw drops. He knows he's saying this in front of his queen's second in command, right? But when I look at Bael, his expression is carefully neutral.

My mind wanders at this man's words. Is that why the Queen of Azrea wants Lander, because she thinks she has a divine right to it? To rule mortals?

What does Liam know? He's clearly not a fan of his own queen, and from what I can tell, he's well connected in the Azrean underworld.

We're playing with fire.

I nod placatingly.

Bael steers the conversation back to the task at hand. After filling Liam in on the details, he places my ring on the desk between them. I struggle not to lurch forward and grab it.

"Until I found her," he gestures to me, "she'd been working for the Lander crown."

I chew my lip nervously, watching his explanation unfold.

"Oh?" Liam says, picking up my ring and rotating it slowly to examine it. "A magic wielder in Lander?" his eyes drink me in. "You must be a keeper, then?" he snorts derisively.

I swallow hard. Does everyone in Azrea know about keepers? We're supposed to be elusive and secret.

Rather than elaborating, he leans forward. "Why does this warrant my help?" he says, looking back to Bael.

"We need you to unlock the magic in her ring." Bael points to it.

"So, your precious king won't do it for you, then?" Liam smiles at me as he puts down my ring to steeple his fingers. He turns to Bael next, a taunting smile curling on his lips. "And this is something that the queen's favorite bird can't solve on his own?"

I brace myself for Bael to launch himself off the table at the insult, but he doesn't. Instead, he narrows his eyes, his jaw ticking.

"We came to you because you can get it done," he says, his voice gruff.

Liam lets the compliment settle between them, and the sacrifice to Bael's pride is clear. Liam smirks as he leans back in his chair, playing with a large ring on his middle finger.

"And you came to collect on the favor I owe you."

Bael nods, taking a measured breath. Out of sight, I wring my hands in my lap. What favor is he talking about?

"This is way more than what I owed you. You know how this works." Liam rolls up the sleeve of his right arm and holds it out.

"What do you want? Choose something that I can actually give you." Bael snaps, drumming his fingers on the armchair.

Liam smiles, his eyes alight. "I'll unlock the magic in her ring," he picks up my ring again, "if you get me *wraith blooms*."

Bael narrows his eyes, a tick in his jaw appears. "What makes you think I can give you that?"

There's clearly something I'm missing.

A slow smile curls on Liam's lips. "I think you'll find things are clearer when you go."

Bael clears his throat, bringing attention back to him. "Fine." He yanks up his sleeve. He grips Liam's arm across the table, and when their arms touch, they both grunt. After a long pause, they both let go. A thin black band forms on both of their arms. I catch several on Liam's arm; are those bargains that he has with others?

And what's a wraith bloom?

Bael gestures for me to stand.

"Looks like we're going to the *Theater of Souls*."

Chapter 11

"Who was he?" I ask as he pulls me back into the rocking boat. The water sprays mist on us as we take off toward the harbor docks.

"Someone we want on our side. He's itching for a fight with the queen," he says, rubbing his elbow where his mark hides under his sleeve.

I can see that now. Liam doesn't even try to hide his disdain for his queen, or my king for that matter.

My mind runs through the possibilities. Is he a gang leader or an assassin? If he operates out of a gambling den, he must be shady. So what does it mean now that Bael owes him?

What can Liam do that Bael can't?

We sit in silence, both replaying the interaction. This is *another* step back. Now we're stuck retrieving some flowers for him before he can unlock my magic. Frustration wells up inside me.

I suddenly hate being this close to Bael, stuck in the confines of this damn vessel. A sudden thought occurs to me.

"Can't you fly us across the water?"

83

He turns toward me, his eyes a dark pool.

"Liam maintains a ward around his den that I can't fly through."

He's powerful enough to maintain a ward, even in Azrea? That must be why we're coming to him for help.

I focus on the waves as they hit the hull of the boat and watch the dock come back into view.

After everything I've seen tonight, I allow myself to feel pity for Azreans. I already knew their queen was power-hungry, but I didn't know it was against her own people.

And Bael's role in all this isn't black and white. Before I met him, I thought I understood who I was dealing with: the queen's loyal second in command. Spending more time with him makes me less confident about what I thought I knew.

***

Once we're back on the docks, we retreat to an alley nearby. He launches off the ground and we take off into the night. The wind rushes past us, my heart beating even louder in my ears than the beating of his wings. We leave the lights and the smog of the city behind and head toward the shadowed landscape of the Forbidden Mountain.

Moonlight streaks across rolling fields and forested hills, except one hillside. We turn toward it, swathed in dense fog. I squint into the night, attempting to pick out any shapes in the void. As we hover, I catch sight of a shimmering pool of inky black water.

When we land, the ground is soft and plush under my boots. I turn to get my bearings, expecting to take in the sweeping view of the harbor city below, but I can barely see through the mist.

"Can you see anything?" He asks quietly.

I shake my head. "Nothing but the fog."

Everything about this feels wrong, but I force myself to stay calm. We have a job to do. It's eerily quiet, void of any nocturnal creatures. The only sound is the gentle lapping of dark water along a sodden shore I can barely see.

I feel Bael come to stand next to me. "Wraith Lake," he says.

"It's so dark here."

"It's the queen's magic."

I gulp, feeling my heart beating louder in my ears. Then I feel it; the low, vibrating hum of magic is like bees buzzing around a hive.

How much magic is the queen using here, and why?

"So, where are we?"

"This is the Theater of Souls. It's the most dangerous graveyard in Azrea."

"Dangerous? Since when are graveyards dangerous?" I attempt to wheel around to face him, but he gently grips my shoulders and turns me around, the lake now at our backs.

Instead of answering me, he asks, "Do you trust me?"

Once again, he's avoiding the answer to the question I've asked. Irritation prickles at me, but so does his warm breath in the shell of my ear. It sends a shiver down my spine.

No, I don't trust him, but what choice do I have?

"Just get me out of here in one piece," I whisper, as if speaking louder may awaken something around us that I certainly want to leave alone.

He points in a vague direction, since I can't discern anything in front of me. But when he waves his hand, the fog dissipates as if pulling back a thick velvet curtain. We're standing at the top of a hillside covered in wild grass.

That's when I see the remains of a long-abandoned amphitheater sprawled out below us. Grassy ledges are carved out of the surrounding hill in concentric half circles, and gravestones of various sizes and states of decay line up neatly like theater seats. In the middle, tall grass and forest vines weave around the stone pillars of an empty stage, the roof long since crumbled.

The dead now take over what once was surely a significant landmark. The air goes still as if the hillside is holding its breath, watching to see what we will do. It's like a thousand eyes are upon us. The vibrations of magic are suddenly so intense I can feel them in my chest.

I don't want to go anywhere near this place.

Bael gestures for me to follow him as we maneuver slowly down the slope. I fight every instinct to turn and run, but where would I go, back to the creepy lake? Either way, I need him to fly me out of here when we finish whatever we're doing.

"This used to be an amphitheater?" I ask, as a distraction.

He nods as he walks next to me. "They say a tragic accident started it all," he says as we walk around a row of headstones. "The actors playing lovers fell to their deaths during a performance. Strange occurrences started after that and rumors spread that their magic had seeped into the ground. Eventually, the amphitheater fell into disrepair. It stayed that way for years until the royal family repurposed it as a graveyard."

"This graveyard is for Azreans?"

"Not just *any* Azrean," he says. "Only the magically powerful."

I think back to what I saw in the gambling den. "What makes some Azreans more powerful than others?"

He pauses before replying. "Proximity to the royal family."

I frown, struggling to follow.

"The Azrean royal family possesses *arcana* magic, the source of all magic in Bayfe. According to lore, it stems from an enchanted deck of cards, and two cards were given to each ruler," he continues.

"Azrea and Brevalin?" I guess.

He nods. "Each royal family has a duty to provide their kingdom with magic, in Azrea's case, air magic."

I frown. "So the royal family fuels their own people's power?"

He nods. "It's what the Night Waltz was originally for, the annual festival to replenish air magic for the Azreans."

"What did they use air magic for?"

"Mostly what you saw in the gambling den, levitation. But they used to possess speed and strength. Now," he looks off into the distance, "most things are now done either manually or with smoke."

Then it clicks. "When Queen Roma took over, she did the opposite."

"Yes. It's part of what makes her so…" he trails off.

"Hated?" I ask.

He nods.

"So, when the king died," I start, trying to put the pieces together.

"His arcana magic died with him. It can only pass to the next ruler by blood," Bael answers. "All Azreans have left is this warped, weakened version provided by their queen."

We continue on while I let those facts sink in. I look around, wondering the significance of this site. Maybe the queen is hiding something here. My heart races in my chest and my palms sweat. To refocus, I turn my attention to what Liam wants us to retrieve.

"What's so special about the flowers in this graveyard?"

He snorts. "They're illegal and highly dangerous."

"Why does he want them?" I prod.

"They absorb magic in the soil, and this is the only known location they grow."

I see now why Liam wanted us to do this; the blooms are valuable. Why couldn't he retrieve them himself?

"What can you do with these blooms?" I ask slowly, though not expecting an answer.

"They mimic other magic."

Then it hits me. Liam is trying to mimic King Adrian's keeper magic in order to unlock my ring.

When we reach the row of graves farthest from the stage, I'm so wound up that any sound would send me scrambling back up the hill. But instead of walking toward the stage, which I assume is our destination, Bael points to a structure set back from the ruins. Though half hidden among the overgrowth, I see a mausoleum, glimpses of richly carved marble columns visible through the tangled greenery.

"Who's buried there?"

"The late King Lewis." He takes a deep breath, "Queen Roma's husband."

★★★

The mausoleum is derelict up close. Despite the expensive stone used to build it, it's weathered and stained with a large chunk missing along the corner. The overgrown foliage is so thick in some places that it makes the building look bloated.

Bael makes a beeline for what I assume is the door. He deftly steps over an exposed root, which I promptly trip over. After untangling my limbs, I take his extended hand and brush the dirt from my pants. He turns to face me.

"Here." He kneels and holds his palms out, gesturing to me to stand on them. "I'll give you a boost."

"What? No!" I hiss, putting my hands on my hips. My gaze travels upward. It has a gabled roof, the slant is so steep I'd break my neck sliding down it. "Why do we need to go up there?" I point to the roof of the mausoleum, assuming it's nothing more than thick vines.

But then I see it. A glimpse of shimmering, iridescent flowers clustered at the highest point on the roof.

"Why can't we just grab blooms from anywhere else?" I wave my hand around.

"Do you see them anywhere else?"

I swallow as I glance around. Unfortunately, he's right.

"Fine, but can't you just fly up there and grab them?" I protest.

I see the shifting of his shoulders that I now recognize as him unfurling his wings, at least trying to unfurl them. When he's unsuccessful, he looks at me expectantly.

So, no flying then.

"You can climb, right?"

He chuckles. "You're lighter. I'd make the roof cave in."

"What about if I help you?"

This time he laughs. "Oh, you'll give me a boost, then?" He quirks an eyebrow. "Go on, I'll step on your hands. But I'm pretty sure I'll crush them."

I huff, then look up at the structure again with unease.

"The sooner you climb up and grab them, the sooner we can leave. Or we can stay here all night debating."

Finally, I concede. This is an awful idea. "Put your hands here." He points to his shoulders. I step gingerly onto his palms and rest my hands on his shoulders. He launches me up above him with surprising strength. I leap up, scrambling for purchase until I find a cluster of vines thick enough to hold my weight. I flail ungracefully until I finally jam my feet through the tangle of branches.

Gripping the vines, I slowly haul myself up like a climber scaling a rock face. The stone beneath my feet *isn't* solid, cracks and holes are hidden underneath the tapestry of foliage. The vines sag under my weight as I get closer to the top and I do my best to ignore the swooping feeling in my stomach. It feels like any moment, I'll fall through. Spotting the blooms, I mentally calculate how far I need to reach to grab them. It's a stretch but I don't dare climb any higher.

"How many do we need?" I shout down to Bael, my voice wavering.

"Grab a handful."

I exhale and swear under my breath before reaching above my head. I'm not close enough, only my fingertips brush the silken petals.

I push myself up on my toes, propelling myself up a little higher. When I finally grab a stem, I pull it down with me. Despite significant resistance, the stem snaps in my hand but I lose my foothold. I claw against the vines, desperate to hold on, but the roof gives way beneath me. Despite the tangle of vines, I fall face first through a hole in the roof and into the crypt.

I roll onto my back, wincing. It's dark and damp here. Moonlight not only shines down from the hole I fell through, but through holes all over the ceiling. The roof is barely intact, no wonder I fell through it.

Trepidation snakes down my spine as I get to my feet. Thankfully, the ground is soft, damp dirt, but debris litters the floor. The structure's magic is deceptive; it appears much smaller from the exterior than it really is. Inside, rows of plaques cover every wall, perfectly spaced and stamped with dark bronze letters. There must be dozens of bodies in here.

If the queen shields this place from the rest of Azrea, surely someone in the royal family would notice, right? They no longer have access to the resting place of their lineage. But I guess that's only one thing on a long list of things the queen does that I'm sure others disapprove of.

If the Azrean royal family doesn't have access to this place, then I certainly shouldn't.

I scan the floor, looking for the flower I dropped. Somehow it ended up on the other side of the room and I stir up dried leaves and dust motes on my way to reach it.

The moment I curl my fingers around the flower, an eerie feeling runs right through me. I'm certain that someone is watching me.

"Bael?" I say, my voice wavering. I shove the bloom into my pocket.

I wait in tense silence, my heartbeat pumping in my ears. To distract myself, my eyes rove over the names etched into the plaques. The most prominent plaque has a bejeweled symbol of a serpent.

King Lewis Barlow, beloved ruler of Azrea.

Nearby is a large stone pedestal with the bust of a young man, hidden in an alcove. That must be of the late king.

What do I know about him? Not much beyond dying young.

I study his features for a long moment, the curve of his nose, the strong brow. It's familiar somehow, though I can't place why. I don't think I've ever seen the likeness of the young king.

But seeing his face makes being here feel even more inappropriate.

I shouldn't be here.

I'm about to shout when I hear something that sounds distinctly like a cough. Panic rises in me unbidden. A curious breeze starts at my feet. When I take a step back, the wind increases and picks up debris. It swirls up to my knees, then expands to the entire room.

That's not good.

Chapter 12

I step toward the door, leaves and debris thrashing in the wind. A horrible grinding sound of stone on stone erupts from the walls. It must be caving in on me. Is this how I die? Crushed to death with a bunch of—

"—Mira!"

"Bael!" I shout, but the noise drowns out my voice.

He staggers into view but doubles over. He clutches at his chest.

"What's happening?" I swat away errant debris.

A crackle of magic like a lightning bolt streaks across the room.

Bael is on his knees now, writhing. The wind solidifies into a dark cyclone, obstructing my view.

My eyes dart to the door. I could run, I could save myself. I have no loyalty to Bael. But seeing him there, in the eye of a storm, I can't walk away. I need him right now, though I loathe to admit it.

Without rational thought, I brace myself to run through it. The wind rushes in my ears and it drowns out everything else.

I grab Bael's arm and tug hard.

"Bael!"

He looks up at me, his dark eyes endless pools. For a single moment, it's like he sees me for the first time. He opens his mouth as if to argue, but he closes it again. He nods once and lets me tug him to his feet. His breath is ragged, and he stumbles, but I push him through the storm.

We both scream when the wind rushes past us, but he makes it to the threshold. He turns to grab my hand, intent on pulling me through with him. When another loud crack sounds and lightning shoots across the room, I stop just short of the door. I can't help it, I'm rooted to the spot. I barely notice him shouting as a wave of nausea overtakes me. My vision turns black.

***

The rain pelts the darkened windows as we shuffle down the corridor. My eyes try to adjust to the flickering light of the sconces; I've just awoken from sleep. Elyse clasps my hand and tugs me along, following Dane. I recognize where we are, but we're not allowed to play down this hall. When we reach a large door, Dane turns to us and kneels down to speak to us.

His face wrinkles with concern.

Something is wrong.

"I need you both to be brave." He searches my face, then my sister's. "Can you do that?"

He's scaring me. I look up at my sister, who's frowning, too. But she nods, so I do, too.

Dane nods and stands, opening the door and lets us in.

We pass guards by the door into a dim room.

The king sits on a leather armchair near a roaring fire. His jacket is speckled with raindrops and his hair hangs limp on his forehead. When he turns to us, he manages a smile, but it doesn't reach his eyes.

He stands and gestures for us to come toward him.

"Girls," he says, leaning forward as we approach.

"Something happened tonight." He clasps his hands and leans them on his knees. "Our beloved queen has passed into the realm of the saints."

I don't know what that means. I swallow and look at my sister. She looks as confused as I am. I turn to look at Dane, who moved to stand behind the king.

"She has passed away," Dane says solemnly.

Elyse and I both gasp.

The queen is dead?

"And your brave mother fought alongside her, but she too followed the queen into the realm beyond."

My ears ring and suddenly I can't focus.

I didn't heart hat right.

The queen died. But not my mother.

I look back up at Dane, his eyes betraying unshed tears. When he nods, a sob escapes me. Elyse squeezes my hand, and I feel her shaking.

She can't be dead. My mother can't be dead.

I need her.

"But in this time of grief, I want you to know how brave your mother was. Do you know what a Keeper of the Ward is?"

I can barely hear over Elyse's quiet sobs. Wiping the snot from my nose, I shake my head.

"It means a protector of our realms. Your mother had a special title that tonight I'm giving to both of you."

He turns to Dane, who retrieves something from the table near the fire.

He hands them to the king, who holds his palms out to each of us. There's a ring in each hand.

"Take them, girls. They're made from your mother's ring. If you promise you'll use it to protect our realms, then you'll make fine keepers of the wards."

Without hesitation, Elyse and I nod.

The ring is too big for my fingers, but it's warm. I cling to it tightly when Dane leads us back to our beds.

If I hold it tight enough, maybe my mother will come back.

***

"Mira." Bael's dark eyes swim into my vision, widening as I meet his gaze. "Can you hear me?"

Waves of panic crash into me. Something forced me to relive my darkest moment, the moment my world turned upside down. The moment I lost my mother, and realized that I didn't even know her. I didn't even know what a keeper was.

When I breathe, it comes out in short bursts. I can't seem to get enough air in my lungs. Sweat breaks out across my forehead. The walls feel like they're closing in and I'm suddenly surprised that I'm still on my feet.

I buried that memory so deep that it's like reliving it again.

Suddenly light-headed, I don't think I can stay upright.

"Just breathe. Come on," he says, tugging my arm.

But my legs are impossibly heavy.

Bael tries to guide me out the door, but when I don't budge, I feel my feet lift from the ground. Strong arms wrap underneath my knees and around my waist, and my head lists until it's leaning against his chest.

I should pull away, but right now, I can't. I need something solid, something tangible. Something to remind myself of my reality.

We emerge into the cool night, and I feel the wind cool my flushed skin. I greedily suck in the cold air, and my lungs constrict before they fully expand. He sets me down, and I bend over and brace my knees, unsure if I'll fall over or vomit.

"Sit. Breathe. You look like you'll topple over at any moment."

He sits down next to me and leans his forearms on his knees.

I take a deep breath, hold it, then release it before I sit next to him on a soft patch of grass. We sit until I stop shaking and my breath returns to normal. I finally focus on something other than the thrashing of my heart, and that's the buried memory. I hate the way old feelings crawl up my throat, suddenly desperate for release. But I don't give voice to that.

I want to ask what happened back there, but I don't even have the energy right now to ask.

"Why did you do that?" he says sharply.

"Do what?" My voice comes out raspy.

"Help me? I didn't coerce you."

I frown. Since when does someone need to be coerced to help someone?

"Don't get me wrong, I still despise you, but I think helping you isn't the worst thing I could be doing."

This earns me a huff.

We sit in silence while I process everything. My mind replays the memory.

Finally, he gets to his feet and extends a hand toward me. I let him pull me to my feet.

THE QUEEN'S CARD

The trek back up the hill is much harder, but I'm eager to distance myself from the theater. I can't shake the feeling that every spirit in this graveyard watches us as we pass.

The lake is just as it was when we arrived, partially obscured by the dark fog. When Bael's warm hands grip my waist, I welcome the touch, even from him.

I'm ready to put this place behind me.

Chapter 13

"Come sit; you need something to eat." We're back in his living room, where he fetches a blanket from an armchair and wraps it around my shoulders.

I nod, too tired to argue. I settle down on the floor in front of a fire, the flames licking at the kindling in the hearth. Bael puts the flower I stole in a cup with water on the mantle. The petals are a little wrinkled, but reflect the glow of the fire as if wet with dew.

My mind reels over everything tonight: meeting Liam, visiting the Theater of Souls, the ensuing panic attack, and the visions of my worst memory. Anxiety grips me all over again, and I feel a cold sweat blooming despite my proximity to the now-roaring fire.

With everything that happened tonight, was it worth it for just one flower? Could Liam unlock the magic in my ring? I loosen my grip on the blanket and look down at my hands.

Bael returns a few minutes later with steaming mugs of tea and biscuits with jam. He sits down on the floor next to me.

"What happened back there?" I ask, a shiver passing through me at the thought of the biting wind.

"I think we tripped a ward."

I nod, chewing.

"So that's why Liam wanted us to get those blooms, because it's insanely dangerous?" I ask between bites.

He nods. "He's too smart to attempt it himself."

We both snort at that.

There's so much I don't understand about Azrean magic, like how the queen can still wield any at all, albeit a warped version of it, after her husband died. And why did Bael tell me all this? I'm still his enemy.

I want to ask him about it all, but tonight is not the night. The warmth of the fire and exhaustion threatens to pull me under at any moment.

I lean my head back against the couch cushion and close my eyes. But I feel him watching me, which I confirm when I open my eyes. His expression is serious.

"In the mausoleum, you froze..."

I chew my lip, resisting the urge to shrink in on myself. "Just lost in an old memory." Silence passes between us, and I watch the fire dance in the hearth.

He leans forward, grabbing his mug from the end table and, taking a long sip, says, "I know what that's like."

I don't reply, but I nod, wondering if his memories are as painful as mine.

Although I don't mean to, my gaze wanders back to him. I take in the sharp lines of his profile. I can't help but wonder, are the rumors of his ruthlessness true? He's stubborn and short-tempered, but enough to tear out a mortal's heart?

"Go on," he says, not turning to face me. "Ask."

"Ask what?"

"Whatever it is you're thinking."

I pause. What do I want to know? What if this is the only time I get to ask?

"Why do you hate King Adrian?"

He grinds his jaw, his hands curling into fists. "Your king is selfish. You don't know what he's done."

I want to defend my king, but from what accusations I don't know. Every king makes decisions for the good of his kingdom, and I expect him to be no different.

"You can't just fling insults and not back it up," I say. "What did he do?"

"He blackmailed my father."

"What? Why?" I blurt.

Who is his father, some Azrean noble? Why would King Adrian blackmail him?

"I—" He grunts but doesn't finish.

The coercion. He can't speak of it, can he?

"—It's not just my father," he says, rubbing his arm with agitation. "All of Azrea hates him. The queen uses *your* king as the excuse to siphon their power."

"What?" I say, taken aback. "Why would she say that?"

They hate each other. Our realms are enemies. And the king is mortal. Why would he know anything about magic beyond keeper magic, let alone how to siphon it? But that explains why Azreans hate mortals; they're resentful because they think we're the reason their queen steals magic from them.

That couldn't be further from the truth.

"Where do you think he got your keeper magic from?"

This stops my racing thoughts. I stop and gape at him. I know so little of keeper history, but according to lore, keeper magic came from the saints, not Azrea.

THE QUEEN'S CARD

But Bael doesn't stop there. He barrels on. "He hasn't given you your magic, and yet an Azrean can unlock it?"

"Liam hasn't unlocked it yet," I snap.

"When he does, I think it'll prove a point, won't it?"

I sit silently, my mind trying to make sense of it all. If Liam unlocks it with a wraith bloom, does that make the magic in the ring Azrean? Even if it is, that doesn't mean it's *stolen*, right?

I don't know what to believe.

I lose myself in the flickering of the flames in the hearth. The air is tense between us until I feel my anger ebb away. I certainly don't agree with his assessment, but I can understand his anger.

"You know, I'm not as wretched as you think I am." His words startle me and my gaze snaps to him. In the firelight, his eyes are somber. For a moment, I see what he hides behind his carefully constructed mask: sorrow.

"I don't think you're *that* wretched," I mumble. I meant it as a jab, but I'm surprised that I mean it.

He's no saint, but I see there's more to him than just his reputation and his demeanor. He's fueled by the same thing I am: protecting his loved ones. And although I won't believe him until I see my magic unlocked, he's under her coercion.

He smiles sadly. "I would if I were you. But I'm not. Just desperate."

"Well, that makes two of us," I say, taking a sip from my mug.

For the first time, the silence that hangs between us is not tense. It's not comfortable either, but it feels a lot like comradery. I'm under no illusion that it's anything other than temporary. He marked me, but right now, it appears our interests align. We're both trying to thwart Queen Roma's plans.

He's certainly the last person I'd imagine similarities with.

My mind replays the riotous emotions that bled out of me tonight. I had to relieve my worst memory that put my vulnerability on full display for him to witness. But, I've seen his vulnerabilities, too. His queen keeps him in line with coercion magic.

He's still irritating and argumentative, and there's no proven validity to the prejudice he holds against my king, but he may be of more use an ally than an enemy, at least until I can get back home.

When our tea is long gone and only biscuit crumbs remain, I feel myself begin to succumb to the siren song of sleep. With heavy lids, I climb onto the couch and feel a warm, soft blanket draping over me. My eyes flutter momentarily, and I see Bael retreating to his room.

***

The next day we leave the treehouse just as the sun comes up. Perstow is loud and bustling in the daylight. And although the bright, late-spring sun shines the same as it would in Lander, it couldn't be more different. The sea air carries the scent of something rotten, and debris and dust float around in a cloud at our feet. I shove my hands into the pocket of a pair of borrowed pants; ones that Bael spelled to fit me. I'd much prefer my own, but it's certainly better than putting back on my dirty clothes after a bath this morning.

We pass men in stained trousers and coats shuffling toward the buildings where black smoke bellows and curls into the air. Carts and carriages roll across the cobblestone roads, and children dart in and out of the flow of passersby.

Bael is mostly silent next to me, his features pulled taught in worry. It's been twenty-four hours since the queen threatened him. Do we really stand a chance at getting my magic and saving his lover in the next two days?

We wind through the crowds until we're standing in front of a squat brick building that spans an entire city block. It's noticeably cleaner than the others, albeit still dusted with soot. Three men in velvet waistcoats loiter outside a lavish front door, set back from the road and lined with perfectly trimmed hedges. Two young men in matching burgundy jackets hover near the gilded iron doors.

What is this place?

A clean black sign with gold lettering spells *Thistle & Rose, A Gentleman's Club*. My stomach drops.

A gentlemen's club?

Bael smirks at my reaction.

It must be exclusive if first impressions are anything to go by. Without hesitation, Bael gestures me forward along the neatly manicured path. The other patrons spot Bael and scramble out of the way, one of them tripping backward into a hedge. The doormen look to each other for guidance, at a loss for protocol apparently. By the time Bael and I reach the doors, they hurry to pull them open.

We step into a large foyer at the base of a large, wooden staircase. A chandelier hangs overhead, the light from the candles so dim that everything is cast in shadows. Two attendees in uniform shuffle up the stairs immersed in quiet conversation. Bael seems to know the way because he wastes no time ascending the stairs to the third level.

I follow him down a hall with ornate dark green walls lit with sconces, evenly spaced between expensive-looking paintings. Through the last door on the right, we find ourselves walking into a dimly lit room. Liam's office on land is opulent, with dark wood paneling and deep purple wallpaper. When we stop just short of the dark wooden desk, he looks up at us.

I take a nervous breath and inhale the scent of parchment and charcoal. I can't read the expression on his face until he turns and pulls the dark curtains open to reveal the afternoon sun. My eyes drink in the daylight and the view of the crowded streets below.

"So?" Liam says, dropping the quill in his hand and snapping the leather-bound journal on his desk shut. "Did you get them?"

Bael produces the single flower, wrapped gently in a white handkerchief.

Liam frowns. "Just one?" He plucks the flower by its stem and holds it up to the light. When the sun hits it, it looks solidly white, so different from the pearlescent sheen it holds in the dark.

"That's all we could get," Bael confirms, stepping back and putting his hands in his pockets. "And the ring?"

Liam twirls the flower in his fingers for another long moment before turning back to us. He reaches into his pocket and pulls out my ring, holding it between his thumb and middle finger.

"She's not dead, so it looks like I'm right," he says casually, handing the ring to Bael.

I snatch it out of his grip and jam it back onto my middle finger. Wait a second—was he talking about me?

Bael shrugs. "You were right."

I turn to Bael and although I don't say it, I glare at him.

Liam chuckles to himself watching our exchange. "You didn't tell her of the risks?" He tsks.

Bael feigns disinterest. "I tested it first. The moment I lifted the ward, she could see through it."

I hate that they're talking about me right in front of me. And did he use me as bait to test a ward?

"How'd you do it?" Bael asks.

Liam lets a smirk curl on his lips, pleased at the tension in the room he created. "Bael," he grins, "never underestimate what I can do."

***

"I could have died last night?" I seethe.

We barely made it out the club's front door before I rounded on him. Last night was traumatizing enough, and there was a chance I wouldn't make it?

"Believe me, I made sure you wouldn't before we stepped foot through the wards."

Oh.

An awkward silence descends between us.

"What would have happened?" I ask.

"You don't want to know," he says, his hands back in his pockets. "But it's safe to say you're the only mortal who's seen the Theater of Souls in a long time."

I let out a long breath.

Let's hope Liam was successful in unlocking my magic. This had better be worth it.

Chapter 14

I follow Bael as he turns and strides down the street. The streets are busier now, the noise deafening after the quiet respite of the club. Tucking his hands in his pockets, he keeps his gaze straight as passerby avoid getting too close to us. As usual, I struggle to keep his pace, made more difficult because I'm still trying to take in Perstow in the daylight. The sun is in full view now, but the warm beams of sunlight don't banish all the shadows. There's a distinct negative energy lingering everywhere we go, evidenced by the cracks in the building facades we pass and divots of missing cobblestones in the streets.

When we pass a cobbler shop, a strange feeling creeps down my spine. It feels like someone is watching us. When I turn to look, the name *Olsen & Sons* is etched in scripted lettering on the storefront window, with several pairs of men's leather shoes on display. It seems innocent enough, until I spot a stocky man with a thick, brown beard leaning against the window frame, his eyes on us. Then two other men appear behind him, folding their arms across their chests.

Why are they looking at us?

I clear my throat to get Bael's attention.

"I think they're staring at us," I say, gesturing toward the stop.

Bael tilts his head just enough to verify, before his lips purse. He shakes his head and grabs my elbow, tugging me forward.

He pulls me into a pub a few doors down.

The door slams shut so loudly behind us that everyone in the pub turns to stare. It's still early for a pint, but there are several occupied tables of men with rolled up sleeves, wiping soot off their faces. As we weave around the tables and settle into a table in the corner, I can feel the tension radiating off of Bael. Those men in the window put him on high alert. We sit for a few moments before I can no longer stand the silence.

"Why were those men staring at us?" I ask, leaning forward and looking toward the door. I assume they're not *just* cobblers.

Bael rolls his shoulders out, but it does nothing to loosen his stiff posture.

"They're getting more brazen," he says more to himself than me.

Before I can ask anything else, the door swings shut but doesn't draw attention like we did. But it doesn't matter, we're both on high alert. We turn to see the same two men from the cobbler's shop appear on the threshold. They are both about my age, with large muscles and severe haircuts. One towers over the other with a lean frame, a dark cap half-covering his eyes and a toothpick hanging from his lips. The other, stocky with big muscles, smirks as he sticks a clove cigarette behind his ear.

Bael tenses as my gaze wanders down to their shoes. Despite their rough attire, their shoes are spotless, a deep brown leather with crisp, clean lines embroidered in intricate patterns. What kind of thug has perfect shoes? One that works in a cobbler shop.

When they stride up to us, Bael feigns nonchalance, but I can see the tick in his jaw. He leans back, leaning his arm against one of the empty chairs as the pair approach.

"Bael," the taller one says, stopping way too close to our table.

The other stands shoulder to shoulder with him, blocking out the door. He's blocking our exit. His gaze roves my face before it stops and lingers on my hand. My ring suddenly feels hot and I quickly hide it under the table.

Bael doesn't answer, he barely acknowledges them beyond a head tilt.

"We saw you going to the *Thistle & Rose*."

Bael raises a brow. "And?"

The stockier man tightens his hands into fists.

"So, why is the queen's *bird* sniffing around our club?"

Bael laughs but it's void of amusement. "Surely you know better than to question the second in command of your queen."

I suck in a breath. He's baiting them, and his words achieve the desired effect. They both lean closer, the taller man bares his teeth and his companion cracks his knuckles.

"You're lucky the boss says we can't—"

"Oh, *I'm* lucky?" Bael is on his feet in the next moment, his fist gripping the taller man's coat. They're nose to nose now with Bael at least a head taller. They stay that way for a long moment, fury rolling off of both of them in waves. The tension is so palpable I want to sink into the corner and disappear.

"If your boss has a problem with me, tell him to find me himself. I don't talk business with *children*," Bael finishes, releasing the man so suddenly that he topples backward into his companion's chest.

The man steadies himself, his eyes like daggers as he dusts himself off. Behind him, the stockier man cracks his neck and stares, but doesn't make a move to get closer.

THE QUEEN'S CARD

"Get out of my sight," Bael growls.

Both men grit their teeth, their fists as their sides before they turn and lumber across the pub. I don't release a breath until I see them disappear through the door. When I turn my gaze back to Bael, I realize the pub has gone still; every patron, including the bartender, swings their gaze from the door back to us.

Bael rubs his hand along his jaw before gesturing to my seat. I sit back down, not realizing I had even stood up.

He takes his seat again, then gestures to the bartender. The older gentleman with gray stubble behind the bar nods once and appears a few moments later with a short glass of liquor. He sets it in front of Bael who nods a quick thanks.

"Anything for the miss?" The bartender inclines his head to me, his demeanor carefully respectful.

I shake my head. He nods, then turns on his heel to resume his place behind the bar.

"Who were those men?" I whisper as I watch Bael take a long sip.

"Liam's men," he says, tight-lipped. "I'm surprised they have the guts to approach me at all."

I frown. "But we just saw Liam, he was pleased to see us. We brought him what he wanted."

Bael snorts. "Doesn't mean he told his cronies what he's up to."

We sit in tense silence for another moment until a man in a dark jacket emerges from the shadows and approaches the table. Bael inclines his head with wariness, but not hostility. The newcomer doesn't spare me a glance, but instead leans down to converse with Bael. My eye catches a puckering scar just behind his ear. A curious place for such a deep wound. Desperate for a distraction, my attention strays to a hushed conversation between two men at a nearby table.

109

"I don't blame them. We don't need him sniffing around us, either. He's her thug."

Are they calling Bael the queen's thug?

"She's already bleeding us of our magic and for what, Lander? The mortal realm is useless."

"But at least she'll stop terrorizing us for a while."

My eyes widen, but when I glance back at Bael, he's still deep in conversation. I turn my attention back to my eavesdropping.

"How hard is it to make mortals bow? They're weak."

"I don't know, but she won't stop taking from us, you know that. We've all seen her temper. She'll level their entire island if she doesn't get what she wants."

The other hums in agreement.

I'm *shocked* they'd discuss this so close to Bael. Do they really think he wouldn't pay attention?

I watch the man who spoke with Bael stride across the pub toward the door before turning my attention back to the men.

"I barely survived last year's Night Waltz. We can't keep up at the docks and my wife is out of work. She can't sew anymore without her magic. Her fingers swell so much that—"

Bael sets his glass down on the table hard enough to bring my attention back to him. So, he *had* heard them. I tense, waiting for a reaction. I glance back at Bael, his posture still stiff, but he no longer looks murderous.

I want to keep listening to the conversation behind me, but they've moved on to safer topics. I busy myself with staring at the ring on my finger and processing what I heard. I don't agree with what the men are saying. They're worried about their magic when mortal lives are at stake. But I can at least empathize with the hardships they live with under their queen's reign.

Bael's eyes rove over me and I squirm under the scrutiny. When I look up again, he looks inquisitive.

"Why is protecting mortals so important to you?"

It's a simple question, but it catches me so off guard that I'm at a loss for words. He didn't react like I thought he would.

I mull over my answer. I'm still mortal, but when I earn my magic, then it'll be my duty to protect them as a keeper. But Dulci is also my closest friend. When I have my magic, I can do more to protect her. I would happily protect anyone I love.

"Because they need protection."

He lifts his glass to his lips and takes a long pull from his drink. Then he inclines his head toward the rest of the pub.

"So do they."

I frown. "But they see you as the enemy, don't they?" I whisper.

"Yes, but they're desperate. And I understand what a caged animal will do when it's backed into a corner."

I replay his words until he finishes his drink. When we take off back toward his treehouse, I can't help but see Azrea just a little differently.

Chapter 15

I twist my ring in circles on my middle finger, watching Bael from the kitchen window. He's on the ground, chopping wood in the rain brought on by an unexpected storm.

With his shirt off.

Not that it matters to me, because it *doesn't*.

Since we returned from our trip to the gentlemen's club earlier this afternoon, I've been too nervous to attempt magic. Instead, I've been questioning if bypassing the king's approval to earn the magic was the right call to make.

What if it doesn't work?

If it does, how do I wield it? Can I harness it in time to help me thwart Queen Roma's plans?

What would my mother think about this? I'm sure she's rolling in her grave as we speak; watching me work with the realm's sworn enemy to unlock the keeper magic in my ring. But I force the thoughts from my mind; I can't change how I got here, all I can do is move forward.

He brings the ax down onto the stump of wood with a crack. He shakes his head, droplets of water spraying everywhere. From here, I can see a lock of hair fall into his eye. He bats it away, the gesture more charming than it should be. As if sensing me, he looks up. Our eyes meet, and despite the overwhelming urge to look away, I don't.

He smirks.

My cheeks heat, and I spin on my heel. I stride back into the living room to perch on the arm of one of the faded armchairs. I've been avoiding the inevitable for too long.

I can't let anything else distract me, least of all him.

No, I need to test out my magic.

I force myself to stop fidgeting, and instead close my eyes and concentrate.

My mind wanders immediately, focusing on the rain which is now a gentle patter sweeping across the windows. I take another deep breath and try to clear my head.

My fingers tingle, like warming up by a fire after a day in the snow. But then they throb. I open my eyes and look down. My fingers drip magic like purple candle wax.

Horrified, I shake them, but the motion is like breaking a dam. Unbidden, magic shoots out of my fingertips.

It sprays across the room, saturating the rug and splattering on the floorboards. I run through everything I know about our keeper magic, but suddenly I realize there are gaps in my knowledge. What happens when it hits the ground? Am I going to fall through a giant hole in the floor?

I look around for something to stop the flow but I can't even think straight.

I hate to admit it, but I need to find Bael. I have no choice.

As if thinking about him summoned him, the front door bursts open and Bael, in all his rain-soaked glory, touches down on the threshold and tucks his wings in. My eyes drink in his exposed chest. Strong pectorals glisten with droplets of water.

My *god*, why isn't he wearing a shirt?

A light dusting of dark hair trails down his stomach, and an unwanted warmth blooms in me. When I meet his gaze, I want the ground to swallow me whole.

"Mira?" he asks, his face showing his concern.

"Help!" I bluster, ignoring the heat on my cheeks. Purple magic continues to cascade onto the floor.

"Cast something," he says, closing the distance between us.

"What?" I shout, distracted. I shake my fingers again and droplets cover the legs of my trousers.

"Try to cast a ward," he says calmly. His large hands are suddenly on my shoulders, gripping me firmly.

I swallow down the anxiety. I don't know how to do that.

"Close your eyes and concentrate. Picture the magic, then *will it* into existence."

"Ok," I say, adrenaline making me shake. I squeeze my eyes shut and picture watching Ambrose the night he cast a protective ward on the Carriage House. His magic, dark orange, spread from his fingers to the building. It looked like a soap bubble, shimmering around the edges. I picture my magic, dark purple, escaping in a steady stream to encircle the room.

I hear him gasp.

I open my eyes to see us standing in a protective ward, an iridescent soap-like bubble covering the entire room. My fingers still drip, but I no longer care. An excited laugh escapes from me.

I did it.

He surveys the room in wonder and when he finds my gaze, his lip curls into a smile. Suddenly, all the air has gone out of the room. We're suspended in this moment, just the two of us, the room nothing like it was a moment ago.

Slowly, so slowly, his hands leave my shoulders and travel up to my cheeks. They're rough and warm and he's achingly gentle.

It must be the adrenaline and the unbridled joy of getting what I've wanted for so long. That's surely what's making me giddy and light-headed, because my stomach flips and my breath hitches when his eyes land on my lips.

He flashes a genuine smile and I stop breathing.

He has two dimples.

Ugh, have mercy.

Who is this man in front of me, the man I loathed not so long ago? When did loathing turn into…something else? Tolerance? Less hatred?

Maybe it was somewhere in the chaotic journey it took to get here, to get exactly what I've always wanted. Maybe it was when I saw more of myself in him than I anticipated.

I'm not as wretched as you think I am.

His thumb grazes my bottom lip and my mind races. All at once, the ward falls away.

Just like that, it breaks the spell between us. He clears his throat and takes a step back.

"You have magic now, Mira," he says. "Now, let's see about controlling it."

★★★

"Watch it!" He ducks, and a glass explodes on a shelf behind him. The shimmering outline of my meager ward fades.

"Sorry," I say, but it's half-hearted. We've been at this for hours and I'm no closer to replicating my earlier ward, or anything as controlled.

I wipe the sweat from my forehead. When I survey his living room, it looks like it's not faring much better. We'd moved the bulky furniture against the wall to make room to maneuver. Still, with my magic's erratic behavior, it bounces off the walls and ricochets into everything, particularly every glass object in this room.

He perches on the arm of one of his leather chairs and sighs. "At this rate, who knows how long my house will last?"

I collapse into the chair on the opposite side of the room, conceding.

He drums his fingers on his thigh, assessing me. "Maybe casting a ward is too advanced right now. Why don't we try something smaller?"

Instinctively, I open my mouth to argue. But something's changed between us; a new, uncertain path laid out in front of us. Certainly not *friends*, but not quite enemies. Maybe being combative isn't helping. He did help me control the flow of magic when it came shooting out of my hands. It's considerably more solid now, the texture more like the ribbons I've seen Ambrose and Elyse wield so many times.

Maybe I need to trust him, if only for the next two days. He unlocked my magic, even if it served his own purpose. Plus, I clearly need his help, and skirting around the truth won't solve either of our problems.

"I don't know much about keeper magic beyond making and protecting wards," I admit, fidgeting with a loose thread on my borrowed shirt. "My sister made it clear it's knowledge earned once I have my magic."

He frowns. "Well, that doesn't matter anymore; you have it now. It's time to move forward, not to look back."

I chew my lip. He's right. If I have what I want now, does it matter how I got it? And now that I do, they have to let me into the keeper ranks, right?

So why does this win feel so hollow?

By now, I can feel my magic gathering in my fingers, which makes me nervous. It's erratic, like trying to will a lightning bolt into striking where you want it to.

"Take a break; maybe we're overthinking it. Then we'll try again."

And we do; we spend the evening trying, but it's just as frustrating and fruitless as before. Plus, I'm not used to this helpful side of Bael.

It's unnerving.

I wander to the bath to have the privacy to think. As I scrub away several days' worth of grime, I run through the day. Gaining access to my magic is a miracle, but it's nothing like how I'd imagined. Neither the situation I unlocked it in, nor the unexpected problems in controlling it. It's unpredictable and about as controllable as a forest fire. And we're running out of time.

Not to mention the royal wedding; it's only a few days away. It looms over me, dread threatening to drown me. The list of things to accomplish before then keeps growing: harnessing my magic, helping Bael free his lover, a woman who surely doesn't know the lengths I'm going to save her. I squash down the petty jealousy that seems to come out of nowhere. I don't even know her, but I do know what it feels like to be controlled by a monarch.

Besides, rescuing her isn't even the only thing I still need to accomplish. Bael still needs to fly me back into Lander and execute a plan to save the princess from whatever attack Queen Roma has in store. A plan I don't have yet. The more I think about it, the more impossible it seems. I can't do it even if I had an entire year to do it all.

※※※

That night, Bael makes roasted meat and savory potatoes, perfectly seasoned with crispy edges. I stopped braiding my hair in the bathroom mirror the moment I smelled it. I can't concentrate on an empty stomach, not when the meal smells like that.

We eat in silence; confusion and a newfound nervousness around him tugs at every part of me. Something has been lingering in the back of my mind that I've avoided bringing up: his plan to rescue his lover when the queen gave him three days to find the caves.

I know harnessing my magic took precedence, but based on how slow progress has been, this might be as good as my control will get.

When I've eaten my fill, I sit back and watch him, waiting for the right moment to bring it up. His gaze is far away, and I wonder what he's thinking about. He must sense me staring because his eyes find mine.

"Spit it out," he says, lifting an eyebrow.

I chew my lip for a moment before speaking. "Have you thought about your plan to rescue her?"

"Rescue who?"

I furrow my eyebrows. "The woman the queen is holding hostage in the castle."

He blinks at me.

"The *someone* you love?" I prod.

"It's my—" he sucks in a breath, "—I can't tell you who," he grunts, "but I can tell you it's not a lover."

"Oh."

This shouldn't be a moving-mountains kind of revelation, but this causes a traitorous feeling to bloom within me. I dismiss the feeling immediately. I'm just surprised, that's all.

THE QUEEN'S CARD

We sit in awkward silence. I realize he can read my expression when he cocks his head to the side.

I clear my throat to ruin the moment, desperate to stop the heating of my cheeks.

"So, what's your plan to rescue them?"

"I fly us in. I can't hide you from her wards, but I have a distraction in mind. The moment we step foot in the castle, cast a protective ward, then we'll find them."

"Wait, I thought you could do that?" I raise my eyebrows at him. "When I tried to stab you with a fork?"

I'm rewarded with a real, genuine smile.

It leaves me speechless.

I meet his gaze and an uncomfortable knot forms in my stomach. That was a *new* smile, one I haven't seen on him yet. I banish that train of thought immediately.

What has gotten into me?

Then the smile fades. "I can only cast a ward for myself."

I pause to consider. "So, you're breaking me in so that I can protect who we're breaking out."

He nods.

"And what kind of distraction do you have—?"

"—I've got it covered," he interrupts, holding up his hand.

I frown but continue with my list of questions. "Ok, so when we get in, how do we find them?"

"I'll be able to sense them."

"And the queen, she'll be there, won't she? What if she sees us? What happens if she coerces you again?"

"I don't know," he says quietly. "But I've got you now. We need to watch out for each other."

I've got you now. My stomach flips, but I blow out a breath to refocus. This mission, this piecemeal plan has to work, because we can't afford to lose.

"And this fulfills our bargain?"

He pauses for a moment before nodding curtly.

Good. Then as soon as we finish this, I'm leaving at the first opportunity.

But if we work as a team, we could both get what we want, right?

Chapter 16

The next day passes in a blur of purple magic. I'm struggling to keep a ward intact for longer than a few moments, and I don't know how to keep it around someone who will run alongside us.

My mind has already sifted through the worst-case scenarios of this plan. What happens if we can't reach the castle? What if the queen finds out?

Bael is no longer in Lander looking for the caves. In fact, he's actively defying her and breaking someone out of her clutches. If we're caught, I'll never make it back to Lander. Any hopes I have of saving Dulci would go up in flames.

By the time the sun sets, I'm an anxious, pacing mess. Bael watches me from where he sits in an armchair, spinning a coin. My thoughts spiral, and I don't realize he's standing right behind me until I almost barrel into him.

"Sorry!" I hold my hands up in alarm. "I didn't realize—"

"—It's ok, I thought I should stop you before you wear a hole in my floor," he says, taking a step back and turning toward the stairs.

"Come with me," he says, ascending the steps. "I want to show you something."

I follow him up the smooth wooden steps along the far wall of the treehouse. At the top of the landing, it's clearly his domain; an ornate sleigh bed takes up most of the room, with a dark gray blanket tucked perfectly around the mattress. And it smells like him.

I gulp and hurry to cross the room, intent on following him through glass doors to a balcony, but something tacked to his wall makes me hesitate. It's small and rectangular.

It's a tarot card.

The Hanged Man.

What does that mean? When I hear the glass door slide in its track, I swivel my head. Bael pokes his head in and sees what caught my eye. He frowns.

"I see you found my *gift* from the queen."

I turn to look at it again.

A man hangs upside down, suspended by one ankle. His expression is curiously serene.

"What does it mean?"

"Martyrdom," he says with disdain. "She says it's the role I'm *destined* to fulfill."

When he sees my horror, he chuckles sadly. "Don't worry, it's just an ordinary card."

An ordinary card with an awful warning behind it.

When he turns away, I take that as my cue to follow him through the glass doors. We step out into the cool air and the firm grip of his hand finds my shoulder. He leads me away from the railing to a recessed alcove along the exterior wall.

"Wait here," he says, turning abruptly and disappearing through the balcony doors.

THE QUEEN'S CARD

I grip the textured bark of the wall behind me. From this vantage point, we're still well hidden among the thick canopy of forest, but the wide expanse of the night sky opens up before us. It's breathtaking.

He drapes a thick, soft blanket around my shoulders and gestures for me to sit down. He sits down next to me, though without a blanket, resting his forearms on his knees. We're so close that I can feel the heat of his thighs against mine, even through the layers of fabric. We say nothing as we gaze into the limitless darkness above us.

I lose myself in the moment, tucked into a tiny space in an enemy land with a man so formidable I'd never have guessed at the gentleness he's displaying now.

"It's beautiful," I say finally. "Thank you for bringing me up here."

I don't turn my head but I can see him nod. "I thought you needed a change of scenery."

I nod and tilt my head back, closing my eyes. I bask in the silence between us to be alone with my thoughts.

"Tonight's the strawberry moon." He says softly.

It pulls me from my moment of quiet contemplation. I finally look over and I see him watching me.

"What's a strawberry moon?" I ask.

"It's the last full moon of spring, but that's not what makes it special. Tonight, it'll hang the lowest in the sky that it's been since Queen Roma took control of Azrea. Plus, it's indescribably beautiful."

I blink and search the sky, only just realizing there's no moon.

"But I don't see it."

He's still looking at me for a long moment before pointing to the horizon. "That's because we're out here to watch it rise."

I sit back, trying to get comfortable, but the gnarled bark of the tree scratches at me. I turn around, paying attention to it for the first time.

When I run my hands along the ridges, I realize it's not the same as the trees nearby with smooth bark.

"This tree is different," I say, surveying it.

"That's why I chose it. You can find beauty in the most unexpected things. Those are the things that I *guard* with my life."

The declaration stuns me. It's so unexpected coming from him, but I'm learning that unexpected is exactly what Bael is. Even though it melts away any hint of playfulness from the moment, it stirs something within me. My heart constricts in my chest and I pull my hand away, suddenly aware of his eyes on me. I shift a little, burrowing further into the blankets.

"Are you comfortable?" he asks.

I nod.

"Then settle in. The moon should rise soon."

A few minutes later, we both spot a sliver of pink just cresting over the horizon.

"There," he says.

I watch, enraptured, as the largest moon I've ever seen rise until it clears the tops of the trees. He's right, it's *breathtaking*. I study the curious hue of pink, which reminds me of…my eyes find his mouth.

"It's like you could reach up and touch it." He says, pulling me out of my traitorous thoughts.

We watch the sky together in contented silence. After a while, he holds his hand up and twirls his fingers lazily. Shadows twist and curl into the night air. I watch the movements with more curiosity than fear; but was it that long ago that he used those to bind me? He catches me looking but doesn't speak.

"Why did you tell me about Azrean lore, about the struggles of the people here?"

He takes a long moment to think before responding. "I wanted you to know the truth. You'll be the first keeper who knows."

Oh. I'm not sure that there isn't an ulterior motive here, but if what he's saying is true, then there's a lot more to the tension between the realms than I thought.

"Why do you want to be a keeper?" he continues.

The question stuns me.

It used to be such an easy question to answer. It's because I'm meant to be one. My mother was one, my sister is one, and I'm going to be one.

But now? With everything I've been struggling with, maybe I won't be.

"I'm expected to."

He lifts a hand to run across his stubble, his eyes assessing me. I can't help but shift a little under his sudden scrutiny. I avoid his eye contact in case he asks me to elaborate, but when he speaks again, it's not to question my answer.

"Do you want to try casting again?"

I frown. "Not particularly. I know exactly what'll happen."

"Maybe the change of venue will help?"

Frustration wells inside of me. I'm fully aware of my shortcomings and I know how much is at stake just as much as he does.

"What is it?" he says quietly. "What's stopping you?"

What's stopping me from pouring every ounce of hope into getting my magic under some semblance of control when I know I'll fail?

Guilt.

Resentment.

Doubt.

It's all there, hanging heavy on my shoulders. I blow out a breath, annoyed and loathe to confront them now.

I close my eyes and picture where I'd be right now if I hadn't fallen into Bael's path. If I hadn't *run* directly into Bael's path. I'd be back in Lander Castle, sullen and miserable about being left behind, but at least I'd still be at Dulci's side. My rash action separated me from her, leaving her vulnerable.

I bypassed earning the king's magic, is that why I can't control it? Am I even a keeper?

If I had stayed, would I have ever earned it? I don't know if my king trusts me. I don't know why he hasn't given me my magic yet. For so long, I resented my sister because I assumed my lack of magic was at her insistence. Maybe I haven't lived up to some unspoken expectation of hers for how I should fall in line.

What if I wasted my time here? What if Bael was right and our keeper magic was stolen from Azrea? Does that mean the mortal king could be responsible for what the Azreans claim he is?

I shake my head. He isn't, he can't be.

None of this changes what I'm duty bound to do; I need to get home to keep the queen from enacting her threat. If I have the magic, I need to force it to work.

"You know, I thought all keepers were the same."

When I meet his eyes, his expression is soft.

"You don't think that anymore?" I ask.

He looks up at the sky, his arms resting on his knees.

"You're different."

I swallow a growing lump in my throat. Before I can ask him to elaborate, he turns to me. "Give me your hand."

He takes my hand and places it in his open palm. I feel the warmth immediately and his fingers twitch slightly under mine. I tense, instinct telling me that we're too close.

"Now, clear your mind. Nothing else exists but you and your magic."

I stiffen, suddenly fully aware of everywhere our bodies touch. There's no way that I can just imagine him not here. But I try anyway. In my mind's eye, I picture my magic; the same deep purple that flowed from my fingers.

"Now picture it wrapping around your fingers. What does it feel like?"

I obey and picture just that. I can practically feel the subtle tickle against my skin, light as a feather.

"Like silk," I say. It reminds me of what it feels like when I walked through my sister's ward to visit Dulci in her chambers.

"Now open your eyes."

When I do, I let out a surprised bark of laughter. My magic, just as I imagined, weaves in between my fingers.

Completely under my control. A wave of pure joy sweeps over me.

"But how...?" I ask, wiggling my fingers and watching my ribbons respond.

He gently removes his hand from underneath mine, and I try to ignore the sudden rush of cool air along my knuckles.

Giddiness and excitement overwhelm me. I drop my hand into my lap and let the tendrils dissipate.

"It's yours now, remember? Only you can control it."

His eyes darken when they land on mine. A slow smile curls on his lips and both dimples show.

Without realizing it, I raise my hand to brush a strand of hair from his eyes. He follows the movement of my fingers.

I blink at the sudden proximity and drop my hand. But he leans in, slow and purposeful.

My breath hitches when his scent envelops me and our lips are so close that if I lean in any closer, I'll shatter the barrier between us.

We're so lost in the moment that when footsteps race up the stairs, it's too late to run.

Chapter 17

Bael stands so quickly that by the time I tumble toward the door, I see nothing but a blur of black feathers. The force of his wings spreading almost knocks me back, and I scramble to untangle myself from the blanket. His wings stretch and flex, covering the entire length of the glass doors. I swallow when I realize he's shielding me from view.

I hear several pairs of heavy footsteps coming closer. Bael's voice is an authoritative boom.

"You dare enter my home?" It drips with venom.

Goblins snort and shuffle in reply and my heart sinks.

"Mistress says—" one starts.

"—the Raven's in trouble," another goblin says.

Bael tenses. "Excuse me? I'm not in trouble—"

"—they mean with me!" Queen Roma's voice is shrill with fury.

Although I still can't see anything, I can feel her presence immediately. It feels like ice water freezing me in place.

"Raven." The single word, spoken like in a discordant key. She doesn't even use his name. "You didn't think I'd check up on you?"

He lets out a slow, controlled breath out through his mouth. "You gave me three days—"

"—silence!" she snaps. "Your queen is speaking. You lost the ability to argue when you defied me. Again."

Shadows explode from her fingertips and the force is so strong it blasts the glass from the balcony doors. Bael takes the brunt of the assault, grunting when glass shards rain down on us. But he only grips the doorframe harder, his back muscles straining with pent up fury.

"Leave—us," he snarls. To my horror, blood drips from cuts on his wings onto the wooden balcony floor.

"Us?" the queen says.

The shadows swirl at his feet and encase him until he's lost in the darkness. Before I can scramble back, he shifts into his raven form.

He screeches and flies straight toward her, his talons poised to rip and tear.

But time slows down. With a sweep of her hand, Bael stops mid-flight. She catches him in midair and clutches him under her arm. He's frozen, solid as a stone.

I shriek.

The last thing I see is the wicked curl of her smile before the goblin guards descend.

"I see he's got a pet now. Guards, seize her."

***

Everything is cold. My fingers feel numb, like they're submerged in Perstow Bay in the middle of winter. Something drips down my spine, and I vaguely register my cold sweat. I barely stay upright, leaning to one side until I hit something solid. Pain shoots down my shoulder. I blink awake and reel back, and a melodic laugh pierces my skill.

I see her standing before me: Queen Roma of Azrea. Her features are much more severe up close. Her fair skin and dark hair create a stunning contrast that's beautiful on anyone else, but not on her.

Tendrils of shadow form solid bars that cage me in.

Where am I?

My hands tied behind my back, I'm bound to a chair. I must have slumped over in my chair and hit the bars.

I blink several times until frayed, fading tapestries come into focus. They cover rough-hewn stone walls, and a worn rug covers most of the floor. To my right is an ornate armchair perched atop a small dais. This can't be the dungeon. Is this the queen's receiving room? Straight ahead is a small balcony that shows dusk approaching.

How long have I been here?

When I finish scanning the room, that's when I see him. A raven statue sits perched on the top of a vanity below a gold gilded mirror, wings still outstretched as if in mid-air.

Something stirs in my chest, a powerful tugging. My heart thuds so hard that my breath hitches.

Is that Bael?

I scan the statue's eyes and see nothing, but somehow, I can't look away.

What if it *is* him?

"What do you think, Mirror? Do you think she's ready to talk?"

I snap my gaze to where the queen hovers a few steps away, speaking to the mirror above the raven statue. From here, all I can see is a murky, swirling fog.

"She appears awake, Your Highness," a low voice says. I stare until a face appears within the mirror's surface, though it's too faint to pick out any real features. Shadowed eyes meet my gaze, and without meaning to, I startle. The queen follows his gaze to me. She takes purposeful strides to close the distance between us, then leans down when she reaches my cage, as if to talk to a wild animal.

"Aren't you an interesting little specimen?" The queen cocks her head to the side. "Pretty enough, I suppose. But that can't be the only reason my raven took you."

I swallow, a lump catching in my throat.

"So, what can you do?" She stands and appraises me, speaking more to herself than to me. "Why would he take you?"

I subtly test my restraints.

She clicks her tongue in annoyance. "Nothing to say, then?" She leans down again to get eye level with me.

Without warning, she forms ribbons of shadows that shoot between the bars of my cage. They swirl around me and melt with the bonds that keep me in my chair. They tug at me, forcing me to stand and I tighten every muscle to resist being yanked forward.

Agonizing seconds pass as I fight her will. When I look at her, she narrows her eyes. She realizes it the same time I do; I can resist her coercion.

She strides forward and plunges her hand into my cage. Grabbing my left arm, she pulls me toward her. It burns from every point where my arm touches the bars, but it's not the agony that makes my heart stop.

It's the moment she sees it, my keeper ring.

"A *keeper*?"

She pulls the ring off my finger but her eyes land on the mark.

"And he *marked* you?"

Suddenly she releases my arm, and I pull it back.

"So, that's why he took you." She turns to the statue on the vanity, slipping my ring into the pocket of her dress. "Very clever, Raven, thinning out the ward magic." Her eyes travel up to the mirror on the wall. "Mirror, can I control her?"

"No, Mistress. She must fulfill the mark's bargain first." The soft voice says.

She hisses in frustration, but my mind is on him.

For the first time, I'm grateful for this mark; it saved me. Even if Bael didn't mean to, he just saved me from being marked by her instead.

"So, what should I do with a Lander keeper?" She drawls, turning back to me. Slowly, her eyes rove over me and a smile forms on her lips. "You can tell me where the entrance to the caves is." Shadows spill from her hands to the floor. They race across the distance between us, slipping through the bars and curling up my legs.

Thrashing in my seat, I try to kick them away but they slither up my body. "I don't know where it is." I grit out.

The shadows slow their ascent when they reach my chest.

A few tense seconds pass, then they squeeze me. My mind is sluggish, desperately sifting through options, but I come up short.

Desperate, my eyes dart around the room. We're the only two people here, except for Bael and the mirror, but neither will come to my aid. Maybe I can use something as a weapon?

Her eyes flash menacingly as my gaze turns back to her. "Tell me your name, child."

Fighting against her shadows is bringing me dangerously close to passing out.

"Mira." I say, tight-lipped.

"Mira," she says, "do you know why I *hate* keepers?"

My pulse thrums loudly in my ears. I shake my head, still fighting the shadow's tightening grip.

"Because they're mortal. They'll always be mortal. A spelled ring changes nothing, does it? A wall could do what keepers do, your wards are apathetic excuse for magic." She sneers at me.

My breaths are quick now and I'm desperate to get air into my lungs.

"And without this," she pats the pocket holding my ring, "you're useless."

I know I shouldn't listen to her. I shouldn't let it get to me. But to hear her give voice to my own thoughts; it's like a punch to the gut.

If I'm not a keeper, then I am no one.

Angry tears well in my eyes. Elyse and the king didn't trust me enough to give me keeper magic. I'll never be one of them.

"I should have known Adrian would still try, though."

I barely register her statement through my spiraling thoughts. She's referring to the king. What is she talking about?

"You're going to bring me to the caves. We leave for Lander tomorrow, just in time for the royal wedding."

I blink away the black dots crowding my vision. She frowns, still talking to the mirror. "Dammit, Mirror, she's passing out."

Suddenly, a door nearby slams open. I watch the queen turn to take in the newcomer.

A stout goblin comes into view, huffing from exertion.

"What do you want?" The queen snaps.

"Mistress," he pants, "the gates."

"What?"

"—storming the gates..."

The rest of his words fade away as I hear their footsteps retreating.

Exhaustion takes over and I sink back in the chair. In my semi-conscious state, despair creeps in.

Bael and I failed our mission.

THE QUEEN'S CARD

We got into the castle, but I'm trapped here and so is he. I'll never see my home again.

And I failed Dulci and my king. I won't be able to stop the queen from killing Dulci.

I may have magic, but I'll never be a keeper.

Chapter 18

Cold sweat beads on my forehead and my stomach roils, rousing me from unconsciousness. It's nothing compared to what my mind replays.

I've failed everyone: the crown, my sister, and myself.

I tried so hard to be a keeper, making my king and mother proud. I thought this would finally prove my loyalty, but I'm worse off than I was before.

You don't always have to be doing something to make a difference.

Would toeing the line and playing it safe have earned me my magic?

I try to lift my head and my gaze lands on Bael, frozen and placed on a shelf like a bookend.

The tugging in my chest comes back tenfold at the sight of him.

I think back to the night I met him. When we collided, I came so close to hitting the ground that my hair brushed the floor, but he'd caught me. He'd held me, and though I hate to admit it, the attraction was immediate.

He's nothing like I imagined. He's stubborn and self-righteous, but he's also brave. And the gentleness he displayed when we watched the moonrise was the only reason I could control my magic. He's the only one who's taken the time to nurture it.

Just when I thought my world was black and white, he showed me the beauty of the gray.

Another wave of nausea hits, and I think I may pass out again. I force my shallow breaths to steady.

How can I escape this castle? How can I escape this cage?

I can't do it without him.

I *need* him.

Straining with the effort, I lift my head. I stare at his unseeing stone eyes.

Can he see through his frozen eyes? Can he hear anything? Is he conscious at all?

His fate is worse than mine.

I realize I'm no longer tied to the chair when I shift in my bonds, but I don't have enough energy to stand. I wiggle my fingers, desperate to summon it. I know it won't work without my ring.

Come on, Bael. Wake up. I need your help.

I need you.

I picture sending ribbons of purple magic across the room between us. I couldn't conjure them when I faced the queen, but I wish for them more than anything now. Dots fill my vision and my head feels impossibly heavy. It's then that I lose the battle to stay conscious and the world fades to black.

★★★

"Ouch!" *Crack.* "Dammit—"

A strong wind blows across my face. Wings flap, and after a series of cracking and snapping, my bonds release. I slump over until strong arms grip my shoulders and right me again.

"Mira, wake up!"

I smile; my memory conjures his voice so accurately. It's as if he's wrapped around me; I feel so safe that I don't move.

Until I'm shaken violently. My eyes shoot open. He's kneeling in front of me, his features swimming into view. His wings are out, but several of his feathers are smoldering.

This can't be real. He's still a stone statue on her vanity, isn't he?

"How?" I blurt, half-sobbing.

"Your magic," he says, searching my face. Seemingly satisfied, relief smoothes over the lines of his brow.

Before my brain can catch up with my body, I pitch forward into his arms. Elation and relief war within me, and the moment we collide, a bubble within me bursts. He falls back but wraps his muscular arms around me.

Time stops as our eyes lock, then his lips crash into mine.

All rational thought is gone.

He smells just like I remember; coffee and pine trees. I feel him envelop me, gripping me like he's not sure if I'm real. The world could collapse around us, and nothing else would matter except this moment.

He and I.

He's alive, and he saved me.

When we finally part, I'm panting and flushed, the rush of the contact leaves me buzzing. Suddenly, his eyes widen at me, and he drops his hands from where he grips my waist. I scramble off him.

Apparently reality hit us at the same time.

What has gotten into me?

Cool air hits my face but does nothing to stop the furious blush creeping up my neck. I'm hot everywhere and I pointedly look anywhere else but at him.

"Here." He leans down and offers me his hand. Reluctantly, I take it and he pulls me to my feet.

He clears his throat but I still can't look at him. When my gaze lands on our clasped hands, I realize I'm still missing my ring.

"It can't be my magic." My heart sinks as I pull my hand away from his. "She took my ring."

His shoulders fall. "The shadow mark." He points between us. "I cast it as a *fae bargain*, but I can feel your emotions. I knew that wasn't normal," his eyes glaze over as he thinks. "I don't know why I didn't see it before."

"See *what* before?"

He clears his throat, his bright eyes snapping back to me. "That it acts like a mating bond."

"A what?"

"It's old magic," he says, "said to snap into place when lovers declare their..." he trails off.

Embarrassment coils in my gut. He clears his throat, shaking his head. "It's so rare that there hasn't been a mated pair in at least a century. I didn't think I'd be able to," he swallows, "replicate it."

So, it's his magic's accidental bonding. It's a plausible explanation. Why else would we share that moment of insanity?

A curious flutter takes up residence in my stomach, lasting only a moment, before the incessant tugging in my chest appears. I rub at it irritably. He notices the gesture and tilts his head.

"Do you feel it too?" he points to me.

I nod, forcing this feeling away and replacing it with what I should be feeling, which is disappointment. I should care more that it wasn't my magic, that it was this damn bond. It freed him when I pleaded with it. But did it also have to make me jump on top of him?

Even though we now know why we responded like that, I can't look at him without feeling flush. My traitorous mind replays his large hands gripping my waist, and—

Nope. I am shutting down that train of thought right now.

I force my mind to refocus on everything that's happened, remembering the reason for the queen's sudden departure.

"Bael," I say, "she saw your mark."

He blows out a long breath, but I barrel on. "She tried to coerce me to reveal the entrance to the caves. She intends on taking me there…" I look away, remembering what's happening tomorrow.

The royal wedding.

This is a disaster.

He runs his hand along his jaw, agitated.

"Where is she now?"

"One of her guards burst in. He said something about someone storming the gates. I must have passed out."

A thunderous boom shakes the room. A bright orange light passes by the balcony, briefly illuminating the dark sky.

What was that?

We race to the balcony and pull open the doors. The roaring din hits us despite there being nothing below us but dense trees. We must be on the other side of the castle from the front gates because, out of sight, a battle rages; we can hear it all. Grunts, shouts, metal on metal. I can imagine it now, the scene must be bloody. Who's trying to take on the queen's goblin guards? I've seen them firsthand, with their sharp sticks, studded clubs, and dense armor.

"Who's outside?" I ask, looking at Bael, whose lips curl into a sly smile.

"My distraction."

I raise my brows. Who could he convince to storm the gates of the Azrean castle? Unless it's a certain ambitious rebel leader.

"Liam?" I guess.

He nods. I let that sink in.

"What will he do if he gets in?"

Bael runs his hand along his stubble. "He won't, but we'll take advantage of the chaos to get what we came here for."

My mind races at the sudden turn of events. I think of Dulci back in Lander and a wave of panic rushes through me. I've failed every step of the way. The queen's words echo in my head.

Without my ring, I am useless.

But I can't give up. There's so much I don't understand. I don't know if any of what Bael claims about the king is true, if he really blackmailed Bael's father, or if he stole Azrean magic to fuel the keeper's rings, but I will not stand back and let the queen hurt Lander or the royal family. I need to stay the course.

I may not be a real keeper or even have my ring, but I will not let my king down again. I got myself into this mess, but thanks to the shadow mark, I have a second chance.

How am I going to stop her from following through with her threat?

Chapter 19

I turn, ready to walk through the doors, but Bael has something else in mind. Without warning, he scoops me into his arms and runs full tilt toward the balcony.

My protest dies in my throat as he dives over the railing. We plummet through the cool night air, the shouts and cries of the battle at the front gates reach our ears.

In a flutter of wing beats, he rights us in midair. The weightlessness sends me into a momentary panic; I'm convinced this is how I'll die. His muscles ripple and strain under our combined weight on his injured wings. We hover a moment before he drops us ungracefully onto one of the stone patrol paths.

Blood pumps so loudly in my ears that I struggle to stand upright. I gulp down air until I finally steady myself.

"Why didn't we use the doors?" I gasp.

"The guards."

That makes sense. I eye the thick stone battlements around us, wondering where to go from here, but I don't wonder for long. He takes my hand and we race down the patrol path, away from the din of battle, the wind whipping hair in my face.

I should focus on the fact that we're running head-first into danger, but I can only focus on his large, warm hand in mine. My thoughts drift again to how it feels to be held and to have his lips on mine.

I know it's the fake bond that's influencing us, but I can't deny that giving in felt right.

I shake my head to dispel those thoughts and focus on the problem in front of us.

How can we stop the queen? We need to find a weakness and exploit it. My mind conjures her blackened fingers.

Disappointment curls in my stomach. If I had my keeper magic, I could help form a ward. I've never made one, but I've seen Ambrose and Elyse cast them plenty of times. But that's not an option. I have to rely on Bael.

The moment we run under the stone archway back into the castle, two goblins with pointed sticks spot us. Snorting and huffing, they race toward us, and I'm so thankful that their bulky frames make them slow and loud.

Bael unfurls his massive wings, blocking the corridor and shielding me from them. Flustered, I brace myself for a fight. But Bael's arms are up and a torrent of shadows burst from his hands. The goblins barely have time to put up their shields to deflect the onslaught as his shadows lash out in all directions.

An explosion of shadows throws both goblins against the stone wall. They slump to the floor, unmoving. We leap over their bodies and race through a maze of corridors.

We spend the next few minutes running, up a spiraling stone staircase and down a corridor until we reach a set of ornate double doors.

He slams his shoulder into the heavy wood until the doors creak open. With one last look down the corridor, we rush in. It's dark and dusty; clearly unused. But as Bael lights the sconces on the wall, my jaw drops.

Dark blue wallpaper lines the top half of the walls above dark wood paneling. Sturdy wooden bookshelves filled with leather tomes are on either side of a massive fireplace. Above the mantle is an antique mirror with intricate serpents carved onto either side of the frame.

"Where are we?" I ask, turning slowly to take it all in.

"The late king's private study."

It's certainly fit for a king. I spin around to ask why, but he replies before I can speak. "It's the last place the queen would think we'd be. And I need a quiet place to concentrate."

I nod, shoving my hands in my pockets and vowing not to disturb him while he focuses on the task at hand.

Bael brushes dust off a leather couch before sitting down and I do the same, sitting across from him.

When he inhales slowly and closes his eyes, my gaze lingers on his lips. I gulp, trying to dislodge a knot growing in my throat. It's a mixture of anticipation, anxiety, and something else entirely that only Bael brings out of me.

Agitated, he takes another deep breath. When he opens his eyes, I watch him run his hand through his hair. A traitorous thought pops into my head about what it would feel like to run my fingers through it.

He catches me staring and tilts his head wryly.

I clear my throat louder than I intended. "Any luck locating them?" I ask, tucking my legs underneath me just for something to do.

He shakes his head. "Nothing, not even a trace." He blows out another breath.

THE QUEEN'S CARD

Movement distracts me when he lifts a foot to rest on his opposite knee. It's so effortlessly sexy. When my gaze wanders back up to his eyes, they're unfocused. He's thinking, something I should be doing.

I wring my hands, loathing the missing ring. For a moment, when he touched me, when we cast together, I felt the magic bend to my will.

I had control.

Without it, I'm no help to him at all.

I pace the room, my thoughts spinning. I stop in front of the mantle, catching sight of my reflection in the mirror. My curls are a mess and my face is blotchy. I guess stress will do that to a woman.

Before my thoughts spiral, grey swirling fog appears in the mirror. I hear Bael jump to his feet, appearing next to me a moment later. A man appears on the reflective surface, though still obscured by the fog. I can just make out solemn, sunken eyes and the curve of a sharp jaw; a much younger face than I'd imagined.

He also looks vaguely familiar but I can't place where.

When he opens his mouth, it seems like a struggle for him.

Bael beats him to it. "King Lewis?" He leans toward the mirror to get a better look as my jaw drops.

What? That can't be right. Queen Roma's husband is dead. How is he trapped in a mirror?

"Bael," the voice says.

I look back and forth between them.

"You've never shown me your face," Bael says, his voice low.

Bael's position must have required him to interact with the man in the mirror at some point, so the late king must have shielded his face from view.

I have so many questions, but I know now is not the time to ask them.

"You need to stop her." The king must be referring to the queen, his wife.

"We're trying," Bael huffs, "but we can't do it alone. My magic isn't strong enough."

Another pang of shame roils in my stomach.

The king nods slowly, the disdain plain on his face.

"They're in this tower—" The king's voice breaks off and he closes his eyes, wincing.

Is the queen coercing him too?

Bael takes a sharp breath. "Where?"

But I know the king won't answer; I can see that he's suffering.

"It's ok." Bael stops him from trying to say anything else. "Don't give her a reason to hurt you more. We'll find them."

The king's eyes remain closed, his face still contorted.

We freeze for a long moment and when I catch Bael's gaze, I can feel frantic energy rolling off of him.

When the king's expression melts into relief, the agony must have subsided. "Arcana magic is a blessing, not a curse."

We both turn our heads toward him.

"What?" I blurt.

The king's eyes find mine and I shift a little where I stand, uncomfortable with the scrutiny.

"She stole it and warped it." Another wave of pain makes him grimace. "My bloodline's magic." He coughs violently but continues, "Her and the mortal. She'll destroy us all."

Bael nods, running his hand along his jaw.

The weight of that revelation sits heavily between us as the king nods.

"Stole what?" Bael says slowly.

"The card." The king retreats into the mirror.

"The arcana card? It's real?" Bael asks.

But as the fog returns, a scene appears within the reflective surface.

Chapter 20

The flames from the sconces flicker as I stride past. My boots click rhythmically on the stone floor, my pace matching the frantic beating of my heart.

I haven't seen her all day. And now I can't find her.

I certainly don't expect my future bride to be by my side every moment, but even my father noticed her behavior at dinner this evening. My brother, Daniel, did too, but I didn't want to believe him.

She looked nervous, on edge. It reminds me of when we first met and I don't like it at all.

I told him she's not feeling well, but discomfort crawls up the back of my neck at the lie. I don't know what troubles her tonight.

I turn the corner and emerge into the corridor. Father set her up with one of our guest suites. It was the first time I had seen her eyes light up; it was the promise of stability and comfort, especially after everything she'd been through.

The soft curve of her lips when she'd smiled and the way her raven hair cascaded over one shoulder had made my heart stop beating. I had wanted to capture that moment to relive over and over again.

I know she's not used to the opulence. Of course, I'm used to wealth. I'm a prince. I can take care of her.

All I want to do is make her happy. She's so thoroughly ensnared me, and I fear that if I don't keep her attention, she may disappear as quickly as she came. If I'm a hound, she is a fox; equal parts cunning and alluring. A prize I've never wanted so badly.

And she is mine.

By this time next week, it will be official.

I finally arrive at her door but notice it is ajar, soft light spilling into the hall. I stop in my tracks when I hear a male voice speaking in hushed tones. Who dares visit my bride at this time of night, alone?

"I thought you said the magic is in the cards?" *the male voice hisses.*

"He only gave me one card," *she says haughtily.* "But I'm going to siphon the magic."

Realization sinks like a rock in my stomach. She can't wield arcana magic, only my family can.

"That's not what we agreed on, Roma," *he says slowly.*

My heart thrashes in my chest. Agreed on what? Are they trying to steal the magic given to my bloodline?

I push my palm against the door with such force that the door slams into the opposite wall. Standing on the threshold, I see Roma, my Roma, in a red silken robe that trails to the floor.

A young man towers over her, a familiar sneer on his bland, unremarkable face.

Adrian St. James. The vain mortal prince. The heir to the Lander throne.

"Get away from her," *I growl.*

Adrian takes a step toward me, and I don't miss the gesture. He angles himself between me and my bride. Fury boils inside me.

She's not his, she's mine...isn't she?

But is this woman in front of me the Roma that I know and love?

THE QUEEN'S CARD

Did he force her to do this? I can't let myself believe the alternative.

"Roma," my voice comes out in a plea. "I showed you one of my family's cards to prove my love, not so that you could..." I stop talking when I see the irritation in her gaze, as if I'm intruding on her private moment with another man in my house.

A piece of me crumbles.

She doesn't reply, she raises her hands. Shadows hit me square in the chest, knocking me backward. My head hits the stone floor, hard. The last of my heart shatters when my eyes

★★★

King Lewis's face reappears in the mirror, replacing the awful scene he shared with us. I saw it from his eyes, his perspective. How did he share that with me?

As I look into his face now, the anguish is clear in his eyes. He thought he loved her, but she only wanted to steal his magic for her own gain.

Bael and I exchange worried looks, his eyes widening.

"It's in the caves."

"What's in the caves?" Bael says, his gaze snapping back to the mirror.

"What you seek." The king's face freezes before he can continue.

Bael rushes to the mirror and grips the frame. "Your Highness?"

But the king's eyes flicker in alarm before he recedes into the mirror, gray swirls taking his place.

I lean closer. "What happened?"

Bael blows out a breath and takes a step back. "She called him back."

Where does he go when the queen calls him back? How did he get trapped in the first place?

My heart sinks as I watch Bael pace the room, knitting his hands behind his head. "This whole time, I thought it was just stories, that there were no real arcana cards…"

I keep replaying the king's last words in my head, desperate to pull some meaning from it.

It's in the caves. What you seek.

Is he talking about the card that the queen stole from her husband?

Bael's body shakes with frustration. "Every answer just brings more questions."

Taking a step toward him, I answer, "I know."

"I keep…" he trails off, running an agitated hand through his hair. The look in his eyes is familiar. It mirrors my pain.

"Failing," I finish for him.

He nods, and before I realize it, my hand reaches up to touch him. It's that tugging feeling again—it pulls me toward him. I place my palm on his chest. He's warm and his heart beats a steady rhythm beneath my hand. For a moment, I expect him to step away, to put distance between us, because he's letting me see behind the mask. Somehow, I know that at this moment; he doesn't want placating words. He's raw and exposed, so I let myself be, too.

And all I want is something to ground me to this moment, when I'm so close to falling apart.

My mind recalls all the new information about the queen and her twisted, stolen magic. But that's not what turns my world upside down. What I can't stop thinking about is my king conspiring with his enemy to steal magic.

Bael's hands, rough and calloused, reach up to cup my face, drawing me out of my thoughts. He's achingly gentle when he strokes his thumbs across the freckles on my cheeks.

THE QUEEN'S CARD

I close my eyes, his touch distracting. I know the shadow mark acts as a bond that's not there, but I didn't know I wanted it.

What's it like to have a mate? To feel this kind of bond and for it to be real?

He leans down, eliminating the space between us. My breath hitches and butterflies thrash in my stomach at the proximity. My tongue darts out to wet my lips, and as the anticipation grows, I want him so much that I'm a moment away from yanking him toward me.

"What is it?" He says softly.

"What if everything I know," I swallow back the rush of emotions, "is a lie?"

The intensity of his attention is suddenly too much. I open my mouth to take it all back, desperate to rewind this moment, but adrenaline courses through me.

"Even if it is, it doesn't change you."

I suck in a breath at the unsaid words between us.

It doesn't change this, the chemistry between us. The magnetic pull, shadow mark or not, that keeps me by his side.

A wave of anticipation runs through me, and I bite my bottom lip to stop it. His eyes drop to my mouth and suddenly one hand drops from my face. He finds my waist and grips me tightly, pulling me close.

But still I need to be closer.

My eyes widen as his dark eyes alight with want. He must see exactly how I feel, because his voice is husky when he speaks.

"Is this what you want?"

I tilt my head back as an invitation, one hand still holding my cheek. His stubble grazes me as he plants hot, wet kisses down the column of my neck. It sends shivers skittering down my spine, and I can't help the moan that escapes.

"Say it."

"Yes," I say, breathless, feeling heat blooming in my cheeks.

In one smooth movement, he pins me against the wall. His lips are soft, molding perfectly to mine, but his kisses are anything but. His tongue demands entrance, and I immediately comply. The way he explores makes my toes curl and if he wasn't holding me up, I'm sure I'd melt into a puddle right here.

I lose myself to this heated moment of stolen kisses and frantic heartbeats. I welcome this unknown, this oblivion, instead of the reality threatening to shake me to my very soul.

Does everything I've been fighting for, to be a keeper, stand for nothing?

***

We only break apart when another boom shakes the ground under our feet. It pulls us back into the present, the last place I wanted to be.

"We should go," I say, flushed.

"Let me try to find them," Bael nods and closes his eyes. A long moment passes until he frowns and blows out a breath. "I can't sense them at all."

"Didn't the king say they're in this tower?" My chest tightens.

Bael turns to face the door, and I slip my hand in his. He turns back to look at me, another one of his soft smiles curling on his lips. It makes my stomach flip.

"Come on."

When we slip back into the corridor, I immediately realize what we felt when we broke apart. The noise is deafening, high-pitched clanging, and shouts feel disorienting.

Did the battle spill into the castle?

When we reach a set of stairs, we race down them until we emerge into a wide corridor. I stride forward, eager to put the sounds of the fight behind me, but suddenly Bael throws his arm out to stop me. I stop breathing, half expecting the queen to spring out from around the corner.

After a long moment of waiting, nothing stirs, but it doesn't calm my frantic heart. He motions for me to follow and we pass several large windows hidden behind tattered curtains. They flutter as we pass.

Several goblin guards turn the corner and face us before we can take another step.

"Bael!" I shout, but he sees them too.

Bael skids to a halt and doubles back, yanking me down another hall. "This way."

We barely dodge a volley of arrows. Our boots echo loudly as we race down the hall. But then he abruptly changes course. Instead of following the corridor as it curves to the right, he seems to pick a door at random, yanking on the doorknob with all his might.

He pulls me in and slams the door behind him. We tumble into the darkened space in a heap of arms and legs.

Chapter 21

When Bael sends flames to illuminate the sconces on the walls, it's a sight to behold. We step into the foyer of a hauntingly beautiful library.

Three stories of floor-to-ceiling bookshelves have thick wooden ladders on wheels. The vaulted ceilings have a magnificent painting of the night sky. I don't like to read, but Elyse does. If she saw this library, she would swoon.

The door shakes violently on its hinges, startling me. Bael gestures for me to follow him. We race up a staircase that spirals to a second floor balcony. We follow along the railing and I can't help but peer down to where we were moments ago. From this view, we're level with several wide windows, the night sky so dark that we can only see our reflections.

The pounding continues and my mind conjures the frightening image of dozens of goblins kicking the door down.

Along the far wall, we reach an alcove where a stone pedestal holds a statue of a bird. I swallow, discomfort prickling the back of my neck. Surrounding it are heavy, velvet curtains.

The wooden doors suddenly burst open below us. He grabs my hand and pulls me further into the alcove. We listen to the heavy footfalls ascending the stairs.

"What do we do?" I hiss.

But Bael isn't listening. His eyes are darting around the library. Panic rises in my chest. Several goblins reach the second floor landing while a few pairs of footsteps continue to the upper level. They'll be on us in moments if we don't do something.

Can they wield air magic like other Azreans?

"Bael!" This time, it gets his attention.

He squeezes my hand in acknowledgement before he whispers to me, "Wait."

Grunts continue as the guards spread out.

Shit, shit, shit.

I close my eyes, desperate to keep the panic at bay.

"When I give you the signal, run into the fireplace," he hisses.

My eyes fly open, but before I can protest, Bael's wings emerge and he shifts fully into his raven form. He flies to the tops of the massive bookshelves. I cup my hand over my mouth to keep from making any noise as he hovers near the murals on the ceiling. Any moment now, the goblins will spot him. A guard at the top of the second floor landing slams his javelin on the ground several times to get the others' attention.

"The Raven!" he shouts, pointing up.

At least a dozen goblins growl and slam their weapons on the wooden floor in triumph. My breath hitches as I watch them ascend the stairs, hoping to get closer to Bael. I dart behind the curtains and force myself against the cool stone wall, desperate to make myself smaller.

What is Bael doing?

When footsteps stomp right past where I hide, I squeeze my eyes shut and bite my lip. A pair of heavy footsteps stops only feet from where I hide. I think my heart will stop beating.

Long seconds pass, but beyond the curtain ruffling softly, nothing happens.

When the footsteps recede, I allow one small exhale to keep myself from passing out.

Bael caws loudly, and it causes another wave of excited energy within the goblins.

I need to get out of here. What did Bael say?

When I give you the signal, run into the fireplace.

What's the signal? Is this it?

I poke my head through the curtain again and realize his plan. He's distracting the goblins and leaving me a clear path down the stairs.

To the fireplace.

I swallow down the fear. Even if I race down the stairs without goblins pursuing me, what did he mean "into the fireplace"?

He caws again impatiently and I see him swooping and diving to agitate the goblins. They swing their maces and clubs at him. One almost clips his wings.

This must be the signal if there ever was one.

I look down at our shared mark. Do I trust our bond, false or not, to mean his intentions are good?

I have to; it's now or never.

I race through the curtains and bolt down the stairs, taking two at a time. Based on the grunting and snorting, followed by several pairs of footsteps, a few guards spotted me.

But I don't stop until I skid to a halt in front of the massive brick fireplace.

Run into the fireplace.

When I turn, I see six goblins trudging down the stairs, their armor making them clumsy but no less deadly.

I blow out a breath and run at the soot-covered fireplace at full speed.

***

I brace myself to smash into the stone chimney. I should have made contact by now, but I see nothing beyond the blackness of the charred hearth. Then, I feel the tingle of magic.

An illusion.

Brilliant!

I emerge on the other side, standing inside another fireplace. It's a little disorienting; this one is in a small sitting room with a massive emerald rug and a pair of high-backed armchairs. Eager not to discover if the goblins can follow me through, I race through the room into a corridor, then into what looks like a greenhouse.

It's a curious addition to a castle, with walls and a ceiling made up entirely of windows, casting rays of moonlight onto the packed earth.

So far, no one has followed me through the fireplace and I allow myself a long, ragged breath.

How long will it take for Bael to find me? If he knows about the illusion, he must know where it leads, right? I just need to wait for him to return.

I gaze around the greenhouse and wander to a window. I can barely see through the foliage of the plants standing sentinel along the perimeter. An interior courtyard is just beyond, protected by the high castle walls.

A trickle of cold sweat travels down my spine, and I shutter. When I hear a raven cawing, my heart races.

Is that Bael?

But that can't be right, he's still in the library. I walk toward the sound, between overgrown shrubs with branches like arms that move slowly toward me as I pass. I squint in the moonlight, not knowing what I'm looking for. It's quiet; the only sound I hear is my own footsteps, crunching down the path.

What a fate to end up here; stuck in the enemy castle, alone and wandering into who knows what kind of danger. Not to mention the silence forces me to listen to my spiraling thoughts.

I can practically hear Elyse's scolding if she could see me now.

What have you done, Mira? Are you that selfish, that desperate to belong, that you risked your safety and the crown's safety to get your keeper magic? Dulci already has keepers to protect her and we're doing our job. You left.

The guilt crashes down on me like a ton of bricks. Maybe I have been selfish. But if they truly wanted my help, they could have made me a real keeper. If I had magic, which for a fleeting, blissful moment I had, then I wouldn't have gone searching for an opportunity to prove myself.

Maybe it's better this way. Maybe I'm too much of a liability for them to be bothered with. But there's one thing I didn't anticipate when I tangled myself in this dangerous web with Bael and the enemy queen: uncovering just how little we know about the state of the realms.

I thought I knew King Adrian, but what if King Lewis is right? Can I believe an enemy king, dead or otherwise? Maybe it's just the rambling of a heartbroken, jealous husband. And there's always two sides to every story, right? I can't help but wonder.

Another deafening rumble erupts from somewhere in the castle. Swerving to avoid a long vine, I pass a statue partially covered in moss

THE QUEEN'S CARD

and lichen. It's a crying woman, on her knees with her palms up. Her expression is so realistic, so raw, it's as if the sculptor knew her suffering.

I quickly pass, unsure which is worse; my racing thoughts or this garden. It feels like I shouldn't be here, like this is an ugly secret to be tucked out of sight.

A shrill caw cuts through the air, closer this time. I scan the windows but see that none are open. But then I find the source. Hidden among particularly thick overgrowth, I see a statue of a young man holding a sword. The blade appears real, though the tip has broken off. He looks so lifelike that it's as if he's frozen in time, in the middle of slaying an unknown foe.

Hanging on the end is a bronze birdcage with a very realistic raven. So realistic that as I approach, it blinks at me.

I move cautiously; I don't want to scare it.

"It's ok, I won't hurt you," I whisper, reaching out to touch the cage. "How did you get in here?"

Its talons click on the metal perch as it hops from foot to foot.

How sad to see such a creature caged in an abandoned part of the castle. How long has it been here, alone?

I grip the cage with my fingertips, a deep sadness welling up within me. I know what it feels like to be trapped, to be helpless. If there was ever a time that my magic could return to me, that I could get just a sliver of magic back, it should be now, when at least one of us could be free.

I close my eyes and concentrate. What did Bael teach me when we were watching the moonrise?

Picture it wrapping around your fingers.

I pour all of my desperation, my anxiety, all my focus into breaking the lock. The cage shakes beneath my fingers and my eyes fly open, suddenly worried that I hurt the bird.

But when it snaps its beak angrily at something behind me, I turn to see who it is.

Bael stands in human form a few feet behind me, his eyes locked on the bird in the cage.

Chapter 22

"Mira, how…?" He trails off. When Bael turns to me, I see the anguish in his eyes.

I tilt my head, confused.

But before I can ask, he strides right past me to the birdcage and leans in. The raven bristles at the proximity and clicks its beak in warning.

"You found…" He doesn't finish his sentence. When he raises his hand, my breath hitches. What is he going to do? When his shadows surround the lock, I hear a sharp click and the lock drops to the floor.

The bird seizes its moment to escape and bursts through the cage door. I scramble back. In a flurry of feathers, a man appears, unsteady on his feet. Bael rushes forward to help the man stand. The moonlight illuminates his features. With close cropped dark hair and a severe expression, he reminds me of the Prince of Brevalin, Dulci's fiancé.

But it can't be him, can it?

Bael grips the man's face in his hands. They lock eyes before twin grins appear. They embrace and the relieved laughter is music to my ears.

Standing next to one another, the resemblance is obvious. Bael is taller, but possesses the same broad shoulders and dark brows.

That can't be a coincidence. And the way they greeted each other. It's as if...

Then it hits me. It *is* Prince Reid.

And the resemblance...

"Are you...?" I point between them.

"Reid is my brother," Bael says, thumping his brother on the back.

"The more handsome *older* brother," the prince corrects him with a grin.

I stare between them open-mouthed, forcing my brain to catch up with my eyes. How is that possible? I look back at the Brevalin prince, who's eyeing me warily.

"You're one of Dulci's guards, aren't you?" he says.

It's not really a question, I can see now that he recognizes me. Suddenly flustered, I swallow and nod. His scrutiny quickly turns to suspicion and I force myself to focus on the *other* revelation.

I turn to Bael and see him in a whole new light. "Are you from *Brevalin?*"

Bael looks at his brother, then nods.

"Does that make you a...?"

A prince? It's so bizarre that I don't even say it aloud.

He rubs the back of his neck, suddenly uncomfortable. "I have royal blood, but I'm not a prince."

What does that mean? All I can manage is blinking at him, at both of them. I have so many questions. I think back to every time Bael referred to Azreans as *them*, not *us*, and suddenly his desire to defy his queen makes more sense now; Queen Roma isn't his queen at all.

How did she ensnare a foreign royal, prince or not, to be her second in command?

I want to ask him about everything, but I focus on one question at a time; the one that's most pressing.

"How are you here?" I turn to Prince Reid, ignoring the discomfort from his reaction to me.

Bael turns and appraises his brother as if the thought just occurred to him.

"Yeah, how the hell did that happen?"

Prince Reid bristles at the accusatory time.

"It's not like I volunteered," he says, then turns to me. "She took me the night of that party." He looks back at me pointedly.

"How?" Bael prods. "Did you provoke her again? The last time you insulted her, it landed us in this mess."

The prince and I both turn to gape at Bael.

"Seriously? You think it's my fault?" Bael's brother narrows his eyes.

"No one needs you to be the hero, Reid. You're always doing that. Insisting that—"

"Bael," I grab Bael's arm and tug him just out of earshot of his brother. He opens his mouth to argue but I shake my head. Clearly there's some unresolved animosity.

In my periphery, the prince crosses his arms defensively and stares at us.

"You just got your brother back and now you're jumping down his throat?" I whisper at Bael, not caring that right now I'm reprimanding two very important men.

His jaw clicks but he doesn't respond.

"Now is not the time to fight. You two need to work together. We need him."

"I know," he says, exasperated, "but the burden on my shoulders is because of him..." he trails off.

I don't know what his brother did to earn Bael's anger, but right now, it doesn't matter. What matters is that we found him, and we're one step closer to keeping the queen from doing any more harm.

I close the distance between us and put my hand on his chest. He looks down at where our bodies touch, then looks me in the eyes.

"I've been angry for a long time," he says softly.

"I know how that feels. Believe me, I do," I cup his cheek, "but now is not the time," I whisper.

He pulls me close and wraps his arms around my waist.

"Looks like we both have some things to let go."

Tears prickle my eyes and I nod. "Who would have thought we'd have something in common?"

He chuckles softly and gently moves a lock of my hair behind my ear. The touch is so gentle that I lean into it.

"I'm still in the room, you know," Prince Reid says pointedly.

I jump back, so lost in the moment that I forgot he was watching us. Bael doesn't step back, in fact he leans forward as if to pull me close again. When I resist, he sighs and turns to his brother.

"Don't look so smug," Bael snaps.

"I must have missed a lot if you found someone to thaw your icy heart." The prince's words aren't in jest, they're sharp and cruel.

Bael cracks his knuckles, falling right into his brother's bait.

"Ok," I interject, "now that we found your brother, we need to focus on forming a plan. Right?" I turn back to Bael, who huffs but nods.

The prince cocks his head at us. "A plan? For what?"

I blow out a breath. "We're going to take down the Azrean Queen."

Then the eldest prince does something unexpected; he laughs. It's a deep, belly laugh that has him leaning down and choking on his next words.

"You must have lost your mind, brother. There's no taking that witch down."

This is going to be so much harder than we thought.

***

"So, what's your plan?" Prince Reid stares between the two of us, still leaning against the window sill.

Bael grits his teeth. "It's a work in progress."

"Well, it's not like you and I," he points between himself and his brother, "could just stop her. What are we going to do, trap her?"

Though he says it flippantly, I see a flicker of something in Bael's eyes.

"Liam and his rebels are fighting her goblins as we speak. Maybe if we cast enough vines, they'll do most of the—"

"Are you serious?" he tilts his head. "That idea is insane. And do you really trust Liam, of all people?" His eyes trail over to me, and I hear the unspoken words. *Do you trust her?*

Bael folds his arms behind his head and looks up toward the ceiling. He looks one moment away from throttling his brother. "It's not like we had a lot of time to plan, we've spent all this time trying to rescue you—"

"You have no plan at all."

"Well, by all means, if you have a better idea, do tell," Bael snaps, dropping his arms to his sides.

The air is suddenly tense around us when Bael takes a step toward his brother. Have they always acted like this? I admit, my sister knows how to get under my skin too, but in the face of something this important, we wouldn't spend our time bickering.

How long have they been harboring this resentment toward the other?

"Don't pick this fight, brother," the prince says, pushing off from the window sill. "We're not strong enough. We need to get out and go home. Regroup there. Come up with a real plan. Hell, we can bring father's soldiers—"

"I'm not leaving Mira."

I inhale sharply. The brothers are now nose to nose, posturing and scowling, until Prince Reid turns his venomous gaze on me.

"Why?" He says it so quietly, narrowing his eyes as if squinting would help him see what makes me worth staying in Azrea for.

"Have you forgotten that she's the one who found you? I couldn't *sense* you anymore."

Prince Reid purses his lips. "I don't know how her magic works—" He stops abruptly and turns to me.

Without conscious thought, my hand hovers over the spot just below my elbow. His eyes follow the movement to where our shared mark is currently hidden by my shirt sleeve.

In the span of a moment, Prince Reid reaches forward, grabs my arm, and pulls up my sleeve. When he sees the mark, he rounds on his brother.

"You *marked* her? Have you lost your mind?"

Bael grabs a fistful of his brother's shirt. "If you don't take your hand off her right now—"

"She's a keeper, and my *fiancée's* guard! She abandoned her post!"

His words pierce my heart as if it were a dagger. Is that what he thinks? I wrench my arm from his grip, pulling down my sleeve.

Bael winds up to take a swing.

"Stop it!" I snap. Surprisingly, they both pause, though both are so tense they're shaking. "You can tear each other apart when this is all over," I continue despite my cheeks reddening, "but right now, you need to put whatever this is aside."

The silence following my outburst highlights the magnitude of who I just yelled at. Two royal Brevalin brothers; one set to marry Dulci to secure our alliance, and the other—who until recently I hadn't even known existed—is still answering to the enemy queen.

"It's no longer about us, or Azrea, or Brevalin. She'll destroy everyone if we let her leave this castle," I say. To their credit, neither brother argues. "We have no idea what her plan is or what she's capable of doing, so we can't give her any opportunity. She chose to pick a fight with every kingdom in this realm, and she'll doom us all if it's up to her. We need to do something about it."

Prince Reid purses his lips, but doesn't argue with me. "Fine," he turns to his brother, "but your keeper is slowing us down. Can we at least fly up to the roof to cast?"

Bael stares daggers at him.

The prince works his jaw. "Fine, we'll go at *her* pace then."

Another thundering boom shakes the castle. Both Bael and his brother shift and hover in front of me as ravens. I should be used to at least Bael shifting by now, but watching them both do it is unnerving.

Footsteps echo down the corridor and shadowed fog appears, curling along the stone floors.

That can't be good.

Bael snaps his beak at me to get my attention. He tilts his head behind me and races off in the other direction toward the noise, the prince zooming after him.

Looks like it's time to go.

Chapter 23

I race through winding corridors, following the outlines of the two brothers. This castle is massive, and I've lost track of where we are. I only catch my breath when they shift back into their mortal forms right before we reach a corridor that curves to the right. We must be close to the front doors if I can hear the sounds of battle over my pounding heart.

Wheezing, I lean against the stone wall. The prince shoots me a withering glare, as if my weak mortal lungs offend him. But I know what he thinks of me now, I bet he sees his brother's determination to overthrow Queen Roma—without regrouping in Brevalin—as my doing. I watch as he turns back and hisses clipped words into Bael's ears. I want to set the record straight, to tell him that I didn't abandon Dulci by choice, but this is not about me, clearing my name can wait.

Prince Reid strides a few steps ahead of us, motioning for us to stay put as he turns the corner, moving out of sight. Bael stiffens, clearly offended by the idea of taking direction from his older brother, but stays put anyway, stepping in front of me. My stomach does backflips, and my chest tugs painfully. He's positioning himself in front of me to protect me.

The prince reappears and gestures for us to follow. Around the next corner is a corridor that looks down into a grand hall. We race across it, the clanging of metal echoing below. A horrid curiosity forces me to look down as I pass.

When an arrow barely misses my ear and spears into the tapestry behind me, Bael tugs me down below the stone railing. The three of us crawl until we reach the other end of the hall. With our backs against the rough stone, the three of us peer around the corner into the foyer below.

The queen stands with her back to us. Her guards knock several rebels to their knees, binding them with shadows. Their gazes are venomous as they stare up at her. Two of her goblins muscle their way through the crowd until they face their queen, holding someone between them. When they let their prisoner go, the figure lands roughly at her feet. He stands ungracefully, and the sharp features and dark hair are unmistakable, despite a bleeding cut above his eye. He straightens his jacket haughtily and scowls at her, clear hatred in his eyes.

It's Liam.

My eyes widen. So he *did* lead his rebels to attack the castle.

"Why are you darkening my doorstep?" Queen Roma snaps. "Call off your band of imbeciles. I have no time for nonsense."

His hands curl into fists. "I gave you what you wanted," he snarls, "but you never held up your end of the bargain."

Despite the chaos, every rebel in that room snaps their gaze to Liam. In every bruised eye, every tightened jaw, I see the moment they realize that their fearless leader omitted some crucial details from their plan.

I freeze. What does that mean? Is he working for her? Bael stiffens next to me.

"You're lucky that I even considered helping you. When I found you, you were nothing but a common thief with an overinflated sense of importance. Know your place, Liam. Stop this petty tantrum."

"It's not a tantrum, your Highness," he says, his voice laced with mockery. "It's a coup."

Based on Bael's quiet snort, he didn't expect *that*, and, if the growls of Liam's men have anything to say about it, their loyalty is quickly waning.

I expect her to lift her hands and send her shadows to suffocate him on the spot, but she laughs. The sound is like glass shattering, high-pitched and discordant.

"You think you can *dethrone* me?" she says, raising an eyebrow.

He rolls his neck and squares his shoulders as if bracing for a blow.

"How long have we known each other, hmm? Ten years? Long enough for you to know what your queen is capable of. I would have kept my word if you kept yours, but you didn't." The last words escape her lips in a sneer.

He opens his mouth to argue, but tendrils of shadows shoot out and race toward him. They crack the stone tile at his feet, and he jumps back, startled. His rebels thrash in their bonds but the fury rolling off them in waves is aimed at the back of their leader's head.

Liam straightens and turns back to the queen, clearly ignoring the growing rage directed at him from every angle.

The queen stalks forward until she's right in front of him. One long fingertip grazes under his chin before grabbing his jaw in a vice-like grip.

"I know you have a wraith bloom. There's no other way you could have breached my wards without it. But you didn't retrieve them. Your magic isn't powerful enough. No one in Azrea is powerful enough. So, who helped you?"

He narrows his eyes at her. "I'm more powerful than you think."

Shadows form at her fingertips and I watch his throat bob as he swallows.

She laughs and squeezes his cheek roughly as she makes a show of looking down as his rebels, their eyes alight in anger.

He wrenches his head out of her grip and straightens his back, staring at her defiantly.

"You don't deserve the crown you wear," he spits at her, "and I'm going to be the one to rip it from your head."

Before he can take a step forward, she lifts her hands and a torrent of shadows circle him. The darkness grows until it consumes him. Time slows down as I stare at the dark fog spinning around him like a cyclone. When the shadows finally dissipate, I blink several times before deciding that I'm hallucinating. Where Liam once stood, a raven now hovers, flapping its wings erratically.

Liam is another man cursed to shift into a raven.

Bael reaches out and grips my hand.

"I can end your life now," she smirks at the bird.

The bird squawks at the threat, the noise shrill in my ears.

Then she lifts a hand, the curling shadows forming once again. This time, Liam, in bird form, stops cawing. The queen stands that way for a long moment, staring down her submissive raven.

"Call off your pathetic followers and find Bael," she finally says. "He'll be looking for his arrogant brother. And if you see the girl, kill her on the spot."

The bird clicks its beak as his men shout curses at their leader, thrashing against the magic that binds them.

As the raven flies above the foyer, the queen turns to the goblins that linger. "Humans are so tiresome to control. I much prefer the company of beasts."

***

"Why is everyone turning into ravens?" I shout, running up a staircase two steps at a time. We didn't stick around to see which direction Liam flew, we turned back the way we came. Bael and his brother shifted again, leaving me to chase after them through the maze of corridors and up this damn staircase.

I know neither of the brothers can answer me and I watch as their wings flap wildly as we ascend to one of the towers.

Liam is now the third man I've met whom the queen forced to shift into a raven. How many others have turned into birds, and why?

Humans are so tiresome to control.

Now that Liam is under her control, we may not survive long enough to find the answers. The queen said they knew each other, and that they struck some sort of bargain. But Liam hates the queen. Why would he bind himself to her? Was it a deal that turned sour?

Short of breath, I struggle to keep pace. I'm completely out of energy by the time the landing comes into view. The cool air is a welcome relief, and I gulp it down, watching as the brothers fly through the stone archway. Struggling, I follow the princes onto a battlement between two spiraling towers, overlooking the thickly forested front gates, and the site of a losing battle. As we look down in horror, her guards force every one of Liam's rebels to drop their weapons. I can't imagine the fate they'll meet when they're forced into the castle.

Flying over the scene is a raven, circling and cawing mournfully; Liam.

Bael shifts a little closer to me.

"What's going to happen to them?" I ask so quietly I wonder if the wind drowns out my voice.

Bael slides his hand into mine and gives it a gentle squeeze. "We can't worry about that now."

I know he's right, but watching those men dragged into the castle to an unknown fate is awful to watch. Those are her own people.

My mind wanders back to what the queen said to Liam when confronted her.

I would have kept my word if you kept yours, but you didn't.

Whatever it is, I have the feeling Liam will pay for not keeping his word, if not from the queen, then from his own men.

Chapter 24

The air is tense as we stand on the battlement. I fight to keep the rising panic and doubt at bay as Bael lets go of my hand and stands by his brother.

With his posture stiff and his gaze calculating, Prince Reid lifts his hands, aiming them toward the castle grounds. Glowing emerald vines shoot from his fingertips. I step back, startled. Bael turns toward his brother and raises his hands, mimicking the gesture, but when tendrils of shadows race toward his brother instead, I suck in a breath. I watch his shadows snake around his brother's arms, encasing his hands in darkness.

The prince bristles at the unexpected touch, but when he refocuses, a powerful surge doubles the amount of foliage flowing from the prince's hands.

Bael's magic must be strengthening his brother's magic.

I look down in fascination. Rather than a ward that I'm used to seeing keepers cast, the prince creates thick, green brambles that spread out to surround the castle at least two stories high. A sharp crunching noise, like trees snapping, echoes around us as the branches criss-cross into an intricate, living wall.

THE QUEEN'S CARD

When the branches finally stop moving, Bael's shadows snake around them, forming giant black thorns.

Finally, they drop their hands and let out ragged breaths, the task clearly weakening them both. I exhale, not realizing that I was holding my breath.

"Woah," I whisper, staring down in awe.

"Let's see how long it holds," Prince Reid says, his words clipped.

The now-familiar tugging in my chest pulls my attention away. My heart thumps with adrenaline and excitement. It must be the rush of our success. When I turn, Bael must feel it, too, because his gaze is enough to make me melt on the spot. His eyes are like liquid umber, and a small smile forms on his lips.

He closes the distance between us and sweeps me into his arms. I lean into his embrace and wrap my arms around his neck, and the tugging subsides. He grabs my waist and pulls me closer until his hands rest on the small of my back.

My gaze wanders back down to the unruly undergrowth below.

"The vines…"

Bael finishes my thought. "It's part of our green magic."

"And you strengthened it with your magic. Can everyone in Brevalin—"

Bael shakes his head. "I have no green magic. I forfeited it when I pledged my allegiance to the queen."

My heart pangs in my chest. His magic, his Brevalin magic, is gone with the queen's twisted magic in its place? I think back to what I've seen Bael do with his magic. He can glamor himself to look like someone else and he can mark someone for a fae bargain, though in our case, it mimicked a mating bond instead. How powerful would he be if he had his Brevalin magic instead?

A thought pops into my head.

"It was your magic on the beach, right?" I think back to all the time I spent desperately searching for the source.

I watch as a smirk forms on his full lips.

I gasp. "So *you're* the one who tripped me?"

He snorts with laughter. "Yes, I did. To be fair, you were an enemy at the time."

I swat at his chest. "That hurt!"

"I didn't pull you down *that* hard."

But the lightheartedness drains away when I recall the dread and the anxiety that plagued me in those weeks.

"Were you in the ballroom that night, at the party?"

"No," he answers quietly. "I was on the grounds, looking for the caves."

I nod, looking back up into his eyes. How strange to think back to who we were then, enemies with entirely different missions. But are we really that different now, with the effects of a fake mating bond driving our actions?

"You know," he leans in slowly, halting my spiraling thoughts, "meeting you sparked something in me. And it's not just the mark we share."

My breath hitches as his nose gently grazes mine.

"For so long, I was going through the motions. I let the despair make me numb."

I nod, knowing exactly what that feels like.

"What about now?" I ask, my breath hitching.

When he brings his lips just an inch away from mine, I brace myself to get lost in his kiss. I want to lean forward; I want to close the distance between us, but something holds me back. I glance back at Prince Reid, who's loitering at the other end of the battlement, watching us with sharp eyes.

I shake my head and turn back to Bael. It's not just the angry prince that's keeping me from closing the distance between us.

I need distance between Bael and my heart, because I know this isn't real.

It's the shadow mark; I can't let myself forget that.

He must sense my hesitation, because he tilts his head to the side and frowns. "It may have started with the mark, Mira." His warm breath tickles my lips. "But this," he brushes his lips along mine, "is real. At least to me."

My heart thumps loudly in my ears, and the lightness of his touch makes me lightheaded.

"If you don't feel it, too," he finishes, "I'll let go."

Time suspends, hanging in this one moment. A moment where he's giving me the choice; he's letting me decide. Can I blame the bond for what I feel?

The bond may have forced us together initially, but what I feel is beyond the chemistry and the attraction, right? It has to be. These feelings are because I'm learning the real him. The one he hides away to keep those he loves safe.

And in this moment, under the stars, it reminds me of the night when we watched the moonrise. His words replay in my head.

You can find beauty in the most unexpected things. Those are the things that I guard with my life.

It's then that I realize what I want more than anything is to be something he guards with his life.

I take a deep breath, then take the plunge.

The kiss is better than I could have ever imagined, even better than all the ones before. He pulls me impossibly closer as he sweeps his tongue into my mouth to explore. My hands tangle in his hair, and I feel the shiver that travels down his spine. He dips me in a movement so much like the first time we met, a dance for just the two of us. My stomach flips and swoops.

When we part, it's as if emerging from the most blissful dream, one that I don't want to wake up from. He looks down at me with an adoration I can't describe and runs his thumb along my lower lip.

Prince Reid, a few feet away, stares at us, his mouth agape. When Bael turns to him, his arms still around my waist, his brother has the good sense to snap his jaw shut and look away. The moment of bliss is gone, and in the aftermath are the mountains we have yet to climb before this is all over.

I finally pull away, straightening my shirt just for something to do.

Who is this version of me? Until recently, everything I've done so far is to prove my loyalty to my king, to earn my keeper magic. But if there's one thing being in Azrea has taught me, it's that things aren't black and white. What if proving myself to the keepers is no longer the most important thing to me?

Bael and Prince Reid's sudden shift into their raven forms startle me out of my racing thoughts. I blink up at them, confused. The prince takes off toward the castle, flying through an open window. Bael stares down at me from where he hovers, snapping his beak sharply.

Something is wrong.

When Bael flies after his brother, I follow, turning toward the open-air corridor that leads back into the castle. Bael turns his head and caws at me again. Is he telling me not to follow?

"I don't understand!" I shout. "What's happening?"

But the next moment, I lose sight of Bael as he flies through the window.

What happened? He told his brother that he wouldn't leave me behind. He made that point clear when Prince Reid tried to convince him to go back to Brevalin. Panic claws at me. I'm alone. Truly alone, with no Bael and no magic.

Take a deep breath. This is no time to lose my head.

Bael and I are in this together and, saints-help-me, I'm going to finish what I started. So I wait for the inevitable, the tugging in my chest. Then I feel it; I couldn't ignore it if I tried. The wind whips through my hair as I race across the battlement and back into the castle.

The halls are nearly identical to every corridor we've run through. Now is normally when I'd panic, but this time, I focus on the feeling. It tugs me down a corridor to the right, so that's where I run.

The longer I wind through corridor after corridor, the more a sinking feeling takes up residence in my stomach. I know I've found him when I reach the end of a long hall with towering double doors that are ajar. Dark orange light glows through the cracks in the frame. I swallow down my fear.

This place is where Bael didn't want me to go. I stay in the shadows for a tense moment, debating with myself. I don't know what I'm running blindly into, or I'll find on the other side. It could be the queen herself. But I can't leave him. I didn't go this far just to hesitate.

Steeling my nerves, I take a deep breath, and run toward the door.

Chapter 25

The circular room is massive. Thick, jagged stones form walls so high that it feels that I've fallen down an endless well. I swallow when I see the celebration in front of me. From an open, recessed pit in the center of the room, a giant open flame roars. Smoke billows and curls, as if dancing, before escaping out of massive arched windows.

Dozens of goblin guards slam their javelins on the stone, grunting, and snorting with glee. Some dance around the bonfire, their dented armor glinting in the firelight. Shaking, I force my eyes up to take in the raised dais along the back wall. Queen Roma sits on a black marble throne, watching her goblins dance and celebrate.

As if my gaze summoned her, the queen's dark eyes find mine. She leans forward, her thin lips curling in delight. She waves over a pair of guards to restrain me.

"Right on time," she says, amused.

I clench my hands into fists until they're wrenched back.

"Can't stay away, can you?" she says as she stands, leering down at me.

THE QUEEN'S CARD

That's when I notice who's at her feet. Bael and his brother are on their knees in their mortal forms, wrists bound in front of them.

No.

I bite back a sob. She must have realized they cast the thorns.

As she descends the stairs, I catch sight of her blackened fingers. It's spreading to both hands. Does that mean that she's getting weaker?

I try to catch Bael's eyes but the look he gives me is enough to break my heart. He mirrors the sorrow I feel.

I'm sorry, I mouth.

"Wait here," her eyes travel back to me. "I'll deal with you in a minute. But first I'm punishing my naughty birds."

★★★

"This is what happens when you love someone, isn't it?" her gnarled grip wrenches his chin up to look at her.

I choke back a sob seeing Bael on his knees. He furrows his brow in anguish, but it's not just physical pain.

"You did it all for them, right? First your brother, then your mortal?" The queen lets her gaze wander to Prince Reid, then to me.

Bael grits his teeth but refuses to take the bait.

The queen senses it but keeps pushing him. "Tell me, why did you do it?"

At first I don't think she expects an answer, but then she leans down to grip Bael's chin in her spindly fingers, forcing his gaze to meet hers.

"Why sacrifice yourself to save someone else? They'll forget about you in the end. They'll only save themselves."

The queen's goblins continue to dance gleefully around the bonfire, though a few have stopped to watch. A hot tear rolls down my cheek. Now that I know him, I know that Bael is the most selfless man, underneath the commanding presence. The ruthlessness and the secrecy was for survival for himself and for his family.

Does that include me, too? Another tear tracks down the dirt on my face and my vision swims with unshed tears.

"You have nothing to say, hmm?" She grips his chin tighter. "Well then, that deal you made with me to spare your brother? It's off the table now. You went against me, after everything I've done for you. I know you want to take his place, but I'm no longer feeling generous."

"I'd do it a thousand times over," he grunts.

The queen's lips curl into a cunning smile. "That's what I'm counting on."

My heart stops beating. What does she mean by that? I thrash against my captor's grip but he holds me steady. When the queen lets go of Bael and closes her eyes to cast, I know it's too late.

Prince Reid and I are shouting but we're drowned out by the excited snorts and shouts of the goblin guards who slam their javelins onto the stone floor in excitement.

When the queen waves her hand, he shifts into his raven form only to collapse, unconscious. The prince shouts and curses as he looks at his brother and struggles against his bonds.

"Reid, be a good little bird and stop squawking."

Before he can utter another curse, she waves her hand in his direction and in a flurry of feathers, he shifts into his raven form, too. He lets out a near-splitting screech before she waves his hand. He goes limp and collapses on the stairs next to Bael. Two unconscious birds.

"Bring me a cage!" the queen shouts to her closest guard. He stumbles over his feet as he rushes from the room.

"No!" I shout.

"You know," the queen says as stares down at them, "I always liked you both more as birds." She shrugs and sighs. "Just be thankful I spared you both your father's fate."

What did she do to the Brevalin King? Bael said King Adrian blackmailed his father. My stomach sinks. He meant the King of Brevalin. Did Queen Roma and King Adrian hurt him together? Before I can form another thought, she turns her attention back to me. I try to swallow the lump in my throat.

"Mira," she says, "why do you keep turning up?" She takes slow, measured strides toward me.

I bite my lips to keep from answering, determined not to take the bait. Instead, I focus on trying to call magic to my fingertips. I know it won't work. My ring is probably still in the queen's pocket, but I have to try.

"At first I couldn't figure out why some nobody like you, a Landerian *brat*, kept weaseling your way into my plans. You're like a roach beneath my boot."

I swallow but keep my head up.

"But then I saw the similarities."

I can't help the snort that escapes my lips.

She quirks a brow at me. "Oh, you don't see them?" She takes a step closer to me. "I know what it feels like to be out of control. You want your precious keeper magic, don't you? To be one of them? But let me give you some advice. Let it go. You'll never be a keeper." The words are like a dagger straight through my heart. I close my eyes, knowing deep down that she's right.

"Because," her voice pulls me back to the present, "I have plans for you. You remind me so much of myself, of how I would have turned out if I didn't take control of my own fate."

Before I can reply, the queen turns, her shadows circling Bael's unconscious raven form. Suddenly, he grunts, his jaw clenching. When the shadows dissipate, he's back in his mortal form, coughing and gasping.

"Bael!" I shout, my cheeks wet from new tears.

But when he lifts his head, his gaze on me is murderous.

"Bael?" I whimper. He slowly stands and stalks toward me, rolling out his shoulders. When he reaches where we stand, he towers over me. All traces of the kind, gentle man are gone. In his place is the ruthless weapon Queen Roma honed him to be.

He closes the distance and leans down, his eyes staring into mine.

"Bael…"

He grips my throat, cutting off my words.

His wings unfurl behind him.

Everything we worked for, all the feelings that have grown between us, all of it is gone. Hot tears track down my cheeks.

And then my world turns dark as I lose consciousness.

***

My body jerks awake with an unexpected jolt. I pitch forward and by the time my eyes fly open, I feel Bael's large hands gripping my shoulders and pushing me upright.

"Bael?" My voice is hoarse.

I look up at him, but it's not the man I know. In his place is the poor facsimile of the man I share a shadow mark with, hard edges, severe expression, and a lip sneering in disdain.

THE QUEEN'S CARD

I rock as the carriage we're in trundles forward. He lets go of me and sits back down opposite me, acting as if there is no worse punishment than touching me. When I try to move, I realize I'm bound within his shadow bonds once again.

"Bael, it's *me*." I hate the pleading in my voice.

He has to recognize me through her coercion, but when he sends another shadow bond to cover my mouth, I realize it's no use.

Closing my eyes and attempting a deep breath to keep a sob at bay, I lean toward the window. Morning light shines through the bottom of the swaying curtain. That means I've been out for hours. It's already past dawn.

How did we get through the forest of thorns that Prince Reid and Bael created?

Realization hits me. We must be on the way to Lander. Today must be the royal wedding.

Rising panic threatens to take over all rational thought. Bael is now my enemy again. It's obvious in the way that he looks at me. Prince Reid isn't in the carriage with us, though I can hardly imagine he's faring any better. And now, I'm on my way back home but as a prisoner. The irony of finally going back home only for it to be in the *worst* way possible is not lost on me.

I sneak another glance at Bael, who sits stiffly. He catches me staring and narrows his eyes.

"Stop staring or I'll blindfold you," he bites out, his hands gripping the edge of the cushions.

Traitorous tears come loose and trail down my cheeks at his ire. I know it's not him, but I don't know how to get the real Bael back. The Bael I know is no longer here and may never be. I force the despair down as far as I can. When this is all over, if I survive, then I can mourn what could have been, a future with Bael.

I don't know how long we ride in silence as the weight of the inevitable sinks in. We never had a chance, did we? The queen is too powerful. She took him from me in the end, and she'll take Lander. It's been hopeless from the start.

The carriage suddenly stops and I hear the queen's icy voice commanding her goblins, who jump out of a carriage in front of us. I can't see anything but I can hear it, they're attacking the guards stationed at the gates. Tears freely stream down my cheeks now as the sounds of scuffling stop. When the carriage jerks forward once more, I know the path is clear now for Queen Roma to approach the castle.

We stop for a final time, and Bael wastes no time rising from his seat and pulling the carriage door open. Then I'm pulled out of the carriage, and I land roughly on the hard-packed earth. My eyes protest the sudden blinding light of the morning sun. I blink desperately to clear my vision and when I do, I see the worst sight imaginable: my sister and several Lander guards appearing on the threshold of the castle doors.

"Come my pets," the queen gestures to Bael, who hauls me roughly to my feet, "time to crash a royal wedding."

Chapter 26

All I see is Elyse. I writhe against my bonds as I'm yanked forward and thrown down on the castle steps like some pathetic offering. My sister races down the steps to grab me and lift me to my feet. Lander guards spread out, descending the stairs to surround us in a surprising gesture of solidarity. When I'm on my feet, Elyse stares into my eyes, and then along the bonds. Though she can't remove his shadow bonds, she casts a ward just large enough for the two of us and tries to pry them away from me.

"This is the reception I get?" Queen Roma tuts.

With a wave of her hand, Elyse and I watch every Lander guard around us collapse. I try to scream as my sister pulls me close to her, but the shadow bonds squeeze me tighter. Looking around in horror, I can't tell if the guards are still alive.

"Come now," the queen gestures to her entourage, made up of at least a dozen of her goblin guards. I scramble out of the way, taking Elyse with me as they ascend the stairs. The queen passes us and steps casually over the forms of the unmoving guards, Bael in line just behind her. He holds a cage with a raven trapped inside.

It's the prince, his own brother.

They're about to cross the threshold when Elyse and I stumble after them, but when Bael raises his hand, I'm wrenched away from my sister. The ward she cast around us disappears with a pop. Suddenly, I'm back in his bruising grip, being shoved through the front doors of Lander Castle. I shake my head, desperate to loosen the bonds around my mouth. It doesn't work, and I only succeed in tripping as I'm yanked across the foyer toward the ballroom. I silently plead with the saints that my sister evaded capture. As we round the corner, I see her racing toward another wave of approaching Lander guards gathering on the steps.

We cross under the same seashell chandelier I used to admire as we walk toward the ballroom. The guards posted at the entrance straighten at our approach. The queen releases her shadows to slither on the marble floor toward them. Chaos breaks out. Swords unsheathe and the sound of screeching birds pierces my ears. For a moment, I swear I see something flying just out of the corner of my eye. The guards rush forward, their meager shields raised and battle cries on their lips. I want to shout at them, to tell them to run, but it's no use. They don't last more than a moment. Sadness rolls through me in waves when the thud of bodies hit the floor. I stumble over my fallen comrades, choking back a sob.

The ballroom is just as resplendent as I imagined for a royal wedding, which makes this moment all wrong. In honor of joining with Brevalin, fresh greenery covers the room. The smell of pine and orange makes it feel like we're standing in the middle of a forest on a beautiful fall evening. Under different circumstances, it would have been divine.

The dais, now an altar, is at the far end of the room. It's decorated with an arch overflowing with wisteria—a familiar scent in Lander—that adds soft purple to the sea of green.

THE QUEEN'S CARD

Guards swarm us, peeling away from their places along the perimeter to form a shield between us and the rest of the room. This scene is so familiar, it's just like when she projected into the castle to threaten the princess. This time, she's here in person.

My eyes land on Elyse on the left side of the altar, who's in a heated argument with Heath. How did she reach the ballroom before we did?

She points animatedly at us just as screeching erupts from the cage in Bael's hand. Queen Roma turns to glare at it and I catch Prince Reid's beady black eyes.

The raven looking back at me glares and snaps his beak aggressively.

Sorrow seems to wrap around my chest and squeeze. Bael is under her control again and Prince Reid is stuck in his raven form. I'm truly alone.

I wiggle my hands but feel the bonds tighten against my wrist. I take a tentative step forward but Bael yanks me back and I bump against his chest. My breath hitches at the wrongness of it, to be so close to him, but knowing in his state of mind, he may kill me.

The king stands at his throne, Heath closing in on his right. The king's gaze finally lands on Queen Roma, and his lips curl in disdain. She makes a show of scanning the massive room, her gaze taking in the row of Lander guests, shrinking in terror. A wry smile forms on her lips when she spots those in the front row. From here I can see Dane, who's shaking with fury.

Her gaze finally snaps back to the king

"King Adrian," she says airily, "your invitation never made it to me. If I were you, I wouldn't let that messenger live." The crowd murmurs anxiously. "But I would never miss such a momentous occasion."

"You're not welcome here," King Adrian says, gritting his teeth. Heath takes another step toward him, ready to shield him.

"Oh," she laughs, "you don't mean that." She clicks her tongue and the condescension grates on me.

"I do." The king tries to step off the dais, but Heath holds him back. "You will not interfere with this wedding or this alliance."

Queen Roma's false pleasantness vanishes, and, when she smiles, it's all teeth. "But I still have a promise to keep." The malice drips from her lips.

A few Lander guards step toward her but when she lifts an eyebrow at them, they stop in their tracks.

I need to do something. I need a plan. I turn back to look at Bael, who's dark eyes narrow at me in warning. He may be my captor again, but I don't want to hurt him. I know it's not *him*. He can't help his actions under her influence.

Could I slip out of these bonds without hurting him?

I scan the room. I don't see anything within reach, and my hands are still behind my back.

"It seems your daughter will pay the price for you." The queen's gaze lands on Princess Dulci, who stands behind her father in her stunning white gown. "When you stole magic from me all those years ago, you knew what I could make the magic do." Her lips curl into a wicked smile. "But you didn't care, did you? Anything for a chance at magic of your own, right? No wonder you gave the magic to your keepers. They're the ones who bear the curse now, don't they?"

Without warning, my sister and Ambrose shift in a flurry of feathers, startling the crowd. Now, two ravens hover where they once stood.

My jaw drops.

The other keepers, those I consider my *family*, can shift into ravens? How long have they been hiding this? That means that keeper magic *is* stolen Azrean magic, arcana magic. Did King Adrian give them this magic knowing it would curse them?

But as the thought occurs to me, a sinking feeling in my stomach forms. He must have known. He was never the ruler I thought he was, and my loyalty to him ends now.

"That's enough!" King Adrian bellows, his fists shaking with rage. "You will not hurt my daughter!"

His voice startles me back into the present. I need to do something, anything. I lunge forward and plant my feet, yanking hard on my bonds. Bael grunts in surprise, losing his balance. The birdcage swings wildly. I whirl around and kick the cage as hard as I can.

It's knocked out of his hand and clatters loudly to the floor. It clangs loudly, bouncing a few times with Prince Reid screeching angrily. When the door to the cage bends just enough for him to squeeze through, he flies out of it, cawing and shrieking.

The goblin guards nearby shout and rage, waving their weapons. The queen snaps her head toward the commotion and sends shadows flying through the air after the prince. I wonder miserably if letting him go was a mistake as he's engulfed in a cloud of darkness. I'm finally yanked backward and I brace myself to hit the ground, but Bael wraps his massive arms around me. I'm smashed into his chest.

Thrashing in his grip, I wait with bated breath, hoping for the prince to reappear. When he finally emerges from her cloud of magic, he flies straight for the princess. The room watches as he struggles under her coercion. He screeches and changes course and it must be a monumental effort, like he's fighting against a non-existent wind. He flies up and down, his movements jerky.

Beneath the struggling raven prince, Heath gestures from his place next to the king, and the Lander guards descend.

Queen Roma's laugh reaches my ears, even over the growing din.

"Adrian, you know that I have no intention of letting your daughter live."

The words fall over the crowd and, within a single moment, at least a dozen of her goblin guards materialize behind her.

"Seize her!" Queen Roma shouts, pointing to the princess.

Prince Reid caws loudly and circles the air above the crowd as her guards fight against the tide of people. The other ravens take flight—Elyse and Ambrose—and soon, I can't keep track of which one is which. Wedding guests shriek and topple out of their chairs, scrambling to get out of the way. Dulci disappears from view as her guards surround her in a practiced formation. They push the goblin guards back, though more quickly step into their path.

Two Lander guards take off toward a pair of double doors along the back wall, one disappearing through the door and the other propping the door open. They shepherd the crowd out of the ballroom through the doors.

I watch King Adrian gesture to Heath, who races toward the princess.

"Guards, take her down!" the king shouts. Swords draw and soon the sound of metal against metal rings loudly in the room. A melee breaks out in a blur of cobalt uniforms and armored goblins.

The queen lifts her hands up above her head and conjures a swirling cyclone of dark shadows, but before she can aim it at the princess, an almighty screech pierces the air.

Prince Reid hovers above the princess, his battle against the queen's coercion lost. He pecks and rages against the protective ward around his betrothed.

How could that be when the only two keepers in the room are stuck in raven form?

"Reid!" she snaps. "How long does it take to break a pitiful little ward?" Queen Roma curls her fingers into fists.

The pecking and shrieking is insistent, and I watch Dulci's eyes widen at the airborne assault. Lander guards surrounding the ward swat

THE QUEEN'S CARD

at Prince Reid as he grazes the tops of their heads. Taking advantage of the chaos, I slam my heel down on Bael's foot. When he grunts, I kick him right between his legs. As I watch him double over, shame blooms within me. It's a cheap shot, but he's not himself right now. His shadow bonds fall away from my hands and my mouth, and I take off running.

I barely make it more than a few steps when Bael's shadows fly right over my head. A marble column in front of me explodes, and I duck as pieces of stone and dust shoot out in every direction.

Surprised he missed me, I spot someone dart out of the rubble. Then I realize I'm not who Bael is aiming at. A moment later, the protective ward around Dulci falls, mere steps away from the back door.

Oh, no.

Prince Reid in raven form screeches in triumph. I watch, frozen in terror as his body grows to the size of an eagle. Then, he dives directly at Dulci.

Time slows down as I watch Dulci rise from above the crowd, her shoulders clamped in her fiancé's sharp talons. She thrashes in his grip, but if the prince is as strong as Bael in his raven form, then she won't break free.

"Dulci!" I shout, my heart shattering into a thousand pieces.

This can't be happening.

"Good boy," Queen Roma croons as he flies across the room, the princess in his clutches.

"I told your father I'd come for you." The queen lifts her hands as if to embrace the princess.

I can see Dulci shaking from here, her movements are jerky and frantic. Her face contorts in panic as Prince Reid begins his descent. She tries in vain to rip the talons from her shoulders.

Shadows shoot out of the queen's fingers and encase the princess in darkness that does nothing to drown out her screams. The vision of her terror burns in my brain as she disappears from view in a swirling, dark cloud.

Angry tears blur my vision and my breathing is so shallow I worry I'll faint. I barely register a baleful cawing from two distraught ravens somewhere nearby.

Suddenly, the screaming stops.

Anguish crawls up my throat like a living thing.

I failed. Everything I've worked for is all for naught. It doesn't matter if I ever prove my loyalty or earn my keeper magic. I couldn't keep the princess safe. None of us could. She's dying and the king will have no choice but to surrender.

King Adrian bellows in anguish, Heath desperately holding him back. "What have you done to my daughter?"

As Prince Reid lowers Dulci's limp body at Queen Roma's feet, the queen eyes the king triumphantly. "You knew how this would end. Now, kneel or die."

Chapter 27

Words fail me. Rational thought fails me. I rush toward Dulci's body on the ground, crumpled at the Azrean Queen's feet. I grab her shoulders and shake her, desperate to wake her. I ignore the throbbing tug in my chest and sink into all my anger and despair as I hold her.

Please, Dulci, wake up. You have to wake up.

I know it's useless, I have no magic to revive her. When I blink away tears, my eyes trace the outline of her delicate face. She was so full of life and of color, but not anymore.

A sob sticks in my throat; the grief is all-consuming.

She's gone. My closest friend and the future of our kingdom is gone.

But I'd already failed her long before the queen got to her. I didn't stop the attack, instead I'd chased after Bael, thinking that confronting him would be worth leaving her side. Her fiancé was right; I did abandon her. I may not have had my magic to help protect her, but leaving her meant I couldn't help her at all. Now, we're worse off than we were before. The princess is dead, and I can't stop the inevitable.

The bond in my chest pulls so hard that it forces me out of spinning thoughts.

When I turn, I see Bael staring down at me from where he stands next to his wretched queen. His gaze is on me. His jaw is clenched shut and his fingers twitch, as if waiting for his cue to attack.

I suck in a breath. The shadow mark still pulls at me insistently, but it doesn't know the man on the other end wants to kill me.

"Bael!" the queen snaps at him, but her gaze is on his brother as he shifts clumsily back into mortal form. Upon seeing her prone form, Prince Reid scrambles forward to lean over his fiancée. Misery etches lines on his forehead, though it only lasts a moment before all emotion drains from his face.

He's under her spell once again.

His eyes narrow and his lip curls as he bends down to lift her body into his arms, as if he's holding someone he despises. The queen turns her full attention back to Bael. "Fetch me your mortal. I have a job for her."

Oh, no.

Does she want me to lead her to the caves?

I won't do it. It doesn't matter if she forces me. I don't know where the caves are, so I can't be forced to give her any more power than she's already taken.

Bael strides toward me, and I try to swallow down the panic.

I need to run, but I can't force my feet to move. I'm locked in place, terror gripping my lungs and squeezing out all the air. He cocks his head, his neck cracking, as if he's relishing the moment before the kill.

With all the strength I can muster, I turn on my heel and race out of the ballroom. My chest seizes from the bond that attempts to force me to turn around. Heavy footsteps pound the marble floor behind me. When a shiver of dread travels down my spine, it confirms what I already know. Bael is chasing me.

I dodge through the fighting, the battle still in full swing. It spills out into the foyer, forcing me to jump over prone bodies. A large, spiked bat grazes the top of my head, and when I duck, it hits Bael square in the chest. After a furious growl, I hear a sharp crack, but refuse to turn and look as I race up the stairs.

Can I lose Bael in the castle? How well does Bael know the layout since he was here posing as a Brevalin servant? As I wind through the corridors, I come up with my only plan; run until I lose him.

I don't care where I'm going, as long as I put distance between us. I hear his pounding footsteps reach the landing, but then they stop.

My heart skips a beat. Where did he go? Did he stop pursuing me? What would pull him away from a direct command now that he's re-coerced?

I keep going, running down a familiar corridor, straining to hear him. Then I realize where I've gone, to my old room.

By the time I'm turning the knob, my anxiety makes me want to jump out of my skin. As I push the door open, I feel it: the rush of wind and the flap of wings. He'd shifted.

I scream and tumble through the threshold. His sharp talons skim the tops of my shoulders, the sting propelling me forward. I turn and slam my entire body weight against the door. As it locks, his body bangs against it with a jarring thud.

I race across the room and drag my heavy wooden desk to the threshold. I doubt it'll stop him, but it may slow him down. With the desk in place, I slide along the wall until I'm sitting just to the left of the door. I force myself to take deep breaths as he slams into the door, his talons and his beak scraping loudly against the wood.

The bond in my chest pulls painfully, and I rub my collarbone, trying to relieve the ache. It doesn't matter that my life is in danger, the bond reveals what my heart already knows, that I yearn to be close to him. The man outside this door—bird or not—breathed new life into me. Though he started out as my enemy, he didn't dismiss me for my differences. He's seen me at my most vulnerable, and he let down his guard in return. With him, I learned truths I never thought possible, and he stayed beside me while I worked through what it meant for me. Because of him, I'm no longer the woman who blindly follows her king, desperate to belong without the full understanding of what it means to be a keeper.

He's sacrificed so much for me already, even if it's fueled by the shadow mark between us. It feels real to me. And it's the worst kind of torture knowing that although only a door separates us, I can't go to him. Not anymore.

But what if I did go to him? Could I break the queen's coercion on him? It worked when she first brought me to the castle.

I squeeze my eyes shut, struggling to remember how I did it. When I was on the verge of passing out, I called out to him in my mind, willing my magic to find him.

What if I call out to him now?

"Bael, I need you." My voice is thick with emotion. "You need to resist her control. We need to stop her."

I pour my heart into the plea, feeling it with every fiber of my being. Despite knowing that I don't have an ounce of magic to give, I force myself to try.

But when his talons scratch with renewed fervor against the wood, a sob catches in my throat.

It didn't work. Of course it didn't.

Closing my eyes again, I take slow, measured breaths. I need to go on without him.

When my racing heart returns to normal, despite the constant assault outside, I stand and slowly take in the room. Is there anything in here that I can use?

Déjà vu rolls over me in waves. Everything is just as I left it: from the unmade bed to the pile of books stacked on the floor. This is still my room, but it doesn't feel like mine anymore.

The moon is full and bright when I stride to the small balcony. I open the door and let the crisp air envelop me. From here I can see clear across Perstow Bay to the ocean beyond. Have I only been gone a few weeks? It feels like years have passed.

Last month, I wanted to belong more than anything and I let that desire guide my actions. My selfishness led me to follow Bael, and put myself in danger. My sister's words echo in my head.

You don't always have to be doing something to make a difference.

I was so sure that taking action, even if it was rash, would earn me what I wanted and save the realm, but I only made everything worse.

I run my hand along the thick stone railing, still ignoring the scratching of Bael's talons against my door, thankful he hasn't shifted back into his mortal form yet. My gaze catches on a small, painted jewelry box on the top of the shelf nearby. The faded flowers decorating the lid bring a wave of nostalgia; it was my mother's.

What would she think of my choices? I let her down. I let her memory down. Would she be ashamed to know what happens to keepers now that they're cursed to shift under the enemy queen? Although she hid that part of her life from us until her death, I know she was proud of it, at least, that's what King Adrian led me to believe. But now that I've seen what the king is capable of, can I even believe that?

A loud thud startles me as my door shutters on its hinges. I whirl around, the wind whipping my hair into my face. Bael must have shifted back into mortal form. He slams a hand on the door, then rattles the doorknob.

I hold my breath, knowing that at any moment, he'll break down the door. But he doesn't.

"Mira." His voice is strained.

It's like a knife right through my heart. I squeeze my eyes shut to keep tears from falling as he rattles the doorknob again. Why hasn't he just burst through and gotten this over with? When he calls my name again, the rattling stops.

"Forgive—me." His voice is a rasped plea.

Ignoring the little voice in my head screaming for me to stay away, I let myself give into the bond. I take slow, measured steps forward until I'm standing in front of my door. I press my palm against the wood, closing my eyes. It hurts so much to imagine him just on the other side.

"Bael," I whisper, letting the tears fall.

I hear him grunt.

"Mira," he grits out, "*run.*"

"I don't want to leave you," I whisper, tilting forward until my forehead leans against the wood.

A low growl escapes him and he slams a fist against the door, rattling it violently on its hinges. I jump back, my heart caught in my throat.

"Run!" he shouts, clear desperation in his voice.

Swallowing thickly, I turn and run toward the balcony. Could I jump and survive? Three stories is still a long way to fall.

But when the door bursts open, I grip the railing, scramble over the top, and jump.

Chapter 28

The bushes below barely break my fall. I scramble out, pushing away branches that scratch and scrape against my clothes. When I break free, I take off down the manicured path that cuts through the middle of the courtyard. The stones crunch loudly beneath my boots, and I kick them up as I weave around a decorative stone bench. Finally reaching the covered corridor farthest away from my balcony, I hide behind one of the stone pillars that frames the arched entryway.

I allow myself one breath before I peer around the pillar back toward my room. Bael stares at me from the balcony, his hands gripping the railing. I don't know how long he will be able to fight the coercion, but at least he's giving me a head start.

I turn back and duck to hide behind the half-wall that lines the corridor. Then I run. It's an awkward, squatting shuffle, but it's all I can do to keep him from seeing where I'm going. This corridor merges with several others in a grid pattern, some leading to different wings of the castle, while others branch off to other parts of the grounds.

Grunting and stomping tells me the queen's goblins are nearby, but none cross my path. I pass a few intersections with the other corridors, but I stick to the path I'm on, which leads back to the castle, and into the king's favorite gallery. By the time I pull open the door and rush in, my calves are burning from exertion. Spotting an alcove just inside the room, I hide and I force myself to focus.

Where am I going to find the caves that I never knew existed? I know it's not on the beach. I followed those shadows—Bael's shadows—for a week and he didn't find it. Is it somewhere in the castle? I picture each room but nothing springs to mind. What kind of room would house a hidden entrance to secret caves? It must be on a subterranean level. On those floors are the wine cellars, the storage rooms, and the dining hall for the Lander guards.

But there's no cave entrance in any of those rooms, I'm sure of it. I've lived and worked here most of my life, I would know, or would have heard something about it.

Maybe it's not in the castle. Maybe it's somewhere on the grounds.

Are there even caves at all?

I can't outrun my spiraling thoughts. Doubt creeps in like a shadow, casting over everything.

Desperate for guidance, I wonder what my sister would do.

I try to imagine what she'd say to me if she were here. Would she tell me to find Heath? I shake my head. He's dealing with the battle, the immediate threat, so he wouldn't listen to me. I chew my lip, remembering his reaction to my suggestion to move the wedding location. Elyse's reaction to my discovery of Bael on the castle grounds wasn't any better.

If I had earned my keeper magic, would I have chased after Bael when I spotted him in Lander Castle? I doubt it, I would have listened to my sister to keep in her good graces, and I would have convinced myself that I was mistaken. But if he hadn't taken me, I wouldn't have seen what life is like in other realms. I wouldn't have seen the oppression that Azrea faces. My mind replays the conversation from the men in the Perstow pub.

I barely survived last year's Night Waltz. We can't keep up at the docks and my wife is out of work...

Now that I know how the Azrean Queen treats her own people, and how her plan includes kidnapping Brevalin royals.

I can no longer stand by, because seeing Azrea changed me.

Meeting Bael changed me.

I need to stop the Queen of Azrea, or die trying, but how? What would Bael tell me to do, to listen to the late king's advice?

It's in the caves. What you seek.

What I *seek* is something to stop the queen. The late king told us about his wife stealing his bloodline's arcana card, that must be what he's talking about. But why would that be in caves in Lander? Bael didn't think the arcana cards were real, that it was only lore.

What else could it be?

Even if it's the logical conclusion, it doesn't help me wrap my head around it. I know nothing about arcana magic, and I'm no closer to even finding the caves it's supposedly hidden in. If I'm going to stop the queen, I need to see this through, even if that means finding the illusive caves, finding a powerful card, and somehow destroying it.

I blow out a long breath. Where do I go from here?

Suddenly, the ground shakes violently, nearly toppling me over. I grip the wall, my eyes darting around at the gold gilded paintings hanging on the wall.

What is happening?

A thunderous boom pierces the air that's so powerful I can feel the vibrations in my chest. The shaking intensifies, and a stone bust falls from its pedestal. I shriek as it hits the ground. Panicking, I struggle to get enough air in my lungs, and all I can manage are sharp, shaking breaths.

Another violent quake rumbles beneath me, causing a crack to form along the ceiling above me. I dart out of the gallery into the exterior corridor, but skid to a halt. Is it safer in the castle or on the grounds?

Before I can decide, I spot movement in one of the exterior corridors farthest from where I stand. Squinting at the setting sun, I see a figure carrying someone in their arms, lumbering forward despite the ground quaking beneath them. They're walking toward the main branch of the corridors, and could potentially turn toward me.

As if sensing my gaze, they stop in their tracks. I rush back into the gallery, my hands above my head to shield myself from falling debris. Ignoring the pounding of my heartbeat in my ears, I wait several seconds.

Did they see me? What about Bael? Where is he now?

Too anxious to stand still, I peer around the alcove, and through the open gallery door. They've resumed their determined pace. When they reach the main corridor, they thankfully turn *away* from me, in the direction of the courtyard with the royal greenhouses.

Who is that, and who are they carrying?

Deep down, my gut instinct tells me *exactly* who it is.

Prince Reid and Dulci.

Right before I fled the ballroom, I saw the prince lift her into his arms, but I assumed that the queen would keep them in her sights.

I sprint down the corridor, scanning for Bael as I go. I cast a quick thank you to the saints when I catch up to the prince unscathed. He trudges into the courtyard with the night garden and now that I'm close to him, I see that he walks like a man possessed. His movements are jerky, and when a ray of moonlight illuminates his face, his eyes are dark and manic. I duck behind another pillar just as his gaze passes over me.

My eyes land on the woman in his arms. The ends of her skirt trail along the ground, and the breeze rustles her long hair. My heart lodges in my throat. I was right, it's Dulci.

I know he's still under Queen Roma's coercion, but seeing her like this brings on another wave of fury. As I look around, déjà vu creeps in, too. I followed Bael here the night he kidnapped me. And just like that night, Prince Reid heads to the night garden greenhouse, though unlike Bael, he kicks in the door.

He ducks in and disappears and I wait only a moment before following him. When I reach the door, I don't even allow myself time to hesitate. The moonlight isn't bright enough to allow me any visibility inside, so I take a deep breath, and step through the doorway.

But there's no sign of him.

It's just as I remember, a cramped space surrounded by thick, overgrown foliage. Scanning the room, I squint, my eyes glancing over each plant. I let out a long breath, attempting to slow my racing heart.

Where did he go? Surely I would have seen him re-emerge?

Alone again and without meaning to, my mind wanders. Where is the queen right now? She's saints-knows-where, most likely already in the caves, enacting her grand plan. She is the worst kind of enemy; the one that feels a lot like looking in the mirror. Her words echo in my mind.

You remind me so much of myself, of how I would have turned out if I didn't take control of my own fate.

I hate how desperate I am for control. I hate that it's what makes us alike. But not anymore. I'm taking control of my life now.

The identity I wanted so badly isn't what I want anymore. I learned the truth about King Adrian. I've seen what happens to the keepers.

Bael's question replays in my head. *Why do you want to be a keeper?* I was prepared then to defend my desire, but my outlook has changed. I'll never be a keeper, but I never really wanted to be one, did I? Being a keeper won't make me feel like I belong. I wouldn't have even wanted to be one if my mother hadn't been one. I no longer want to belong if that means that I have to pledge my loyalty to a king who willingly gave my sister and Ambrose cursed magic. I don't even know to what extent it forces them to comply with Queen Roma's demands.

My mind replays everything that Bael taught me about Azrean lore and how much Azreans are suffering. Now that I know the truth, that he's a Brevalin royal, I see his true character. He told me he wanted me to be the first keeper who knew the truth.

But this truth doesn't benefit him. Azreans aren't his people. He wanted me to know because it's an injustice. And now that I get to choose who I'm loyal to. I choose Bael, if he can break away from the queen's coercion.

Frustrated, I pace the length of the space, looking in every nook and cranny, angrily swatting away overgrown branches that hang in my way. They couldn't have left this room. I would have seen them.

I stalk to the worktable in the corner, reaching out to grasp the top to look under it.

But my hand passes right through it.

I almost fall forward but then step back and blink. It *looks* like a worktable, complete with discarded tools and small pots. Tentatively, I reach out again, but my hand goes through it.

It's an illusion. Has it been under our noses this whole time? I'm surprised that I didn't accidentally discover it the night I was here with Bael the night he took me.

Cautiously, I take a step toward it, though I still expect to run into something solid. But once I pass through the illusion, where the back wall of the greenhouse *should* be, there is a short corridor illuminated by a single torch. At the end is a set of stairs.

I allow myself one backward glance before I grab the torch from the wall, and hurry down the corridor. When I reach the end, I hold the flame out in front of me, my hand shaking. Below me are steep stone steps descending into darkness. Suddenly, I'm fully aware of my clammy hands, my sweat-slicked forehead, and my shallow breaths.

Pushing away the fear, I take my first step. Each stair is as damp as it looks, and more than once, my feet slip across the slick surface. I steady myself with the equally slick wall, and the smell of stale, wet dirt is overpowering. My thoughts race. How long has this been here, right under our feet? What am I walking into?

Relieved to find hard-packed earth at the bottom, I try to shake off the tension in my shoulders, but it's quickly replaced with something else, dread.

I focus on putting one foot in front of the other. Rather than giving into the growing terror that coils around my lungs, I focus on what I can see and hear. It's pitch black, and something nearby drips. The air temperature plunges the farther I go.

The stillness of the air is stale and oppressive, but the tunnel widens the farther along I travel. It twists and turns, and more than once gains elevation before angling back down. I reach a fork in the tunnel and feel a tugging in my chest. Without giving myself time to overthink it, I choose the path to the left.

When I reach the end of the tunnel, I can hear... shuffling? The tunnel widens into a massive cavern.

This is it; it must be.

I found the Lander caves.

There's an ominous red glow that outlines the stalagmites protruding from the cavern floor. I creep around the clusters of rocks, following the noise. I pass a dark pool on my left, and the inky blackness makes the hairs on the back of my neck stand up. I keep going, bracing myself for the queen herself to emerge at any moment, but as tense moments pass, nothing happens. Finally, my eyes find the outline of a bird hopping across the cavern floor. Before I can get a better look, it spreads its wings, hovers, then flies right toward me.

Chapter 29

I shriek, covering my head from the oncoming assault. To my surprise, the bird flies right over me to perch on a massive rock protruding from the dark water. Water drips from the stalactites on the ceiling, making ripples along the surface.

I squint in the dim light and realize that it's a raven. Now that I know the queen favors ravens, this could be anyone, including my sister or Ambrose.

It turns and stares at me, tilting its head as if trying to figure me out, too. Suddenly, flapping wings echo throughout the cavern. I startle and look around, but I can't tell where the noise is coming from. A dozen ravens appear from the tunnel I emerged from, flying in formation, right toward me. I watch them glide over me, until one by one, they dive into the pool.

Wait. What just happened?

Just as the splashing stops and the water begins to calm, the raven on the rock clicks its beak at me before following its brethren into the pool. I lean forward, my mind unable to make sense of it. I wait with bated breath, but none of them resurface.

Then, the cavern is too quiet. I'm so anxious that I can't stand it. Swallowing, I take a step closer, searching the surface. Suddenly, the tugging in my chest yanks. It wants me to follow the ravens into the pool.

Taking a deep breath, I lean down and dip my hand into the water. The water is warm, and, when I pull my hand out to inspect it, its dry.

It must be another illusion.

Before I can talk myself out of it, I jump in.

***

My body is weightless. I hang suspended in nothing but darkness and struggle to make sense of it. All of a sudden, I'm thrown sideways onto smooth, damp ground. I'm clearly in a different room within the caves, but my entrance was disorienting.

When I look around, I see a massive mirror hanging on the cavern wall. Did I fall through that?

That can't be right.

But as I stare at it, I can see the surface rippling. Gingerly, I stand, rubbing my shoulder, tender from landing on it. I turn, scanning the rest of the room. Candles float near the ceiling, giving an unexpectedly calming glow.

I spot movement in my periphery. Ravens perch everywhere, on the ground, and on ledges that jut out from the wall. They shift and ruffle their feathers as if waiting for something.

One snaps its beak to get my attention, and when I turn to look for it, my breath hitches. It's perched on a rock ledge just above a floating body.

Dulci's prone body hovers several feet off the ground, bobbing gently like a boat in water. Her hair cascades around her as if spread out on a pillow, and her face is so serene that it looks as if she's sleeping. But I know she's not. I followed the prince as he brought her down here for saints-knows-what.

Why did he bring her down here?

I run to her and lean down, resisting the urge to pull her down. I stop myself from touching her, not knowing what would happen if I disturb this strange levitation. I fight back a sob, tears welling in my eyes. I hate what happened to her. She became a pawn for Queen Roma to exploit.

She shouldn't be here, paying for her father's mistakes. I need to get her back to the castle. But can I bring her back and find the queen's card?

And where's Prince Reid? When the raven above her shuffles its talons against the rock, I wonder if that's him. The thought makes me uneasy.

A startled yelp makes me spin on my heel. My sister emerges from the mirror, though she manages to keep her balance. An exhausted-looking Ambrose appears a moment later. I blink several times, until I'm sure it's them. A burst of elation overtakes me.

I race across the cavern and when I reach my sister, we collide, tangling into a heap of limbs.

"Mira?" she gasps. Her arms wrap around me and squeeze all the air out of my lungs.

"Must—breathe—" I pant. She finally lets go, holding me at arm's length to look me over.

"Thank the saints, Mira. We thought we lost you!" She hugs me again, though this time it's gentler. I wrap my arms around her, too, a wave of relief and heartache sweeping through me. I hate to admit it, but it's been hell being apart from her.

When Elyse and I finally break apart, I feel Ambrose's powerful arms sweep me up into a bear hug. I lean into the touch, so grateful for the familiarity.

When he places me on my feet again, the seriousness of our situation falls between us again.

"How are you two still—" I gesture vaguely at them.

"In human form? When we left the ballroom, we both managed to shift back. We saw Prince Reid—" Ambrose's words die in his throat, and his eyes widen.

"Dulci?" Elyse sees her the same time as Ambrose.

When Elyse and Ambrose reach Dulci's side, Ambrose does the same thing I did; he reaches out to touch her hand, but stops himself. Instead, he runs his fingers through his hair.

"What is she doing here?" Ambrose says softly.

"I don't know," I answer as Elyse scans the cavern.

I hadn't had time to think about it, but it wouldn't make sense that he acted under the queen's order. She would never let Prince Reid walk away with Dulci. If we're lucky, the caves we're standing in may still be a mystery to her. Did he find a way out of her coercion? I saw the way he walked, he was still under a spell.

I shake my head, focusing my attention back to my sister. "The queen coerced Prince Reid to chase after her," I say quietly. "He…" another sob claws its way up my throat. I don't want to finish the sentence, so instead I just gesture to Dulci vaguely.

Elyse nods. "Forced him to shift. She forced us, too."

I look at each one of them and remember the curse that they bear for wielding stolen Azrean magic. I can't imagine what it feels like.

"Where have you been?" My sister's voice is thick with emotion.

THE QUEEN'S CARD

I swallow a few times to fight the rising tide of despair. "I followed Bael—the Raven," I say as my sister turns to me, confused. "He took me to Azrea and—"

Her eyes widen. "—Hang on, you chased after the Raven?"

Shame blooms within me, a feeling so familiar. "But he's not—"

"And he kidnapped you?" She holds her hand to interrupt my explanation, which makes me flush with anger. "Mira, of all the *irresponsible* things you could do—"

"I had to do something! You didn't believe me, remember?" I bite out.

Doesn't this sound familiar? An imaginary Bael says in my head. I purse my lips, annoyed that this version of him in my head is right. It's exactly what I chided him for when he reunited with his brother. *Now is not the time to fight. You two need to work together.* I'm sure he'd say it back to me if he were here with me.

I take a deep breath, reminding myself that despite how we got here, the three of us are back together. A long silence stretches between us until my sister speaks.

"I never wanted you to see any of this," she says softly.

"That's why your sister kept the king from giving you keeper magic." Ambrose's voice is equally quiet.

"What?" My head snaps to him.

Ambrose's small smile is so full of pity. I turn back to my sister, the hurt bubbling to the surface once again to the surface.

"Why didn't you tell me?" My voice comes out an octave higher, the onslaught of emotions threatening to pull me under. "If I'd have known, I would have—"

"—You would have done exactly the same thing," Elyse tilts her head, "I know you. A few weeks ago, you wouldn't have cared that we're cursed to follow her command, to shift into a bird. You would have insisted on being a part of it, too."

I press my lips together, fighting back the anger crawling up my throat. Bael's imaginary voice echoes in my head.

She did it for you. She did it to save you from this fate.

My breath stalls. She protected me from cursed magic, and an uncertain fate at the hands of an enemy queen. She made sure that Queen Roma would never control me, even if it meant keeping me excluded from everything.

The ugly truth rears its head. I can no longer blame her for my failures because she's right. If she had told me about the dangers of keeper magic from the beginning, I would have still insisted that she tell the king I was ready to harness it. I was so sure that having magic would make me belong, but after everything I've learned, I'm not so sure. The ache of it twists like a knife.

I can't keep up this vicious cycle of anger and resentment. So instead of arguing, I look her in the eyes.

"Thank you," I whisper. That's all I can manage.

She swipes a curl out of her eyes before enveloping me in another hug.

Without warning, a man's voice says, "What a touching reunion."

I pull away from my sister and we spin around.

Despite the candles illuminating the space, I squint because I'm certain that my eyes betray me.

"Liam?"

He materializes from the mirror with more grace than anyone else I've seen travel through it. Has he traveled here before? A peculiar smile forms on one side of his face as he strides forward to meet me. Ambrose and Elyse bristle next to me, but I hold up my hand to keep them at bay.

"What are you doing here?"

"Relax," he holds his hands up placatingly. "I won't hurt you."

I tilt my head to the side. "Unless you found a way around it, your queen coerced you to kill me, remember?"

Elyse squares her shoulders, and Ambrose steps in front of me. My heart pangs. It's the same way Bael stepped in front of me the night the queen captured us.

"Mira, who is this?" Ambrose says, his voice low.

"This is Liam." I gesture to him. "He's…" I struggle to find the right words.

How would I describe him? A prominent figure in the Azrean underground world? It's not as if I can admit to them that Bael and I asked him to unlock the keeper magic in my ring. Or that as part of the deal, I robbed a grave for wraith blooms he used to storm the castle?

No, if my sister knew what I've been up to, I'd never hear the end of it.

"Not a fan of the Azrean Queen," he finishes for me.

Elyse narrows her eyes, but I know that look. The wheels in her head are spinning.

"And you're not here to hurt us?" my sister asks.

He shakes his head, shoving his hands into his pockets.

"How did you break her coercion on you?" I ask warily.

"I had some help," he says, casually looking between Elyse and Ambrose. "It looks like you two did, too."

"What do you mean?"

"Well, you two," he looks between Elyse and Ambrose, "aren't stuck flapping your wings right now, are you?"

I frown at him. "So who helped all of you?"

He raises a brow at me. "You'll see. But let's just say it's someone who wants the Azrean throne more than I do."

I huff.

I resist the urge to take a step away from him. I don't trust him.

He was willing to betray his own followers to cut some kind of a deal with the queen. I'm surprised he's still alive. If his rebels find him, he'll have a hell of a time outrunning them unless he wants to live as a raven permanently.

He shrugs but continues on conversationally. "Well, what's your plan?"

"Plan?" Ambrose says.

"To stop the queen." Liam states it as if it's obvious. But apparently to Elyse and Ambrose, it's not.

I turn to Liam in reply. "I'm looking for her card. I think we need to destroy it—"

"What card?" Elyse interrupts.

"Her husband's magic—Azrean magic—comes from an enchanted tarot card. She's wielding magic that she's not meant to use, which is why it's so unstable."

"So, you think if we find and destroy the card, we can stop her?" Liam asks.

I nod.

"Ok, but where's the card now?" Ambrose asks, looking around the room.

"I think it's somewhere in this cavern."

Elyse stares at me, incredulous. "Hang on. We're supposed to track down a magical tarot card hidden somewhere we never knew existed? Mira, that's a waste of time. We need to go back up to the castle. Find Heath—"

"You're kidding," I deadpan. "We can't just leave. We have one shot at this. It's up to us to stop the queen."

THE QUEEN'S CARD

A heavy weight hangs between us. I can feel the chasm between us getting wider, with Elyse and Ambrose on one side, and Liam and I are on the other. But there's no time for divisiveness.

We need to work together if we want any chance of stopping the queen. That means I need to convince my sister that she can trust me to make decisions.

"Please, Elyse. I need you to trust me," I whisper. "I need your magic."

Elyse shakes her head. "Our powers stopped working the moment she arrived in Lander."

I turn to Ambrose. "You, too?"

He nods.

"What about you?" I turn to Liam.

"I can't either," Liam says.

"What about the wraith bloom we gave you? Doesn't it mimic magic?"

At this, a sad smile reappears. "You don't think she'd let me keep that, would you?"

Memories rush into place.

"Wait a minute…" I take a step back.

He struck a deal with her. She told him he didn't fulfill it.

"What kind of deal did you—"

But before I can finish asking, he shifts in front of me until he hovers as a raven. A moment later, so do Ambrose and Elyse, clearly against their will.

Is the queen here?

Chapter 30

I watch Elyse flap her dark, sleek wings with a mixture of shock and curiosity. Just as I glimpse into her black eyes, she touches down onto the ground and turns to stone. I yelp, jumping back.

Every other raven in the room follows suit, flying to the ground before turning to stone. The cavern floor is now littered with stone ravens, each frozen in motion. One barely had time to land before shifting, and it looks as if it'll tip over at any moment. The worst part is, they're all facing me, like they're waiting for me to turn to stone, too.

It's like being back in Azrea Castle, in the greenhouse where I found Bael's brother. The stone statues were so lifelike I swore it's like they were staring at me through their frozen eyes. And it reminds me of *him*, of seeing Bael placed on the queen's table like a decoration.

Despair wells up inside of me, a moment from bursting free. My only allies are gone. When I stand up and look around, a dark, looming shadow collides with me. We tumble to the ground, a muscular body on top of mine.

THE QUEEN'S CARD

Bael's face swims in front of me and his arms cage me in. For a moment, the gaze he levels me with takes my breath away. I allow myself one moment of hope that he's in there, that he'll recognize me.

Then his hands find my throat. I gasp as he squeezes, but I suck in as much air as I can. I thrash in his grip, tears welling up in my eyes. All traces of Bael are gone. In his place is the queen's murderous second in command, the man I feared from the very beginning.

My Bael, my protective, brave Bael, is gone.

And this man? He's going to kill me.

I struggle beneath the weight of his body as black dots coat my vision. This isn't just about subduing me. This is how I'll die, at the hands of someone I love.

I hate that it's this version of Bael that I'll see as I take my last breath. The rage and hatred in his eyes don't belong to him.

"Very good," a voice croons. "Now, bring her to me."

It's her. Queen Roma. She's here.

He immediately lets go, snarling at me as he gets to his feet. I scramble away, gasping for air. It burns my throat but I take greedy lungfuls. The reprieve from his grip is temporary, though. Bael leans down and hauls me up by the arm, his grip rough.

The queen stands in the middle of the cavern, surrounded by her frozen subjects. Bael drags me toward her. Her smile is all teeth when he halts in front of her.

She turns and walks toward Dulci's prone form, watching me. With her hands at her sides, she sends shadows to snake around her feet before fanning out, turning the cavern floor into a hazy fog. I know what she's looking for because it's what I'm looking for, too: the missing Azrean arcana card.

When she reaches the princess's body, she leans down, and then lifts her head to address me.

219

"Why are you here, child?" she says, brushing away a lock of hair from Dulci's pale face.

I go rigid, hating her proximity to my friend. The queen savors my discomfort, her lips curling with satisfaction.

I swallow and lift my chin, mustering all the courage that I have. Standing in front of her without magic or any allies makes me realize how naïve I've been. Why did I think I ever stood a chance against her?

"The same reason as you," I answer, forcing my voice to stay even.

"Oh, I doubt that," she laughs, the shadows pausing their exploration of the cavern floor. When she turns back to the princess, my heart lodges in my throat.

"Perhaps you came to see what becomes of your beloved princess?" A shadow shoots from her finger and weaves into Dulci's hair.

My hands ball into fists. When I don't answer, she continues, "I don't have any children." She peers down at Dulci's face. "I don't care for them. They're meddlesome and ungrateful." Her blackened finger traces the apples of Dulci's cheekbones. "But this one," she continues, "she's obstinate. Strong willed and opinionated. She might have made a worthy opponent. Except," she sneers down at Dulci, "she fell right into her father's plan. And he's nothing but an arrogant fool."

I take a step back, the words stinging all over again. She must have seen Dulci just as she sees me, a younger version of herself. A reminder that she hates.

"She's the strongest woman I know," I say, standing up for both of us. She doesn't deserve the queen's vitriol.

"Was," the queen corrects.

I shake my head.

"She did nothing to you," I say.

"But her wretched father did," she snaps. "If I don't get to keep who I love then neither does he. So…where is it?"

My limbs tense up and without my consent, start to move. It's her coercion. I squeeze my eyes shut, fighting to keep my hands to my sides, but it hurts. It's a white-hot burning, not unlike when Bael gave me the shadow mark. I have to resist.

I manage to keep my body rooted to the spot despite the powerful tugging toward her. Finally, the pain recedes and I stumble forward as all the muscles in my body relax.

Did I just resist her coercion?

"Interesting," she says, narrowing her eyes. "What if I give you something you want?" She plunges her hand into her cloak. When something small comes flying toward me, I instinctively hold my hands out to catch it.

Oh, my god.

It's my keeper ring.

Without hesitation, I slip it onto my finger. It feels icy against my skin. My breath hitches in my throat. It's like reuniting with an old friend. But I can't ignore a wrongness that wasn't there before. It's the last reminder of who I wanted to be.

"Now," she drops her hands, "let's try this again. Where is my card?"

Coercion hits me like a punch in the stomach. I double over, the wind knocking out of me.

"I—don't—know," I say through my teeth.

She spelled my ring to make me comply?

I try to wrench the ring off my finger but my vision blurs. I sway on my feet. Blinking rapidly, I force myself to pull the ring off, but it's stuck. I try to breathe through the panic crawling up my throat.

I look down at my finger again, hating the sight of it.

"Liar! Where is it?"

"I—" a fresh wave of agony brings me to my knees. "Dael," her voice betrays her impatience, "make her stand."

His rough hands wrench me up by the back of my shirt. I'm crushed against his hard chest, and his arms banded around me.

Panic threatens to take over. I have nowhere to run, no idea where the card is, and no idea how to destroy it. I scan the room frantically, but all I see is the mirror that I fell through, a dark gray fog swirling within it where there wasn't a moment ago.

The queen closes the distance between us, and her blackened fingers grip my chin. They're freezing to the touch, and it sends a shiver of terror running down my spine.

I need to do something, anything, to stall. Forcing myself to focus, I open my mouth and my words come out as a muffled mumble.

"What was that?" she says, her voice dripping with condescension.

"You'll," I try to inhale, but Bael's vice-like grip makes it hard to breathe, "kill us all."

"Nonsense," she snaps, her piercing eyes staring into mine. "You know, everything I do is for the good of the realm. I will rule it all. It's my divine right."

Liam was right, she believes it's her divine right. He told us when we visited him in his gambling den.

"It's not divine," I take another labored breath, "to steal magic."

She raises an eyebrow at me. "Who told you that?"

I steel my nerves. "King Lewis."

For a long moment she just stares at me, looking like she's one moment away from killing me just to be done with it. But, then her sneer turns into a smile, a terrifying one.

"My late husband's family had no idea of the true power they possessed, but I know what it can do." She gazes around again. "There's a reason that Azrea was blessed with *this* arcana card. It's a part of us, a part of the destiny of our people. Embracing the death of the old ways and rejoicing in the new era."

What does that mean?

"History is destined to repeat itself, my dear," she grins, seeing the confusion on my face.

Without warning, she pulls something from an inner pocket of her robes, in a motion that I've seen before. When she pulls out a card, she spells it to float between us, suspended in midair.

My stomach sinks. I know that card, it's the one that she showed the crowd the night of the party. I hadn't seen the details up close until now. The card shows a raven perched on a human skull. Behind it is a crescent moon.

The Death card.

"Oh, Mira." She clicks her tongue at my confusion. "You still haven't figured it out. This," she gestures to the card floating between us, "is nothing but a tarot card from an ordinary deck. The real one is here, somewhere in these damn underground caves. I can *feel* it."

So she's been hiding behind an ordinary card, a decoy while she tracks down the real arcana card? I purse my lips in disdain. It's not her card to wield, it's King Lewis's family's arcana card. Just because he chose to marry her, doesn't mean she had the right to steal magic from him to suit her own gain. "But it's not yours, it belongs to King Lewis's—"

"I'm better than his bloodline," she snaps. "I can rule better than my husband ever could. I saw the potential in it. They only cared about upholding tradition, the fools. I saw the possibilities, I just needed to get my hands on those cards."

"You can't just *give* yourself magic."

Her laugh is hollow. "Isn't that what you did?"

I open my mouth to protest, but I can't fight the guilt and shame roiling in my stomach. She's wrong. But the thought sticks, and I can't shake it. Before I can protest, a door slams behind us, echoing in the cavern.

We all turn to watch a figure kick up the gray swirling fog at our feet. Her magic must also cause hallucinations because I swear the man striding toward us cannot be who I think it is.

It's the man who is the closest thing I have to a father.

He's also my savior.

Chapter 31

"Dane?" I gape at him, but the tightness in my chest loosens. He's really here, in the caves with the queen and I. He may be mortal like me, but he'll be on my side.

I look him over in his current state. His tailored jacket is ripped across one arm, and his gait favors his right side. It's definitely him, I'd recognize his bright eyes, and kind smile anywhere. Though he's not smiling now.

How did he find us? He must have come straight from the battle upstairs.

He doesn't notice me yet, his eyes are on the queen. When he stops to stand in front of her, his face is unreadable, a mask of cool indifference that I've never seen on him. He slips his hands in his pocket in a falsely casual gesture.

A wide smile forms on the queen's lips. "Daniel, it's been a long time."

Daniel? Why did she call Dane *Daniel*?

He nods curtly. "It has. Exile certainly keeps visits to a minimum."

My mind struggles to keep up with their conversation. What are they talking about?

Queen Roma lifts a brow. "Well, you know why I couldn't let you stay. But I didn't think you'd stoop low enough to seek refuge in Lander, of all places."

He shrugs, but I watch his jaw tick. "Would you rather I went to Brevalin instead?"

She laughs, but it's void of humor. "I figured you'd prefer Brevalin over Lander. Even that mortal's *rock* is beneath you."

When Dane's eyes rove in my direction, lingering on Dulci, before our eyes finally meet. My heart pumps so loudly in my chest that I think the entire room can hear it. I try to convey my confusion in my gaze, and he must understand because he inclines his head to me in a barely discernible nod.

I can hear what he's saying. *Trust me.*

Dane has something up his sleeve.

"I knew it was you the moment I saw the protective ward around the Lander princess," the queen's lip curls. "Then I saw you among them, next to that pathetic mortal you now call your king."

The pieces finally slot into place. I know where I've heard the name *Daniel* before. King Lewis referred to his brother, Daniel, in the flashback he showed me.

Wait. Is Dane the late Azrean King's brother?

Why else would Queen Roma exile him? He must be Azrean.

My eyes widen as I watch him confront Queen Roma. He's also Lander's Head Scholar. So Dane is an Azrean royal who taught King Adrian's keepers how to wield magic, how to wield his bloodline's stolen magic. And yet, he's treated us with kindness, when bitterness and resentment could have easily taken over. He fought for Lander, and he protected Dulci when Elyse and Ambrose couldn't.

"As much as I love a family reunion," he says sardonically, taking a step forward, "I know you're not here for me." He pulls something out of his pocket and holds it up.

This card glows bright white around the edges, but I can't force my eyes to take in the details. Is this the elusive arcana card?

"Stop this charade, Roma. I'm going to take back what's rightfully mine."

The queen sneers. "Oh, Daniel. You never had the guts to challenge your brother for the throne. What makes you think you can now?"

"You've been wielding our bloodline's magic for too long. It's not yours. It was never yours. And neither is Azrea."

"So, you came to tell me in person then, did you?" She narrows her eyes.

"This fight is personal, Roma. I knew the moment I met you. You never cared about my brother. All you wanted was money and power." He lowers the hand holding the card, and the queen watches the movement closely. "Our magic doesn't respond to you. You forced it to submit to you. It's killing you, and I had half a mind to let it." He points to her blackened fingers.

"The magic may not be mine," she says, shadowed fog trickling from her fingertips, "but I deserve it. I'm the rightful ruler of Azrea. It's fate. I've seen it in the cards."

Dane curls his hands into fists. "Your perversion of our magic will destroy the realms. You'll have nothing left to rule but a wasteland. I won't let that happen."

"Then by all means, take it back," she snaps.

She lunges at him, but he's one step ahead. In a flash, an iridescent ward forms around him. Her forward momentum forces her right into it. She slams her hand on it, snarling in fury.

"How dare you!" she shouts. "Give me that card!"

He turns to me and lifts his hand. My heart skips a beat, anxiety at an all-time high. But this is Dane, even if that's not his real name.

I know him. I trust him.

The ward stretches across the space between us. I feel the familiar tickle of magic over my skin as it encapsulates me, too. Bael is thrown back, forced out of the ward.

Relieved, I run into Dane's arms. He feels familiar, even more so than when I visited my old room in Lander Castle. When we break apart, his eyes are frantic.

I don't even realize I'm crying until he swipes at them as they fall against my cheek.

"Mira, I'm sorry for all the secrets, but it was *crucial* that you didn't become a keeper."

I barely have time to register his words when Bael's fists pound against the ward.

"Why?" I ask, my voice wavering.

"No time to explain." His voice is low and urgent. "Destroy the card. Bring Dulci back. You're the only one who can."

"What? How?"

"Use your ring."

"But I can't!" I shout, "It coerces me."

He grabs my hands in his. The moment he does, a warm tingling travels from my fingers to my palms. Suddenly, my ring feels warm against my skin. When I look down, it glows white, then returns to normal.

Is this his magic, Azrean arcana magic?

"It has to be you."

Before I can reply, he shoves the card in my hand, then races out of the ward to face the queen. The moment I feel its sharp edges, a bolt

THE QUEEN'S CARD

of energy shoots up my arm. I freeze, my eyes blurring until a vision appears.

***

The crisp autumn wind rustles the stiff leaves outside. I catch a hint of spiced meat and cinnamon, but my growling stomach is the last thing on my mind.

I pulled The Chariot card again tonight. That means I'm on the precipice of victory.

Tonight I'm finally going to get the one thing that I desire, I'm going to catch the eye of a prince, and I'll say goodbye to the old Roma.

I plaster on a pleasant smile for the young woman sitting in front of me, the king's cousin. She scans the inside of our tent with wariness bordering on disdain. A non-believer, I see.

Her companion, another young woman, lingers by the door, cast in shadow. She wrings her hands nervously.

"Lady Netta, maybe we should come back. The princes will arrive any minute—"

"—I'm not leaving until she tells me my fortune!" the woman snaps.

The reprimand is enough to silence her companion.

"Aren't you going to pull a card?" She directs her ire back to me, but I don't let it bother me.

I clear my throat to refocus and let my fingers hover over the deck. These cards are new, their edges are crisp and the images are heavily saturated with color. It's not like my beloved deck, that I know well enough to read with my eyes closed. I keep it with me at all times, lest Mother try to burn it again. She says we have to use the new ones to look our best, in case we garner the *attention of someone important. That's all that matters to her, gaining respect and favor from the king.*

I pull five cards and place them in a practiced formation, the five-card cross. When I open my eyes, I adjust their placement on the velvet tablecloth. Once I have her attention, I flip over the card in the middle.

The Three of Cups.

Three maidens stand raising their glasses in celebration, flower crowns adorning their heads.

"A joyful celebration," *I say sweetly.* "This means harmony and happiness within your social circle. Expect support and praise from those closest to you."

She looks unimpressed. "That's not about me. It's the king's birthday. Of course it's a celebration. Do another one."

I bristle and take a deep breath. I won't let some royal brat ruffle me. It's my craft, my art form. Just because it may seem obvious to her doesn't mean that it's not without skill or flair.

And it's the only thing I have. If I can't use it to carve my own path, then I have nothing.

"Of course," *I say, feigning meekness, before flipping the next card.*

The Six of Swords, reversed.

A man struggles to row a boat with six swords stabbed through the bottom of the boat.

I tut under my breath for dramatic effect.

"What?" *she snaps.*

I place my fingers on the card and close my eyes, as if I need more time to decipher the meaning. I could interpret it several ways, but I already know what I'll tell her.

"Hmm," *I say.* "This doesn't look good. There are obstacles ahead. You've been stuck in the past and you're running away from your problems—"

She scoffs and puts a hand to her chest. "I'm not running away from my problems!"

THE QUEEN'S CARD

I lower my head respectfully but barrel on. "I'm afraid more turbulent waters are ahead. If you continue to look back, you'll risk jeopardizing your future."

She sits in stunned silence, her eyes wide. Something struck a chord.

Good.

I don't need to tell her the discomfort is often temporary. Instead, I let her think she's doomed. I flip over the third card. Despite the urge, not even a flicker of a grin passes my lips, because I'm a professional.

It's The Moon.

The card shows a full moon with a face on it, peeking down at creatures on earth forlornly.

"Oh, dear," *I whisper ominously.*

"What?" *Her haughty demeanor is gone, replaced with wide-eyed panic.*

"Enemies hide all around you. They lie in wait, luring you in and deceiving you. Fear and anxiety are—"

She stands up so abruptly that the chair behind her topples over.

"Wait!" *I say, dropping my act.* "We still have two more cards! Don't you want to know..."

But all I see of her are her skirts, swishing as she races through the tent flap. Her companion races after her.

I scowl and blow out a breath, irritated. She didn't even pay.

It wasn't always like this. When I was young, I'd watch my mother tell fortunes. The way she'd captivate an audience was the envy of any street performer, but it was never enough to simply be good at it. She wanted more, more money, more recognition, and more respect. All I'd wanted was her love.

I'd long abandoned the hope that I'd be something she'd care about. Traveling around the realms with her, reading fortunes is its own form of punishment. To be present but never seen, never appreciated, wrong no matter what I do.

Now all I want is to be free of her, to leave this version of Roma behind. When Mother told me we received an invitation to work at the King's birthday, I knew my chance had arrived.

I straighten my skirts anxiously.

Without warning, Mother bursts through the tent, her eyes blazing.

Before I can ask, she turns and wrenches the flaps shut, then strides to where I sit behind the table.

"The princes are here!" she whisper-shouts. "Get up!" She tries to wrench me up by my arm, but I stay seated. "You are not messing this up for us. Let me—"

The tent flaps rustle and two guards walk in, each holding one flap open. We both turn to stare. A nervous, giddy excitement bounces around inside of me and I can barely stay in my seat.

Yes, tonight the fates are smiling down on me. The two Azrean princes stride into my mother's tent. The future king is taller than I'd imagined, with long chestnut hair and angular cheeks. He looks around the tent with narrowed eyes.

I stand up and bow low.

"Oh, your Highness," Mother says quickly, dipping into a rushed curtsy. "I'm honored that you've come into my tent. Have you had your cards read before?"

But before he can reply, I turn to the Azrean heir. I dip my head in respect, the picture of meek and humble. "I would be honored to read your cards, Your Highness."

When I look up, I flutter my eyelashes. Sure enough, his dark eyes catch mine and appraise me with rapt attention.

Mother's head swivels to look at me with disgust.

"Not you. I'll do it," she snaps, then turns to address the princes once more.

Embarrassment crawls up my neck and burns my cheeks. My hands ball into fists. She's controlled everything in my life, but I won't let her mess this up for me.

I think of The Chariot card, of victory and willpower. Taking a deep breath, I cast my eyes down, the guise of a dutiful daughter. I can salvage this.

"Of course, Mother," I say. "I only wanted to offer my skills." Wiping my hands on my skirt, I continue, "I'm so eager to prove myself."

"We don't want to waste his Highness' time, would we Roma?" Mother snaps.

The eldest prince bristles. "You don't speak for me or what I deem is wasted time."

I can still feel his eyes on me.

My mother blanches but quickly recovers. "Forgive me, I just wouldn't want her to lead you astray. She's not very bright, at least not in—"

"Has she not apprenticed under you?" he interrupts.

"Yes, she has, of course," Mother blurts, becoming increasingly flustered. "But her skills are dismal at best. She just made the king's cousin run out in tears—"

"You made Lady Netta cry?" The prince turns to me, his eyes alight with mischief. His younger brother snorts behind him with barely contained laughter.

I feel a small smile curling on my lips. An unexpected turn in my favor. I could use that to my advantage.

When the prince sits down on the chair across the table from me, I know I have his attention. My mother continues her drabble, but I drown her out, my attention fully focused on the young man in front of me.

I'll make Prince Lewis mine, starting tonight.

Chapter 32

My mind reels from the vision. How did I do that? It's the third vision I've been able to see, though this one was from the queen's perspective. I know very little about her, but it looks like Bael was right, that she was a fortune teller.

If the vision was real, then I saw the real queen. Skillful manipulation was already a skill she was using. She was focused on catching the future king's gaze, her future husband.

And the sorrow behind the actions, I saw that, too. Her mother was the source of childhood suffering. She was so hell-bent on power and respect, but all her daughter wanted was love. I allow myself one moment of pity for the way her mother treated her, but it's clear that her actions were all her own.

I force myself to breathe.

You remind me so much of myself, of how I would have turned out if I didn't take control of my own fate.

Perhaps this was the moment she took control of her own life.

Queen Roma is still to blame for all the suffering she's caused in her pursuit of power, but for one fleeting moment, I see her. I understand, even if I don't agree. I know what it feels like to have no control over your future. Her words echo in my head again.

You can't just give yourself magic.

Isn't that what you did?

The memory of her quip stings again. My situation is different...isn't it?

I begin to see our similarities. We both manipulated someone into giving us magic that we thought we deserved. She manipulated King Lewis, and I, out of survival, manipulated Bael into making a deal with Liam for my magic.

Magic was meant to make us feel important and worthy. Hers was meant to help her carve her own path, and mine was meant to help me feel like a part of something. In the end, it didn't work, and I won't let myself end up like her.

If Liam had truly unlocked the magic in my keeper ring, it still wouldn't have made me a keeper. I've spent the last several years being resentful of my sister, only to learn that she spared me from the curse. I have to stop blaming her for my perception of myself and my own perceived failures. Not gaining keeper magic wasn't a failure, not when I learned the true meaning behind it.

I'm glad it didn't work. Because magic doesn't make me belong, and I don't need it.

I suck in a breath, Elyse's words echoing in my head, aligning with my own thoughts.

Magic isn't what makes you belong; you already do.

I was so desperate to feel included, but it's not what I truly want. And, although I didn't set out to, I found somewhere else I belong, at Bael's side, if we both make it out of this nightmare alive.

He taught me to look at all sides, that preconceptions often bury the truth. He also taught me what it feels like to be seen.

Forcing my gaze up, I take in the scene in front of me. The queen sends a torrent of shadows that circle Dane. His hands are up, shooting white light to combat her shadows, but the moment they collide, his magic fizzles out like dying embers.

Her shadows quickly close in, and he's visibly struggling to keep them at bay.

Is she so powerful that his arcana magic can't subdue her? Why isn't he casting a ward? I need to help him.

I look back down at the card in my hand. It looks so plain, worn with the edges dog-eared. It doesn't seem like the source of so much anger, greed, and betrayal. I grip it with both hands, and try in vain to rip it in half, but to no avail.

A wretched cry pulls me out of my spinning thoughts. The shadows encasing Dane shift enough for me to glimpse him again. He's unsteady on his feet, one hand clutched at his chest while the other casts. He's clearly hurt.

"Dane!" I scream, taking a step toward him.

But when he looks at me, he shakes his head.

"The ring!" he shouts.

I can't focus. My hands are clammy and a bead of sweat stings my eyes. How am I supposed to use my ring to destroy the card? How will it bring Dulci back?

I stare at my shaking hands. The ring starts to glow. It's faint at first, a soft, white glow, but, in an instant, it blinds me.

"Enough!" Queen Roma bellows. When my eyes recover from the after-image, I see her sneering down at Dane. In a flash and a swirl of shadows, Dane turns to stone. My chest seizes and I swear that my heart stops beating.

"No!" I scream.

THE QUEEN'S CARD

Clutching the card in my fist, I race forward, his protective ward around me popping.

She turns to me, her hands outstretched. Shadowed fog surrounds her, and her gaze is murderous.

"Give me that card!"

I skid to a halt, feeling her coercion like an arctic gale. I clench my jaw, focusing on the gentle heat and the tingling from the magic in the card in my palm. The wave of coercion passes, and I exhale in relief.

Dane's magic must have released the coercion from my keeper ring. I stand up straighter and shake my head.

Her eyebrows raise in genuine surprise. "You dare to defy me? You're nobody," she laughs haughtily. "Some Landerian brat with no magic and no purpose."

I steel my nerves and tip my chin up. She's absolutely right. I am nobody. I know I won't be able to survive her wrath, but I've seen too much. I know too much to walk away.

I think of Bael and his brother, the Brevalin royals stuck under her coercion, forced to do her bidding. I think of the Azreans I met. I even think of Liam, the rebel, forced to turn on his comrades, even if his goals were selfish. None of them deserve to suffer and neither do my people. She needs to be stopped, and, if I'm the only one left standing, then I'll fight her until my last breath.

"Hand it over, now!" She raises her hands, and, in slow motion, a torrent of shadows move toward me. I brace myself for the impact.

But something blocks my view. Bael stands in front of me. He's not facing me; he's not attacking. He's blocking me from the queen's view.

No, Bael, what are you doing?

Suddenly, he's on his knees, the wave of shadows from the queen hitting him square in the chest. I barely register my own screams as I dart around the shadows to look at him. When her magic recedes, I see nothing but anguish etched on his face, and it's his eyes that hurt the most. The dark pools of umber appraise me frantically, as if searching for injuries. It's him, the real him.

Then I feel it, too.

I scream in agony. It ripples through our shadow mark. It's a blinding, searing stab that makes me feel like my chest is being ripped open. I can't stop the overflowing despair welling up inside of me.

This is it. This is the end.

I fight the urge to curl up in a ball on the marble floor and give in. I know my time has come. Instinctively, I close my eyes.

"Bael," I cry out, my hand grasping around until I find his. His hand is warm, steadily enveloping mine.

At least he's here with me, in the end. I feel his hand squeeze mine. I open my eyes, if only to take in the last memory of his face, but when gaze finds mine, he looks down at my arm, right where our shadow mark hides beneath my sleeve. I realize what he's about to do.

"No!" I shout, but it's too late.

His fingers grip just below my elbow. In a flash of blinding, white-hot pain, our shared mark disappears.

"No, no, no!" I scream, panic clawing up my throat. The agony of the queen's magic is receding, but it's all flowing into Bael instead. He pitches forward, clutching at his chest.

"Stop it!" I scream at the queen. "Make it stop!"

My world tilts on its axis. Where I used to feel the bond between us is now hollow. He released me from our shadow mark so that I didn't have to suffer the way he's suffering.

He sacrificed himself for me.

The card he has in his treehouse flashes in my mind, the Hanged Man, *the martyr*, he called it. He said it was his fate.

"Bael," I cry weakly, crawling on my knees toward him. He's coughing violently, his hair hanging limp in front of his face.

I can't let this go on. I have to stop it. He sacrificed for me, and I have to sacrifice for him, for all of them.

Use the ring.

That's what Dane told me. But how?

Chapter 33

"I'll give it to you," I sob, my lungs constricting. She stops her torture long enough to quirk up a brow. It allows Bael a breath, a small reprieve.

I know I'm no match for the queen. I'm the only mortal in the room, but as I look down at the ring that protected me from her coercion, I recall the flash of white, and the tingling I felt.

Dane gave me arcana magic through my ring. I don't know how long it'll last, but I have to use it. I have to try to destroy the card, and hope that somehow, it brings Dulci back.

I look down at it. It may be a physical reminder of my failure to be a keeper, but it's a weapon now. So how do I use it?

"Come here, Mira," she says, beckoning me over.

I force myself to let go of Bael, to stand, and put one foot in front of the other.

"People will only disappoint you," she says as I approach, "but power never will."

When I first met Bael, I thought he would always be my enemy. Our fundamental views on magic and mortals were so different, but

THE QUEEN'S CARD

he's shown me that there is room for understanding and compromise. Despite my rational brain, I fell in love, and love will always be more important than power.

Power was something I wanted, wasn't it? Keeper magic, at its heart, is power. It's recognition and inclusion into an elite society that I was so desperate to be a part of. But I will choose love over power any day. I know that now.

Standing in front of her once more, I desperately wish that I could shield Bael from the agony that thrashes through him. If he were standing here, what would he tell me to do?

I look down at the card in my hand. I try to remember how Bael helped me control my magic the night we watched the moonrise.

Clear your mind. Nothing else exists but you and your magic.

"Now!" the queen demands.

She raises her hands and tendrils of shadows shoot toward me, but I ignore them. In my mind's eye, I picture my magic as the delicate, curling ribbons of purple. Uncertain if I imagined it, I swear I can feel the gentle caress of it as it wraps around my closed fist. It feels just like silk.

Suddenly, the queen is shouting, her voice high-pitched and frantic. I feel the sharp edges of the card in my hand as I crush it. But the ring burns hot against my skin, and instinctively, I open my cramped palms.

When I open my eyes, the queen is pointing at my hand. Something feels gritty against my tender palm. Looking down, I realize the card is nothing but ashes slipping through my fingers. Weak purple tendrils twirl around my fingers before disappearing.

A keening scream fills my ears. Her shadows retreat from around my feet, coalescing into a whirling cyclone around the queen.

"You insufferable little cretin!" she screams, lunging toward me. I stumble back, just as she falls to her knees. Through pockets of swirling black shadows, I see her face contorted in rage, but she's no longer the all-powerful sovereign hell-bent on taking over the kingdom. She cradles one arm in the other, and I watch in horror as the skin on her neck turns black, as if her own shadows are consuming her.

She lifts her head defiantly, her eyes piercing. With one last shriek, she collapses onto the cavern floor, the shadows spinning and tightening around her. Her cyclone of shadows finally explodes in a cloud of darkness. I sink to my knees, covering my head, terrified the cavern walls will implode.

But as the wave of residual magic, ice-cold and pitch black rolls over my back, it finally dissipates. The candles illuminating the room flicker to life again, casting a warm glow back into the room. On wobbling legs, I force myself to stand. Where the cyclone of shadows was is now a discarded pile of clothes and a blackened, ashen husk of the former queen of Azrea.

Too shocked to comprehend, I stand frozen, gaping at the scene. When my ring burns too hot on my finger, it forces my focus back. I wrench it off and drop it to the ground, where it glows white before disintegrating.

My breath comes out ragged, and I lean down, my hands on my thighs, trying to calm my racing heart. Is it over?

"Mira." Bael's voice is gravelly as if from disuse.

I whirl around to look at him.

Bael. *My* Bael.

I run back to him, dropping onto my knees in front of him. He reaches out, cupping my cheeks with his hands. Those eyes, so full of anguish, look at me like I'm the air he breathes. I smile, a sob escaping me.

When our lips meet, it's like coming home again, but when he deepens the kiss, it's not gentle. It's heady and consuming. His fingers

THE QUEEN'S CARD

tangle in my hair, and I can't help the gasp that escapes me. Nothing else matters. I have him back.

When we finally come up for air, I bury my face in his neck.

"You did it," he whispers into my ear.

"No, we did it." I sniffle, relishing his strong arms around me.

Curious shuffling erupts around us but I don't let go. I lift my head to watch each of the stone ravens shift back into living forms. They immediately take flight, escaping through the mirror, leaving only three, who shift into human form: Elyse, Ambrose, and the prince. I reluctantly pull out of Bael's arms, pointing to them. He struggles but gets to his feet.

When Elyse spots me, she and Ambrose race toward me. I'm tackled and let out a relieved sob, squeezing them back.

It's only when we break apart, that I realize there are two figures still frozen.

We all turn back to look. My eyes bounce from where Dulci lay, prone on the floor, to where Dane kneels, his body frozen in stone.

Ambrose swears, his body going rigid. He races across the cavern to kneel by his father. My heart hurts, it's a visceral ache. The ravens shifted out of their stone forms when the queen died. So why didn't he?

Tears well in my eyes as I walk up behind him. Ambrose holds his father's shoulders, resting his forehead on his father's and closing his eyes. Long, agonizing seconds pass, and I feel his heart breaking. I place one hand on Ambrose's shoulder and squeeze.

"We're going to figure this out," I whisper as Elyse joins us.

Movement behind us draws our attention up as Prince Reid, exhausted and unsteady on his feet, pulls away from his brother's embrace to approach his betrothed.

Princess Dulci lay prone on the floor, no longer hovering ominously. He sinks to his knees in front of her, his shoulders slumping. He strokes her hair from her face, before cupping her cheek in his palm.

"Dulci," he murmurs, his hands roving over her. "Wake up, please."

I remember Dane's words. *Destroy the card. Bring Dulci back.*

When I destroyed the card, shouldn't it have woken her up?

We all watch with bated breath as he shakes her, gently at first, but she doesn't wake. As long, tense moments pass, his attempts get more frantic. I take a cautious step forward, but Bael holds me back.

I turn to him, frowning. Bael jerks his head toward his brother and I watch as Prince Reid leans down, placing a tender kiss on Dulci's forehead, then her lips. The silence in the cavern is deafening. How will a kiss wake her up if his other attempts failed.

I bounce on the balls of my feet, anxious and worried. I can't lose two people tonight.

Finally, Dulci gasps, and a relieved cry escapes from my lips. Prince Reid bends down, nuzzling his face into her neck before scooping her up into his arms. Her laughter is like the tinkling of a bell.

She survived.

I feel Bael's warm arm wrap around my shoulder and pull me close.

Chapter 34

The sunrise casts a hazy pink light through the giant windows of the scholar's tower. It feels the same here; the same stuffy air, the same dusty tomes, the same well-worn worktables and lamps. But it's not the same. I'm no longer the same.

I wander to the window to look out over the water. Only a month ago, I was scouring the beach, following sentient shadows. I was so desperate to prove myself, so worried about the queen's threat, but I had no idea of the magnitude of the dangers that lie ahead. I had no idea the part I would play in unraveling everything I thought I knew. Nothing turned out as I thought it would. I didn't get what I thought I wanted, but I'm not powerless. I'm not alone.

I watch the waves crash against the rocky beach and what's left of the jetty. After the queen unleashed her ground-shaking, twisted magic on the castle last night, it destroyed most of the only strip of land that connects us to the rest of the continent. I'm sure it's not the only damage sustained.

For reasons I still can't fathom, the man who I grew up with was the one who knew the true danger Lander was in. My heart pangs when I think of Dane, who's currently still frozen in stone in the caves under Lander Castle. He was looking out for me, for us, all along.

I'm just a mortal, but for the first time in my life, it made me useful. He and Elyse kept secrets from me, kept keeper magic from me, though I'm sure they didn't anticipate that I'd run off and follow Bael. But he had faith that I would be willing to see the real problem, that the late Queen of Azrea's reign affected more than just the realms that she threatened. Her own people were suffering.

When soft footsteps echo behind me, I already know who it is.

My sister comes to stand by me, and we watch the seagulls swoop over the beach. Finally, I turn to ask something that's been gnawing at me.

"Did you know that keeper magic was stolen from Azrea?"

My sister frowns, then nods.

"I didn't know until after King Adrian gave it to me. It felt like something was wrong though..." she trails off, looking outside the window again.

"Why didn't you tell me?"

When she refocuses on me, a sad smile forms. "I wanted to protect you, Mira. This wasn't your burden to bear. But before I could speak up, the king gave it to Ambrose, too. As soon as I found out, I told Dane."

I frown, picturing my sister having to deal with this burden without me. Perhaps she's still dealing with it. I haven't wanted to ask if the magic in her ring is still warped from the queen, or if she's still forced to shift into a raven. "You could have told me," I say softly, "but I understand why you didn't."

She reaches out to grab my hand. "I'll always look out for you." Concern crosses her face, then she frowns again. "Mira, about the Raven—"

"It's *Bael*, actually," a low voice says just over her shoulder.

THE QUEEN'S CARD

A grin spreads across my face. I lean to the side to watch Bael approach. He's pale with purple bags under his eyes, but I see the warmth in his eyes when I meet his gaze. I race into his arms and immediately I'm enveloped by his comforting scent. I take a long breath, savoring the closeness, almost forgetting my sister is in the room. When he pulls away, I notice his eyes travel back to my sister.

I turn and introduce them. "Elyse, this is Bael."

My sister stiffens and doesn't make a move to shake his hand. Bael, to his credit, takes it in stride, and inclines his head toward her. "I can promise you, I'm no longer the queen's second in command."

"He's Prince Reid's younger brother," I add. "He's a prince of Brevalin."

Elyse's jaw drops. "How?" She pauses, searching for the right word. "We didn't know the prince had a younger brother."

Bael shrugs. "Because it's not my title. Brevalin only recognizes one heir. Lander's standards may consider me a prince, but at home, I was training to be my brother's Second in Command."

"How did you end up under the Azrean Queen's command?" Elyse asks.

Bael lets out a long sigh. "That's a story for another day."

I gently squeeze his arm, and his soft smile, the one he saves for me, dances along the corner of his mouth. Warmth blooms in my cheeks. Elyse must notice the intimate moment, because she says a quiet goodbye and leaves.

"She'll come around," I whisper as Bael strokes my hair.

Content to be alone with him, I wriggle in his grip until I face the window. His powerful arms wrap around me from behind, and I sink into the touch. How strange that other times that he's held me like this, I was terrified. But he was under the queen's coercion then. Not anymore, this feels safe.

We stand like this for a long time, and I savor the feeling of his heartbeat and the steady rhythm of his breathing. However, it doesn't stop the inevitability of spiraling thoughts. There's a void in my chest where the shadow mark had been, where our *bond* had been. It doesn't matter that it was mimicking a mating bond. It was real to me. Without it, I feel hollow. But I don't dare voice it.

I know the sacrifice that he made was for me.

My mind conjures the tarot card hanging from a frame in his loft. The Hanged Man, the martyr. He's sacrificed for those he loves countless times, for his brother, and now for me. I just hope to one day do the same for him.

"What are you thinking about?" he asks, finally breaking the silence.

"I keep replaying last night in my head and I'm trying to make sense of it…" I trail off.

"How you destroyed the queen's card?"

I nod. I feel the rumble of his chest as he thinks. I turn, craning my head to look into his eyes.

"The moment Dane touched my hands, the queen's coercion in my ring melted away. I felt his magic. I think it was his bloodline's magic, his arcana magic. And when he handed me the card…" I remember the tingling in my hands and how my ring glowed white.

He tilts his head, looking at me curiously. "He must have lent you his arcana magic in order to destroy the card. He completed the rune in your keeper ring."

"But I don't understand why *he* couldn't do it? Why couldn't he destroy the card? It was his family's magic that she stole."

He pauses to consider. "It was a twisted version of his bloodline's magic. Arcana magic can't be used against itself, at least not by those of the royal bloodlines. At least, that's what the lore says. It keeps Brevalin and Azrea from conquering each other."

I frown. "But why me? Why not Elyse or Ambrose?"

"They're keepers," he says simply, "her warped magic affected them. But not you. You're—"

"Mortal." I say, finishing his thought.

Dane told me it was crucial that I didn't become a keeper. Is that because he knew he would need a mortal to wield his arcana magic and destroy the card?

"So why not any other mortal?"

Bael shrugs. "I don't know, but he trusted you. He knew you would do what's right. And in any case," he whispers into my hair, "you were the right one to do it."

I ignore the shiver down my spine from his warm breath on the shell of my ear. When I turn, I search his eyes. "Why do you say that?"

"Because you're the only keeper who was willing to see the truth."

"I'm not a keeper."

"No, I guess not," he agrees. "But that's because you saw what it meant to be one. You saw the suffering in others and did what needed to be done."

"Dane put a lot of faith in me."

"For good reason."

I swallow thickly. My eyes automatically look down to where I know our mark no longer is. My mark is gone and my ring is gone.

I've come full circle, and now I'm back to being mortal. I've seen and heard more than I ever realized I'd been missing, and now I see a different future ahead of me.

"Mira?" he says softly, breaking me out of my thoughts.

I crane my head back to look at him again.

"Do you know why each royal bloodline is said to have two arcana cards?"

I shake my head

"Arcana magic requires balance. And I fear that when you destroyed one of Azrea's cards last night, it's going to have disastrous consequences, even if that scale seems like it's tipped in Brevalin's favor. But we have to restore the balance somehow. I don't know how, but we have to, before it's too late."

I swallow, feeling my heart start to race. I open my mouth, but nothing comes out.

I recall something the queen said.

History is destined to repeat itself.

"Something is coming, Mira, and we need to be prepared." He squeezes me tighter but my stomach sinks at his words.

Something is coming…

To Be Continued…

Reviews help indie authors like me reach new readers, and if you loved this book, it would mean the world to me if you left a review!

***

CAN'T WAIT TO SEE WHAT HAPPENS NEXT?

This is the end of *The Queen's Card*, but Mira's adventure is far from over! Dive into *The King's Card*, book 2 in the *Fairytale Tarot* series now!

THE QUEEN'S CARD

***

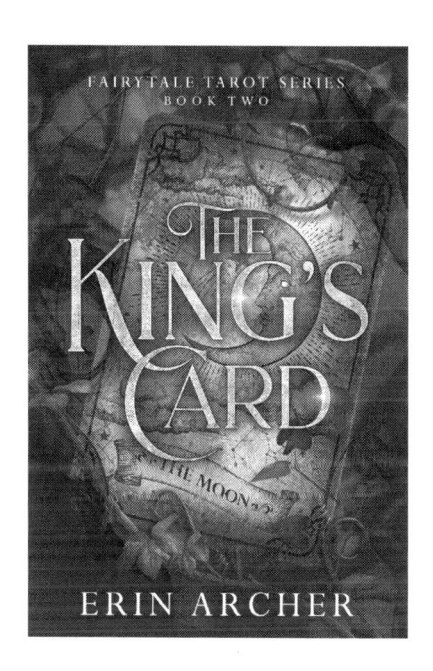

JOIN MY NEWSLETTER & KEEP IN TOUCH!

Do you want a free, *exclusive* bonus scene from Bael's perspective? Sign up at AuthorErinArcher.com/Newsletter to get email news from me and I'll send it to you! You'll also stay in-the-know about my releases. Also, come find me on Instagram @AuthorErinArcher and Facebook @AuthorErinArcher.

Acknowledgements

To my readers: I have no words to express my gratitude that you gave this book a chance, so the most heartfelt thank you will have to do. You helped me achieve my dream.

To my incredible critique partner, Rachel. Your wise feedback, willingness to brainstorm, and unwavering support is the reason this book even has an ending. Cheers to all the books we'll write together!

To my wonderful author friend, Annah. Thank you for always making time to sprint with me, it's my favorite part of the day. You always help me see the bigger picture.

To the incredible writing friends I made along the way: Heather, Kelli, Hannah, Nour, Laura, & Annie. Thank you for being there for me. I can't wait to see what you accomplish! A special thanks goes to my wonderful writing friends Malina and Aphéira, who graciously beta read for me. Your insightful feedback and encouragement had a massive impact on this story.

To my ARC readers: you took a chance on me and my little book, thank you for trusting me! Shoutout to Jessica, who supported me right away as my first reader. I can't wait to read all the romantasy books with you!

To my editor, Sarah: this book wouldn't be half of what it is without you. Your guidance and advice were paramount in making this story the best it could be. I am eternally grateful, and I promise to study dialogue punctuation before book 2 :)

To my cover artist, Fay. You understood my vision right away and you brought it to life. I am still in awe of your talent. Thank you!

About the Author

Erin Archer writes fairytale retellings and fantasy romance.

Originally from Seattle, she traded gray clouds for sunshine, though she still pines for the rain, the mountains, and the coffee. When she's not writing, you'll find her binge-watching *Outlander*, playing *Stardew Valley* with her husband, or snuggling with her band of rescue dogs.

If you want to know more about Erin's new releases, sign up for her newsletter at AuthorErinArcher.com.

Made in the USA
Middletown, DE
08 September 2025